WALTZING WITH THE EARL

Catherine Tinley

HarperCollins
PUBLISHERS
Since 1817

Published in Great Britain 2017
by Mills & Boon, an imprint of HarperCollins*Publishers*
1 London Bridge Street, London, SE1 9GF

© 2017 Catherine Tinley

ISBN: 978-0-263-92566-1

Our policy is to use papers that are natural, renewable and
recyclable products and made from wood grown in sustainable
forests. The logging and manufacturing processes conform to the
legal environmental regulations of the country of origin.

Printed and bound in Spain
by CPI, Barcelona

Catherine Tinley has loved reading and writing since childhood, and has a particular fondness for love, romance and happy endings. She lives in Ireland with her husband, children, dog and kitten, and can be reached at catherinetinley.com, as well as through Facebook and @CatherineTinley on Twitter.

Waltzing with the Earl
**is Catherine Tinley's enchanting debut for
Mills & Boon Historical Romance!**

Visit the Author Profile page at millsandboon.co.uk.

To my parents, Sheila and Tommy, with love.

Prologue

London, 1814

Leaning against a gilded column, the Earl of Shalford coolly observed the revellers at Lady Jersey's party. The elegant ballroom was thronged with gentlemen and ladies of every age, shape and demeanour, all determined to enjoy the evening. A country dance was in full flow, and the sight of tittering ladies and merry gentlemen leaping and capering around the room seemed, at this moment, the height of absurdity.

'Adam—so this is where I find you. Ogling the ladies, eh?'

The Earl regarded his younger brother with disfavour. 'No, I shall leave that to you, Harry. I am leaving.' He wrenched his long frame upright.

'So soon? But the night is barely begun—and you are promised to dance the cotillion with Miss Ross.'

The Earl shrugged. 'I shall apologise—a sudden indisposition, I think.'

'You are not indisposed—well, not unless one counts this unseemly languor. Come now, Adam, there are lovelies to be danced with, flirtations to be had. You are too staid for your own good!'

'Not staid—bored. Not one of these ladies has the power to hold my attention. I dance with them, then immediately forget them. I cannot choose between them.'

'Then do not choose. Simply enjoy the moment. We have been out of mourning for Papa for months, yet still you act as though…'

'As though I were still mourning him? You need not worry, Harry. Papa is gone. I have accepted it. The Earldom—and all its responsibilities—rests on my shoulders.'

'It must not be a burden, Adam. You can still enjoy life.'

'I do, Harry, I do. I just do not enjoy—*this*.' He indicated the crowded room. 'Give me an evening with friends instead—with people I know and wish to talk to.'

'But your friends are here.' Harry indicated a corner near the supper room, where a group of young men were indulging in drinking games with Lady Jersey's potent punch.

'Perhaps I am not friendly enough tonight. Have a good evening, Harry. Flirt with as many young ladies as you can manage. Keep up the Fanton name.'

Harry shook his head. 'Adam, this is not good.'

His brother, unheeding, left with a slight wave of

his hand. He spoke first to Miss Ross, who looked disappointed, then made his farewell to their hostess, Lady Jersey.

As Adam slipped out of the room, Harry spoke softly, though he knew his brother could not hear. 'I wish I could lift your spirits, Adam, but if pretty girls and dances can't do it then how can I?'

Chapter One

B<small>UXTED</small> House in Half-Moon Street was a neat, elegant townhouse, ideally situated between Curzon Street and Green Park. As his coach stopped outside, Colonel Sir Edward Wyncroft glanced around. Late morning meant the street was busy with delivery men, street sweepers and errand boys. The smell of spring was in the air, mixed with the usual London odours—chimney smoke and horse manure.

A lean, sprightly gentleman, with intelligent blue eyes and dark curls showing only a hint of grey, Sir Edward had an easy gait, and his youthful looks belied the fact that he was now in his fifth decade.

Surrendering his hat and cane to the footman, Sir Edward addressed the butler, whose name, he remembered, was Biddle.

'I believe your master is expecting me, Biddle?'

'Indeed, Sir Edward. I am glad to see you again, sir. Please come this way.'

Sir Edward followed him to the breakfast room,

where Mr Frederick Buxted, an affable, portly fellow in his middle years, was demolishing a selection of cold meats and rolls with coffee. Rising as the butler announced his guest, he shook Sir Edward's hand and bade him join in the spread.

'No, no, Freddy, I have eaten already. Can't get used to these late hours, you know.'

'Ah, yes,' said Mr Buxted knowledgeably. 'No doubt you rise early in Venice?'

'Vienna, my dear boy, Vienna,' said Sir Edward. 'Yes, I can't abide sleeping late. Got to be up and about, you know. Army habits. Too much to do.'

Buxted eyed him suspiciously. 'You know, I never *did* understand why you stayed in the Army after Maria died. The ladies said you couldn't bear to come home without her.'

Sir Edward, with some difficulty, conjured up an image of his long-dead wife. 'She was a beauty, my Maria. But that wasn't it. I'm an Army man, Freddy. And besides, there was no reason to come home then.'

'No reason? What about your daughter?'

'Now, Freddy, don't be a gudgeon! You know little Charlotte was with us when her mother died. She was such an easy, contented little thing, and her nursemaid was devoted to her. What was I to do—open up the house and let her rattle around in it with a legion of servants? No, she was better with me.'

'Better with *you*?' spluttered Freddy, almost choking on his coffee. 'A life travelling around war

zones and foreign cities, in goodness knows what
danger?'

'Oh, there was never any danger. She stayed safe
with the Army families, far away from any action.
Well, most of the time.' His brow creased. 'There
was that time in Burgos…and once when we had
to hide in a cellar. But my Lottie has the heart of a
soldier—no airs and vapours from her. We took her
home sometimes, when Maria was alive, but Maria
didn't like us to be apart.'

'Yes, but she was never here long enough.'

'True.' Sir Edward looked pensive. 'After Maria
died I established Charlotte with her maid and a gov-
erness in Madrid, then Florence, and now Vienna.
I sent her to a good school there—she has just finished, in fact. Though, of course you are right. She
needs to see London, and she needs English ladies
around her.' He eyed Buxted keenly. 'How is your
family? Mrs Buxted? Your daughters? Both girls
are out now, I think?'

'Yes, and all are well. Louisa and the girls are
still abed, as they were at Lady Jersey's rout last
night. A chance for me to enjoy a quiet breakfast.
Not that—I mean, of course I *prefer* to have breakfast with my wife—it is just—'

'Yes, yes, I too have a dislike of listening to nonsense too early in the day. Actually, I had hoped to
ask a favour of you, Freddy.'

'Of course, of course, Edward.' He glanced towards the door. 'That is, anything in my power…'

'It is the Corsican, you see.'

'The Corsican?' His eyes widened. 'Napoleon?'

'The very man. Fact is, he is to be exiled. Elba, you know. All agreed this week.'

'Yes, of course. The news reached us here in London a few days ago, though we didn't know where he was to go. Just grateful the war is over, really.'

'Well, Castlereagh doesn't like it, but the Czar must be magnanimous. I'm with Campbell, who will stay to see it done.'

'Er...quite, quite. Important business, that.' Freddy adopted a knowing look.

'Indeed—and delicate. Can't let that little upstart think he actually *was* an emperor! The thing is—I think it is time Charlotte came home to England. I'm going back to Paris with the Foreign Office chaps. Everything seems to be settling down, but I wouldn't trust the French—not suitable for her at all.'

'No, no!' said Buxted, much struck. 'But is there no one—?'

'No one in London I would know and trust like you, Freddy. You're Maria's cousin, got two daughters of your own. Seems an ideal situation for my Charlotte.'

'Yes, I see, but—'

'You needn't worry. She won't give you any trouble, Freddy. She is not one of those demanding females. Quiet little thing, but got a good head on her shoulders, my Lottie. In fact, shouldn't be surprised if you *like* her, Freddy—everyone does.'

'But for how long would we be expected to have her?'

'Not more than a couple of months, Freddy. You know how it is with these things—hard to tell.' Freddy nodded sagely. 'It will be my last mission, though. After making sure Napoleon is safely on his way I'll need to tidy things up—regimental business, you know—then I'll be coming home for good. The job is done and I'm looking forward to retirement.'

'To be sure, yes. But—'

'And don't worry, Freddy, I'll stand the blunt. You won't have to lay out a penny on her behalf. I shall arrange her pin money, but I will need to stable Charlotte's mare with your horses, if you are agreeable?'

Mr Buxted, his shoulders slumped, could not object.

'Then it is all settled! I shall ask Charlotte to write to your wife to confirm the date of her arrival.'

Sir Edward, entirely satisfied, took his leave without further ado, leaving Freddy Buxted with the happy duty of informing his dear wife Louisa of their impending guest. He sank back in his seat as the enormity of his task slowly dawned on him.

'For this,' he muttered to the empty room, 'I shall need the assistance of a power greater than myself.' He raised his voice. 'Biddle! *Biddle!* Oh, there you are, man. Get me some ale!'

A little over three weeks later, on the date appointed in her polite correspondence with Mrs Buxted, Miss Charlotte Wyncroft arrived at Buxted House. She was accompanied by her groom, Joseph, leading a fine bay mare, her abigail, Miss Priddy—who was also Joseph's sister—and an enormous number of trunks and bandboxes, piled high behind the coach.

'Finally, Priddy, we have arrived!'

'Now, then, Miss Charlotte, no need for over-excitement.'

'But, Priddy, this is *London*! You know how long I have wanted to visit England, and especially London. It is hard to call oneself English when England is a distant memory. *Ooh*, there are my cousins— what attractive girls!'

Charlotte peered out through the carriage window, trying to see everything without making it obvious that was what she was doing. Two young women stood with their mama at the top of the steps. Both looked fair, pretty and elegant.

As the carriage door was opened Charlotte overheard snatches of their conversation.

'Mama, what a lot of luggage!' exclaimed the younger-looking Miss Buxted.

Faith was her name, Charlotte remembered from the letters she had exchanged with Mrs Buxted these past weeks. A pretty young lady with blue eyes and flaxen curls, she was a paler imitation of her older sister. She glanced anxiously at her mother and sister as they stood waiting for their guest to mount the steps.

Miss Henrietta Buxted, at twenty, was two years senior, and was stunningly beautiful. Guinea-gold curls, wide blue eyes and a stubborn chin—she would be much sought after among the young men, if Charlotte was not mistaken.

Henrietta sniffed. 'I hope she will not be an *inconvenience*, Mama.'

'Charity begins at home,' said Mrs Buxted.

A stout lady on the shady side of forty, with a certain hardness about her eyes and mouth, she still showed faint traces of the former beauty that, Papa said, had attracted young Freddy Buxted to offer for her.

Standing stiffly in a burgundy Norwich crepe round gown, she remarked, 'I still don't understand how your father agreed to this. To have an unknown girl foisted on me, when I have two daughters of my own to see settled… It is beyond belief!'

Mr Buxted, who had been standing quietly behind his wife and daughters, looked alarmed. Muttering what sounded suspiciously like, 'Fortitude!' he stood his ground.

Charlotte glanced at Priddy, who looked shocked. Did Mrs Buxted and her daughters think she could not hear them?

Schooling her features into a polite smile, Charlotte tripped lightly up the shallow stone steps.

'Mrs Buxted, I am so happy to be here. Thank you so much for agreeing to let me visit. What a beautiful house! And these must be my cousins.'

'My daughters, Henrietta and Faith.'

The girls made their curtseys.

'It is lovely to meet you all! Mr Buxted!'

'Do call me Uncle. I should happily be your uncle. I'm so glad your father agreed to let you visit.' Mr Buxted, moved by Charlotte's enthusiasm, gave her an avuncular kiss.

'Now, now, Mr Buxted—Uncle! I can imagine quite well that my father pressured you into it. He normally gets what he wants.' She leaned forward, and added with a twinkle, 'It is what makes him such a good colonel.'

Mr Buxted laughed, at which his wife and daughters looked quite startled. He stepped back and made a study of her.

'Well,' he pronounced, 'you look *nothing* like my dear cousin Maria.'

'Yes,' she agreed. 'She was a famous beauty, was she not? I am thought to favour my father.'

Henrietta sighed dramatically. 'To live without a mother. It must be so sad for you.'

'Not at all!' said Charlotte cheerfully. 'I don't really remember her. She died when I was six, you see.'

'But you have not had the guiding hand which

every young lady needs,' offered Mrs Buxted evenly. 'Growing up without a mother, you must lack the wisdom only a mother can offer.'

'Oh, probably,' agreed Charlotte. 'I do not think I am very wise sometimes.'

'Then perhaps,' offered Henrietta, 'we may help improve your mind during your visit.'

'I wouldn't be sure of that,' said Charlotte sorrowfully. 'I was a terrible student. I finished school last month, thank goodness, and I did try to be sensible and obedient, but I admit I found it a struggle sometimes.'

She twinkled at Faith, who—thankfully—returned an understanding smile.

'Reverend Welford—our chaplain in Vienna—has quite given up on me, but says he likes me as I am. I do find it hard to be *good* sometimes. But I do try.'

Ignoring Henrietta's gasp of shock, Mrs Buxted inclined her head. 'Well,' she said, her mouth a thin hard line, 'we shall see.'

'I am glad,' said Henrietta to her mother, 'that our cousin is *dark*-haired—not fair, like me and Faith.'

'Why does that matter?' asked Faith, perplexed. 'Besides, Charlotte has blue eyes like us.'

'She will be described as a petite girl, with a good figure, striking blue eyes with dark lashes—the Buxted eyes—and unfashionably brown hair. She is *pretty* rather than beautiful, Faith.' Henrietta sounded exasperated at her sister's dim-wittedness.

'It means that I will still be known as the beauty of the family—although Charlotte is pretty enough not to discredit us.'

'And she is elegant,' agreed Mrs Buxted, her eyes sweeping over Charlotte's stylish blue pelisse, worn over a pretty figured muslin gown.

Charlotte stood in astonishment as they openly discussed her. In Vienna this would have been considered shockingly rude.

'Yes, yes,' said Mr Buxted, 'I am sure you will all get on famously. My love, I shall leave you to get better acquainted with our little niece. I shall return for dinner.'

With this decisive pronouncement, he left, nimbly avoiding the train of footmen carrying Miss Wyncroft's baggage into the rapidly shrinking hallway.

'Mrs Walker, our housekeeper, will show you to your room.' Mrs Buxted indicated a plump, middle-aged lady, standing by the staircase. 'I am sure you will want to rest a while after your journey.'

'Not at all, for I have travelled only a few hours today. We broke our journey in Godalming last night, rather than arrive with you in the evening.'

Mrs Buxted blinked.

'But of course I should like to freshen up. My abigail, Miss Priddy, will assist me.'

Miss Priddy, who was standing in the background clutching Charlotte's small jewel case, bobbed a curtsey to the Buxted ladies and joined her mistress in following the housekeeper—and two footmen,

laden with trunks—up the wide staircase. She was
a thin lady of indeterminate age and wore a plain
dimity gown in a sober Devonshire brown, buttoned
up to the neck. She had been with the Wyncroft
family since before Charlotte was born—initially
as maid to Charlotte's mother.

Charlotte's room was bright and spotlessly clean,
with a comfortable bed and a small fireplace. It was
decorated with pretty green hangings and over-
looked the street. Charlotte graciously thanked the
housekeeper and the two footmen, who then left to
fetch more baggage.

Charlotte waited for the door to close before
crossing to the window. Down below, it seemed all
of London was passing by. 'Oh, Priddy. I knew it—
this will be interesting.'

'Now, Miss Charlotte.'

'I declare, I like my Uncle Buxted. And Miss
Faith seemed friendly.' She frowned. 'I'm not sure
about my Aunt Buxted and Miss Henrietta. They
are shockingly plain-speaking—but perhaps ladies
are different in London. And did you hear what they
said as we arrived? They don't really want me.'

Priddy threw her a sharp look, but said nothing.

Charlotte stretched her arms above her head, glad
to be out of the rumbling carriage at last. It had
taken over a week to travel from Vienna, by easy
stages. Joseph, who had criss-crossed Europe many
times, had organised the best inns and the safest
routes. Although peace had been declared, there

were still pockets of trouble in France, and they had been accompanied on their journey by armed outriders.

Charlotte gazed thoughtfully at her abigail, who had opened one of the trunks and was tutting at the creases in a white silk gown.

'I have met many ladies of the *ton* in Vienna, and in Brussels, while their husbands were engaged in meetings, but I do not recall any who seemed so stiff—or so blunt—as the Buxted ladies. And everyone welcomed visitors—*always*. Are things so different here, or is it me they do not like?'

'You are in London now, miss. This is the heart of English society. Many things will be different. They have never met you before, so they cannot truly dislike you. Once they learn to know you, they must like you.'

'Oh, Priddy, I do hope you are right. I am so happy to be in London,' said Charlotte with a contented sigh. 'I have waited for this for so long. I've had years of parties and dinners with English people visiting Vienna, talking of things I knew nothing about—the English weather, the royal family, the countryside. Now I am finally in my home country. It is a new adventure, and I aim to make the most of it. All will be well, I am sure.'

Chapter Two

Charlotte spurred Andalusia to a canter. The breeze stung her cheeks and the afternoon sun sparkled on the Queen's Basin as she cantered through the meadow, savouring the exhilaration in her veins. At the end of the open field she slowed the mare to a gentle trot, allowing Joseph to catch up.

'I'll say this, Miss Charlotte,' said the groom who had taught her to ride amid Wellesley's Portuguese campaign, 'you know exactly how to handle her.'

'Yes, you enjoyed that, didn't you, Lusy? Just a pity we aren't allowed a full gallop,' said Charlotte, leaning forward to pat the mare's neck. 'I suppose we should be getting back, Joseph. We are to have visitors this afternoon and I am a little late.'

As they moved through the park towards Half-Moon Street Charlotte reflected on her first week in London. The Season was now in full swing, but Mrs Buxted disapproved of the 'carousing' involved. House parties, assemblies and balls were only to be tolerated, she had pronounced, in order to find suitable marriage partners for her daughters.

In her first two seasons Henrietta had been restricted to small gatherings and an occasional visit to Almack's. Not this year. Faith had shyly confided to Charlotte that 'Dear Mama' disapproved of some large social occasions, but with Henrietta still unmarried—and yet so beautiful—Mrs Buxted had conceded she might have to relax her normal strict avoidance of parties, balls and routs.

Privately, Charlotte had wondered *why* Henrietta was still unwed, despite being so beautiful. Had she spurned offers of marriage? Surely she had *had* offers?

'Mama wants only what is best for us,' Faith had said, 'which is why she wants us to beware of heedless pleasure. But I confess I am enjoying the silly vanities of ball-gowns and assemblies.'

'And so you should,' Charlotte had replied. 'For it is wonderful to dress up and go to parties. I declare there is a certain excitement about knowing one is going out, in planning what to wear and getting ready. I think many men feel the same, for they spend a lot of time on their hair, and their neckcloths, and their boots. At least, Papa does.'

Charlotte had been excluded from all the evening outings so far. As Mrs Buxted—a stickler for propriety—had explained, dear Charlotte had not yet been presented at Court. She was therefore to be excluded from large balls and routs, though she might attend small, informal events. Charlotte had heard this with great disappointment. She had been looking forward to many things in London—including *ton* parties—and had certainly not expected her life to be quite so restricted.

On her first evening in Buxted House, it had been made clear that Charlotte was to adapt to the needs of the family.

'Miss Charlotte,' Mrs Buxted had said. 'I am a straightforward person, and I pride myself on my honesty. We are well thought of in London. You are a Buxted by blood, although somewhat diluted by your father's family, the Wyncrofts, who were of lesser birth. I cannot imagine what your childhood was like, being raised by a widower in the train of the Army!'

Charlotte had opened her mouth to defend her darling papa, but Mrs Buxted had been insistent.

'No, I do not wish to hear what you have to say. You are in my charge now, and you will submit to me. I expect the highest standards of behaviour from you. I have spent many years preparing my girls for London society, and no one—least of all a nobody from Paris, or Vienna, or wherever you have been—will risk their future. Do you understand me?'

'Yes, Aunt.' Charlotte, chastened, had had no choice but to submit.

Her heart had sunk. Her time in London was to be a more rule-governed existence than the life she had lived abroad. This visit to London—that she had looked forward to with such excitement—would be more of a trial than an adventure, it seemed.

Her hopes of building friendships with her cousins also looked likely to be dashed—Faith was sweet, but slow-witted, and Henrietta seemed proud and vain. Their mother was probably well-meaning, but ruled the household with a will of iron.

Charlotte, unused to being disciplined quite so forcefully or bluntly, reminded herself that as a young person, and a guest in her aunt's house, she must be ruled by her aunt, no matter how much she hated it. She'd had no idea this would be her life here when she had persuaded her father to let her come. Now all she wanted was for Papa to rescue her from Buxted House.

Her eyes misted as she thought of Papa. There had been many times when they had been apart, but never for three whole months, and never with the sea in between them. He felt much further away than he had ever been. She cried sometimes, when feeling low, but always tried to cheer herself up again.

I'm trying to enjoy this, Papa. And I am trying to behave. But I miss you.

So far, she had done *quite* well. She had submitted to having a maid accompany her each time she left the house—apart from her morning ride, when she was accompanied by Joseph. General manners and conversation seemed little different, so she had avoided her aunt's criticism there. The toughest challenge so far had been a surprising one—she was expected to avoid seeming knowledgeable, and not to hold an opinion on anything of note.

'For a lady,' Aunt Buxted had advised, 'must not set herself to be higher in knowledge or understanding than a gentleman. Our weak feminine brains cannot cope with the complexities of knowledge, and to pretend to be well-informed is an unfortunate and unnecessary affectation. There is nothing worse than to be thought a bluestocking!'

This Charlotte found difficult. She was accustomed to the company of political and military men and women and had a great interest in politics. She also enjoyed reading.

Still, to please my aunt, she thought, *I can try to be dumb and stupid—at least while she is present. Papa would laugh if he saw me.*

Entering the house, she mounted the stairs, intending to go straight to her room to change. On the way, she heard Mrs Buxted's voice coming from the drawing room.

'Oh, where *is* the wretched girl?'

Charlotte hurried inside, her heart suddenly pounding. Mrs Buxted and her daughters were seated in full splendour—the mother on a throne-like winged chair, the girls on matching French *chaises*. The room had been redecorated recently in the French style, with delicate-looking gilded furniture and in colours of yellow, straw and gold. Faith had an embroidery tambour in her hand, while Henrietta was reading a book of sermons. They looked extremely proper.

Three pairs of eyes turned to her.

'Ah, *there* you are—and still in your riding habit. Go and change into something more appropriate. Quickly, girl! They will be here soon!'

'Of course, Aunt. I am sorry for being late.'

As Priddy helped her don a pretty half-dress of pale blue muslin, with a fashionable hem-frill and satin ribbon, Charlotte wondered aloud why her aunt was so anxious today. 'For we never had this much fuss for any of the other visitors I've met this week.'

'I'm sure I couldn't say.' Priddy sniffed. 'But some of the servants seem mightily interested in the young gentlemen visiting today.'

'Two brothers, Faith said—Adam and Harry Fanton. I know little about them.'

Priddy began tidying Charlotte's hair. 'One should never listen to gossip, but they say Mrs Buxted has her sights set on these gentlemen for her daughters. The elder—called Adam—is for Miss Henrietta—him being the Earl of Shalford, with an estate bordering the Buxteds'. They say he is on the lookout for a rich wife.'

'Oh! I am sure my aunt will be glad to see Miss Henrietta well settled.'

'Hrmphh! Well, your hair will just have to do.' Priddy stood back to admire her handiwork. 'Why did you go riding just before meeting visitors? Your face is quite red, girl.'

'Oh, do stop fussing, Priddy.' She flashed her abigail a quick smile before hurrying downstairs.

Too late!

As she approached the room she heard male voices. Pausing in the doorway to take in the scene, she was completely unaware of how fetching she looked, with her cheeks flushed and eyes bright from exercise. The ladies were still sitting stiffly, and had been joined by two handsome men—one in a coat of black superfine that looked moulded to his body, the other in regimentals. They rose immediately, and Mrs Buxted made the introductions.

'Miss Wyncroft, may I present the Earl of Shalford and his brother Captain Henry Fanton? This is Miss Charlotte Wyncroft. Her mother was Maria Buxted—my husband's cousin. Miss Wyncroft has been living abroad with her father, Colonel Sir Edward Wyncroft.'

Both gentlemen were tall and broad-shouldered, and it was clear to see they were brothers. Both had thick dark hair and handsome, striking faces. The Earl looked slightly older—maybe approaching thirty. His eyes were a piercing grey, and he observed Charlotte coolly. The Captain, in contrast, was all smiles. He showed a marked resemblance to his brother, though his eyes were blue, not grey, and he was perhaps a little shorter.

They made their bows, the Earl formally and unsmilingly and the Captain with a decided twinkle in his eyes. He spoke first.

'How long will you stay in London, Miss Wyncroft?'

'I am not certain. My father, you see, is in Paris.'

At this his brother, who had retaken his seat beside Henrietta, looked up. 'He is with Castlereagh?'

The Captain laughed. 'My brother knows them all, Miss Wyncroft. He has taken up his seat this year and finds he has a taste for politics.'

'I too, have an interest in politics—though I know little about what goes on in the Palace of Westminster. My education has been on the continent— we lived in Austria most recently—and I am sadly lacking in knowledge of our own internal politics, save that which we poor *émigrées* must pick up from our visitors.'

She turned to the Earl, who was listening with attention.

'I was with Papa—and Lord Castlereagh—until two weeks ago, when I left for England.'

'My cousin has not lived much in England, Lord Shalford,' said Henrietta. 'She is quite the foreigner.'

'You must excuse her tardiness,' added Mrs Buxted. 'She was out riding and has yet to learn the importance of being ready for expected guests.'

Charlotte, unusually, was for a moment lost for words.

The Captain came to her rescue. 'Oh, a lady after my own heart, then. I know what it is to enjoy a good outing on a dry, clear day such as this.'

Charlotte smiled gratefully. 'Indeed, I enjoy riding immensely, and I miss it when I have not been out for a few days. My Uncle Buxted has kindly stabled my mare.'

'You have brought your own horse, then? From Austria?' Captain Fanton gazed at her intently.

'Yes, though we got her in Spain. Her name is Andalusia—and she is a darling.'

'I should like to see her. My brother and I ride most days. Perhaps I—or we—could accompany you on one of your rides?'

'You can—if you can keep up.' She twinkled at him.

'That sounds uncommonly like a challenge, does it not, Adam?

'Indeed.' The Earl removed a tiny speck of dust from his sleeve.

'I admit I cannot resist a challenge. I shall call upon you tomorrow, Miss Wyncroft, if you are amenable.'

'I don't think I am amenable at all, but I shall ride with you tomorrow, Captain Fanton.'

Captain Fanton dipped his head in appreciation, while his brother crossed one muscular leg over the other and remained silent.

'Faith enjoys riding—do you not, Faith?' Mrs Buxted interjected loudly, drawing all eyes to her younger daughter.

Faith, unfortunately, had just taken a small bite of cake, and almost choked at her mother's question.

After some coughing, and sips of tea, she recovered enough to confirm that, yes, she enjoyed riding.

Charlotte refrained from raising a brow. The Buxted ladies' idea of riding was no more than a sedate walk, from what she had seen. On two occasions, when the family had had no evening engagements, Charlotte and her cousins had gone for an early-evening ride to Rotten Row in Hyde Park.

The Buxted horses were staid and placid—Papa would have dismissed them immediately as packhorses—and they had not even broken into a trot. Both Henrietta and Faith seemed decidedly nervous around horses. Their ride had not been at all energetic, and Charlotte, who had a great deal of liveliness, had found it frustrating.

Their evening promenades were simply a chance to see and to be seen. Many members of the *ton* were usually there, and Charlotte had been introduced to some of the Buxteds' acquaintances. Today, however, was her first encounter with the Earl of Shalford and his brother.

As Henrietta engaged the Earl in quiet conversation, and Mrs Buxted talked briskly to the Captain and Faith about mutual acquaintances, Charlotte took the opportunity to study the two men a little more closely.

Lord Shalford—the Earl—was tall, dark and distant. His demeanour was disengaged, verging on bored. His grey eyes had displayed complete indifference to Charlotte, which amused her. He was listening politely to Henrietta, though. Charlotte suppressed a smile. The Earl clearly preferred sedate, dutiful, blonde ladies, who arrived on time and were fashionably pale.

The Captain seemed much more likeable. His open countenance and smiling blue eyes reminded her of many young officers she had met through her father's career. Since her seventeenth birthday, when she had been home from school, she had acted as her father's hostess at dinners, parties and even a grand ball. It felt strange to act the debutante again—although here in London that was exactly what she was.

Lord Shalford addressed his hostess. 'We have come today with a specific purpose in mind.'

'Adam, *must* you be so formal?' His brother laughed.

'It seems I must, Harry,' replied the Earl. 'As you may know, Mrs Buxted, since my father's death last year I have been busy with paperwork, death duties, and ensuring that my father's—that is to say, *my* estate—is well-managed and that I understand its workings. As the eldest son I had naturally already had some dealings with my father's steward, but I still have much to learn.'

'Indeed—and I am sure the estate is safe in your more than capable hands.' Mrs Buxted showed a smile which did not quite reach her eyes. A gleam of curiosity lit them, making her look strangely calculating for a second.

'Well, only time will show. But to the purpose of my visit today—'

'Yes, *do* get on with it, Adam.'

The Captain made a childish face at Charlotte, whose eyes danced in mischievous response. Their exchange was noted, causing Charlotte a moment's discomfort as the Earl's grey eyes pierced her with a keen glance.

She raised her eyebrows, undaunted, though she was assailed by the unexpected memory of old Lord Carmby, an arrogant diplomat who had crossed Charlotte's path in Vienna. His caustic put-downs had alienated all who knew him there. He had once called Charlotte *'a forward, opinionated brat'* when she had daringly questioned his views on a political matter. Luckily, Papa had not been within earshot. *Hmmm…* She hadn't been made to feel like a child for a long time. Anger began to burn in her chest.

'Now we are out of mourning, I think it is important for the family—indeed, for everyone at Chadcombe—that we resume normality. My father was ill for a long time, and as you may know my mother died three years before him. So I have decided to invite a small party of friends to Chadcombe after Parliament rises. My great-aunt—Miss Langley—has kindly agreed to act as hostess. I would be delighted if you and your family—and your guest, of course—' he glanced at Charlotte '—would agree to visit.'

'Visit Chadcombe?' Henrietta came to life, an excited smile lighting her face.

Mrs Buxted sent a quelling glance to her elder daughter. 'Of course we should be *delighted* to visit Chadcombe. It is an age since we were in Surrey—almost a year ago, I believe. We have not visited Monkton Park since last summer. To stay in Chadcombe would be unusual, since our estates are so close together, but we are grateful for your invitation.'

Henrietta explained to Charlotte. 'My grandfather's sister left Monkton Park to us two years ago. It adjoins Chadcombe's lands to the east.'

Mrs Buxted continued. 'We inspected the place when my aunt died, and have visited occasionally.' She turned to Lord Shalford. 'We could not call on the third Earl—your father—because of his illness. Monkton Park is a pretty little estate, though we prefer our main home, near Melton Mowbray. Monkton Park has been left to whichever of our daughters is married first, although the old lady positively *doted* on dear Henrietta.'

Henrietta smiled slightly.

'Of course that question has never been in doubt, for Henrietta is the elder…and so pretty. My aunt clearly intended *she* should have the estate. And so she shall—just as soon as she is married!'

The room was silent. Charlotte looked down at her own hands, which were clasped so tightly the knuckles were white.

Aunt Buxted, oblivious, continued after a pause. 'I shall of course check with Mr Buxted, but I am almost certain we have as yet no fixed engagements for July.'

Henrietta said nothing, but Charlotte, glancing across, saw a triumphant gleam in her eyes. This, then, was what she wanted.

'Excellent,' said the Earl. Turning to Henrietta, who quickly adopted an innocent, guileless expression, he added, 'And you, Miss Buxted? Will *you* be happy to visit my home?'

'Indeed I shall, Lord Shalford.' Her voice was quiet, well-modulated, gentle.

The Earl nodded approvingly—satisfied, it seemed, with her muted response.

Charlotte suppressed a smile. If he had seen Henrietta earlier, shouting shrilly at Faith about a length of ribbon, he might not be so sanguine. Charlotte had been glad to go riding, simply to avoid the tantrum. Henrietta, she had realised, was much indulged by Mrs Buxted, and as the elder—and prettier—daughter, held prime importance in her mother's mind.

The pliant Faith was expected to sacrifice any treat or privilege if Miss Henrietta desired it strongly enough. Including, it seemed, the chance to marry an earl. Charlotte had gently suggested that Faith be stronger in standing up for herself. Faith, admitting she was easily crushed by unkindness, had vowed to try.

The men took their leave a few moments later, as was correct. The Captain bowed to Charlotte, ex-

pressing the wish to see her again soon, while Lord
Shalford nodded his head perfunctorily. Mrs Buxted
watched closely, her eyes narrowed.

When they had gone, she turned immediately to
Henrietta in triumph. 'My dear Henrietta, this *is*
good news.' She smiled sweetly at her elder daughter. 'We are all included, but it is clear the invitation
is especially for you. If you make the most of this
opportunity, he will declare himself at Chadcombe.'

'Oh, Mama. He did ask me *particularly* if I
should enjoy visiting his home, did he not? Just
think—Chadcombe. The Fanton estate. And I am
to be mistress of it!'

'Now, my dear, do not think you have already
won him. You must secure him first. Though I dare
say any man in England would be delighted to wed
you—with your beauty, your pedigree, and your
ladylike demeanour.'

And your property! Charlotte thought, then
chided herself for being uncharitable. Monkton Park
was clearly part of the marriage deal. And with a
handsome dowry as an added sweetener, Henrietta
would be an attractive prospect to any suitor.

Priddy had told Charlotte already that the Buxteds' Melton Mowbray estate, as well as the townhouse, was entailed on Mr Buxted's heir—a distant
cousin living in Leicester with a wife and a brood
of children—so there would be nothing for Faith
apart from her dowry.

Charlotte reflected that the Fantons did not *look*

as if they were in need of rich wives—they behaved with the confidence of the wealthy, and their clothes were of the finest quality—but money was certainly a consideration for many men looking for a bride on the marriage mart.

She did not know what her own dowry was to be. The question was not one which had much occupied her. But since arriving in London, and seeing the Buxteds' preoccupation with weddings and dowries and money, she had abruptly realised she did not exactly know how wealthy her father was. Living in different places across the continent, they had always seemed to have enough money, and she had never wanted for anything.

Her aunt, it seemed, knew more about it than she did herself.

'I have asked my husband about your dowry, Charlotte,' she had said bluntly after dinner last night. 'He tells me that he imagines your fortune will be modest, due to debts from your grandfather. He believes Sir Edward will have put away a little money over the years, out of his soldier's pay, but he is sure it is not a substantial amount.'

Charlotte had been taken aback by her aunt's frankness. Papa never talked about money, and it had never been clear to her how much independent wealth he had. There was the family home in Shawfield, which she had not seen since she was twelve, and which had been rented out for many years. She vaguely remembered talk of mortgages, and had formed the impression that her grandfather had not been prudent with money—which fitted with the Buxteds' conclusions.

In Austria, Herr Lenz, Papa's man of business, had certainly been exceptionally active on his behalf, but Charlotte simply did not know exactly how things stood. Nor had she thought about it until now. This was the effect of being in England and seeing Aunt Buxted's blatant manoeuvrings on behalf of her daughters.

Papa had made a banker's draft over to Uncle Buxted for Charlotte's pin money and expenses in London, and had offered to pay for the stabling of her horse, though this had been politely declined by Uncle Buxted. Her uncle had written to Papa just before Charlotte had left for England, to say he would not accept a penny for Charlotte's keep, but would be happy to act as banker for her during her stay.

Charlotte wondered now if her uncle had been trying to be kind, if he thought Papa could not afford to pay. Her back stiffened and she tightened her lips.

'Oh, Mama! Did you notice how he looked at me? And how he asked me *particularly* if I should be happy to visit? He had eyes for no one else.'

Henrietta's excited voice brought Charlotte back to the present. Her cousin was flushed with success, and Charlotte guessed there would be little else talked of today.

Suddenly unable to stomach Henrietta's glee, Charlotte excused herself, saying she needed to practise her music. Walking lightly down the stairs on her way to the morning room, which housed a fine pianoforte, she was surprised to see the two gentlemen only just leaving. They had clearly been waiting for their carriage to be brought round. The brothers did not see her, but she was able to hear a snatch of conversation between them as they left the house.

'…guest is a charming girl.'

'Perhaps—though she is a little impudent. Another silly girl, like all the rest.'

'Really, Adam, at least she shows spirit. I cannot understand how you can prefer—'

Impudent? Silly? Such was the Earl's opinion of her? There could be no other possible interpretation.

Oh, I hope he marries Henrietta! she thought, and images of marital disharmony momentarily soothed her wounded pride before she was struck by the ridiculousness of the situation and, laughing to herself, continued on her way.

Chapter Three

***

True to his word, Captain Fanton arrived at Buxted House the next morning on a well-balanced grey stallion. Unexpectedly, his older brother was with him, also mounted on an impressive thoroughbred—though his was all black, and sidling impatiently outside the house.

Charlotte's heart sank. The Arrogant Earl!

'Hold, Velox,' he said, turning the stallion in circles to quiet him.

They had timed their call well, for Charlotte had just left the house for her morning ride with her groom. She was wearing a dashing riding habit in dark blue velvet, finished with fashionable military epaulettes and silver buttons. Her striking outfit was completed by a tall shako set at a rakish angle.

'You look charming, Miss Wyncroft,' said the Captain, his eyes full of admiration as she mounted Andalusia with Joseph's assistance. 'And your mare is a fine specimen. Do your cousins accompany us?'

'Not today—though they did express a wish to ride on another morning. I am sorry to disappoint you. They have gone shopping.'

Though if Henrietta had known the Earl would come...

'Ah, the favourite pastime of females.'

The Earl was all politeness but, remembering his opinion of her yesterday, Charlotte could not ignore the implied criticism.

'Not me,' she said, 'I am most unnatural, I fear.'

Joseph, now mounted, followed them as they moved slowly towards the park.

'What? Do you not enjoy shopping at all?' asked the Earl. 'It seems to me that young women, when they are not flirting or gossiping, are talking about ribbons and hats and fashion plates.'

Charlotte bit back the retort which was on the tip of her tongue, instead asking mildly, 'And do you not take pleasure in seeing a well-dressed lady?'

'Of course. A beautiful lady is an ornament to be admired!'

An *ornament*! 'And can we be more?'

He looked confused.

Amused, she gave him a sunny smile, and he blinked.

'I enjoy dressing well, Lord Shalford—as I think you do, too.' She swept her eyes over his tight-fitting buckskins, well-made coat and highly polished boots. 'In order for we ladies to be well turned out, we do not rely on our tailor and our valet. We must consider, and design, and choose the best fabrics, dressmakers and milliners, and we also have to worry about how things will match. There is no little skill in it.'

He considered this. 'So the enjoyment of shopping is a necessity?'

'In a way. Many ladies enjoy it, but it cannot be described as the favourite pastime of *all* females, for it is certainly not *my* favourite. I had much rather be out like this, riding, than stuck in a haberdashery.'

He looked sceptical, but let it pass.

Captain Fanton, as if surprised by his brother's garrulity, intervened. 'You are certainly unusual, Miss Wyncroft. Tell me, is it because of your upbringing in military circles?'

Charlotte, pleased with her small victory over the Arrogant Earl, smiled at Harry. 'I suppose so. I have been around military and diplomatic families my whole life. I was born in Portugal, and I have lived in many different places. It was, I think, a good childhood—though I don't know anything else.'

'And you speak Portuguese?'

'Yes. I'm afraid I can speak French, German, Italian, Spanish *and* Portuguese. It is a terrible thing, I know, to be thought a bluestocking, when in reality I never *learned* any of them, I just…*knew* them.'

'Perfectly understandable,' said the Captain. 'Fear not, I should not take you for a bluestocking. Why, bluestockings are dowdy!'

Charlotte laughed. 'I must thank you both for including me in your invitation to Chadcombe—even if I may be seen as a bluestocking. I am looking forward to it. It is in Surrey, I believe?'

'Yes,' said the Earl, 'between Godalming and Guildford. There have been Fantons there for nearly four hundred years.'

'Godalming—I stayed at a posting inn there on my way to London. I thought it a most pretty town. They are building a new town hall with a pepper-pot roof.'

'That's it. It replaces the old market house, which has stood there since the Middle Ages.'

'And is your house—er—medieval?'

The Earl's eyes narrowed. 'Now, Miss Wyncroft, I think you are trying to fence with me. Are you asking me the age of the house, or whether it is ancient, decrepit and devoid of modern conveniences?'

She laughed lightly. 'Is it not the same thing?'

'No, it is not—and you know it! To answer both your questions…the original medieval house is now used for stabling. My grandfather built the present house—and nearly went bankrupt doing so. It was his obsession.' His eyes fired a challenge to hers. 'It has modern water closets *and* a new closed oven.'

'I shall simply die from excitement! A *closed oven*! Why, I have never seen such a thing!'

The Captain, observing their repartee with some amazement, said, 'Miss Wyncroft, if I had known you were so interested in domestic devices I should have invited you to tour an oven-maker's or some such thing.'

'Oh, please don't. I much prefer this ride in Green Park. Tell me, Captain, do you spend much time at Chadcombe?'

'I am there when I can be. These few years, since our mother died and our father became ill, have been difficult. I have been away with my regiment for most of the past two years. Much of the burden has rested on Adam's shoulders.'

His brother nodded, acknowledging the truth of the Captain's words. 'My father worked hard to restore our fortunes, and the stability of the estate, but was ill for the last years of his life and unable to give the necessary attention to the estate. My task is to make sure the place can thrive once again. There are many families—not just ours—who rely on it.'

'I just wish you could relax and enjoy life once in a while, Adam.'

'I am content, Harry. I do not need to.'

'Agreed. But you might enjoy it.'

Charlotte felt a twinge of unexpected sympathy. Lord Shalford had put duty first. This she understood. Even if the man *was* horribly proud and judgemental. And arrogant.

The Captain turned to Charlotte again. 'Miss Wyncroft, tell me—when you were with the Army, did you perhaps meet my friend Captain Jack Harris? We served with the Thirtieth, in the Peninsula.'

'You mean Parson Jack?'

'Lord, that soubriquet followed him everywhere! Such a prosy fellow, but with a good heart.'

'In the Peninsula he was always in the company of Captain Burnett.'

'Yes. We three were best friends at school. Did you also meet Major Cooke?'

'I did—many times. He is a particular friend of my father.'

She and Captain Fanton continued to converse easily as they progressed to Green Park, while Lord Shalford remained silent, watching them.

The Captain was keen to establish who Charlotte knew of his military friends, and to share impressions of places they had both visited. Charlotte laughingly fended off his questions, enjoying his relaxed manner and humorous tales. He reminded her so much of the young soldiers she had known in Vienna—they had been like younger brothers to her.

'I remember one time, near Ciudad Rodrigo, when some of my men dressed a pig in full regimentals. Lord, such a to-do! But many are gone now.' He fell momentarily silent.

'Were you at Badajoz, then?' she asked softly, remembering the difficult time during and after the siege.

'Yes, we were all there. It didn't end well.' A shadow crossed his face. 'But let us not dwell on it. Today the sun shines and we are out for a ride. Where can we let the horses have their heads?'

'Well, this is the spot where I usually enjoy a canter—from here to the end of this meadow.'

'Then let's ride!'

The Captain spurred his horse and they all set off.

Cantering easily, the Captain moved slightly ahead. About halfway across the meadow he eased back, allowing Charlotte and the Earl to catch up. Joseph followed at an easier pace. The brothers were both good horsemen, and Charlotte was enjoying the thrill of the ride in their company. Charlotte and the Captain were now neck-and-neck, while the Earl eased back slightly. Somehow, Charlotte reached the end of the meadow first.

'You let me win!' she accused the Captain, as Lord Shalford reached them, two lengths behind. Joseph, on his Buxted hack, was last to catch up.

'I? No!' The Captain laughed.

'I wish you hadn't. I do like to win, but only when I play fair.' She turned to the Earl, tilting her head to one side. 'Don't you think it's terrible when someone lets you win?'

'It depends,' he said, giving her question serious consideration. 'For example, just now I let both of you win.'

His eyes were definitely smiling. Charlotte noticed they crinkled up at the sides in a most interesting manner. She frowned—she didn't want to find anything likeable about the Arrogant Earl.

'Adam, you wretch,' said the Captain. 'You just won't admit you couldn't catch me.'

The men continued with their light-hearted banter as they all picked their way back through the grasses, evoking childhood contests lost and won, and Charlotte felt amused—and a little envious—as she listened.

'How I should have loved to have a brother or sister, to tease and be teased like this!' she said as they paused in their recollections. 'Do you have any other brothers and sisters?'

'We have a sister—Olivia,' said Lord Shalford. 'She is seventeen, and not yet out. She lives quietly at Chadcombe. That is one of the reasons why I have invited you all to stay. I believe she needs the company of women.'

'My papa said the same to me, when we talked about my visit to London. I have no sisters, although my school friend Juliana is almost like a sister to me.'

'Olivia has friends too, but I think—I *hope*—she will enjoy the company of other ladies. Ladies younger than my great-aunt, who is a most admirable lady, but…' He hesitated.

'She is not the best companion for a seventeen-year-old girl,' finished the Captain.

Charlotte reminded herself of the other reasons the Earl had for inviting the Buxted family. This would be a test—to assess Henrietta as a possible bride. Her substantial dowry—and Monkton Park—would surely assist his restoration of the family's estates.

The Earl clearly felt a strong sense of duty to his heritage. Marrying well was a logical step. Henrietta was the right age, of good family, and had a handsome dowry. It was a sensible match, Charlotte thought wistfully. An exceptionally sensible match.

Arriving back at the house after their ride, Charlotte was rather alarmed to find Henrietta waiting for her. Her cousin's expression was grim.

'A word with you, if you please!' she said, turning on her heel and making for the drawing room.

Charlotte followed her up the wide staircase, feeling like a naughty child. She lifted her chin.

Aunt Buxted and Faith were already in the room. Faith looked uncomfortable, but she sent Charlotte a tremulous smile. Mrs Buxted, who was mending a petticoat, lifted her eyes briefly to acknowledge Charlotte, then returned to her work.

'Good day,' said Charlotte, generally. 'Did you enjoy your shopping trip while I was riding?'

'Charlotte!' Henrietta's voice was sharp. She stood before the door, tapping one small foot in an agitated way. 'The servants have let slip that you were out riding with Lord Shalford and the Captain.'

'Indeed I was. There is no secret about it. You heard the Captain arrange it yesterday. I confess I did not realise Lord Shalford would be there.'

Henrietta pursed her lips.

Charlotte removed her hat. There was a gilded mirror above the fireplace. She walked across and smoothed her hair, checking her reflection in the glass. Unfortunately, she had to stand on tiptoes in order to do so, which perhaps spoiled the impression of calm poise.

'I had a most enjoyable time,' she continued. 'They are well-informed and pleasant gentlemen, I think.' She turned to face the ladies. 'You should come next time. You would enjoy the conversation, I believe.'

'You went out riding with *two men*!' Two spots of unbecoming colour had appeared on Henrietta's cheeks and her breathing had quickened. 'I do not know—nor do I *wish* to know—what customs prevail in Spain, or France, or any other heathen, uncivilised place, but in London you would do well to avoid seeming *fast*.'

Charlotte raised her eyebrows, but answered calmly. 'My dear Henrietta, I appreciate your concern, but I was very properly accompanied by my groom, so I believe my reputation is intact.'

'Your—your groom?' Henrietta's mouth opened, then closed again. 'I—I see. I did not know...'

Her eyes darted around the room as she searched for something to say.

'Hrmmph! Well, on this occasion—with your groom—you may have managed to stay on the right side of acceptable maidenly behaviour... But you know I am only trying to help you.'

She smiled weakly, but her eyes told a different story.

Charlotte moved away, placing her hat upon an ornate side table. Her hand shook a little. There was no point in arguing with Henrietta—much as she longed to do so.

'The gentlemen were most disappointed you did not ride today.'

'They were? What did he—they—say? Did he—they—mention me?' Henrietta's voice was small.

'The Earl talked about his sister, Olivia. He hopes for female companionship for her, I think.'

Mrs Buxted, who had held her tongue during Henrietta's outburst, spoke dispassionately to her elder daughter. 'My love, you must befriend the sister. And you *should* have gone riding today. But there is no need to worry about competition from your cousin.'

Charlotte blinked. She knew—and did not mind—that Henrietta was the prettiest young lady in the household. Her golden hair and deep blue eyes captivated attention wherever they went. Strangers sometimes turned their heads in the street when Henrietta passed by. At present, though, her cousin's beauty was somewhat marred by her petulant expression. And for Aunt Buxted to speak so plainly was, Charlotte thought, unnecessary—though hardly surprising.

'I will certainly go next time.' Mollified, Henrietta patted her side-curls, eyeing Charlotte's fashionable habit. 'I need a new habit from Milton's, Mama. Can they make it up in a week?'

'I'm sure they can, if I require it. We shall go to-morrow.'

'Mama,' said Faith tentatively, 'you said *I* was to get a new habit, for my old one is now a little too small. Should I go with Henrietta?'

'No, I do not want her distracting them. *My* habit must be perfect!' said Henrietta.

'But, Mama—'

'Don't listen to her, Mama. I missed the ride today and *everything*. I must have a *perfect* habit!'

'I will take you another time, Faith.'

'Yes, Mama,' Faith submitted, though her voice trembled a little.

Charlotte threw her a sympathetic look.

'Did you arrange to ride with them again?' Henrietta asked Charlotte sharply, oblivious to her sister's disappointment.

'Yes—next Tuesday morning. I said I hoped you would both also ride then.'

'Well, at least you did *something* right.' Henrietta was back at the glass, turning her head this way and that, preening slightly. 'And we shall see them at Lady Cowper's ball on Friday. Oh, but of course—*you* can't come, Charlotte.' She smiled sweetly. 'What a *pity* you have not been presented at Court. You miss all the most exciting parties! It must be so dull—being limited to small gatherings. No routs, no balls, no Almack's.'

'Oh, it is perfectly fine.' Charlotte smiled through

gritted teeth. 'I have much to amuse myself with. I shall probably write another letter to Papa.'

'Yes, and so you should. One must know one's duty.'

'I do—though it is not duty that makes me wish to write to my father. We are good friends.'

'*Friends?* With your father? How strange.' She wrinkled her nose. 'You know, Charlotte, you really should change. You smell of horse.'

'Er...yes, thank you, Henrietta.' Charlotte refrained from reminding her cousin that *she* had intercepted her and delayed her from changing. She picked up her hat again.

'Oh, I do try to be helpful to people when I can,' said Henrietta, with a little flutter of her hand. 'Mama says it is helpful to point out people's flaws, so they may correct them.'

Mrs Buxted nodded approvingly. 'You have learned well, Henrietta. It is not enough to be virtuous oneself. One must also help others where one can. Charlotte, you would do well to take Henrietta as your pattern card. She is a perfect example of a well-brought up noble lady.'

'I shall certainly observe her closely, Aunt Buxted.'

Charlotte left the room quickly, her fists clenched and her heart beating hard. Oh, Henrietta and Aunt Buxted were infuriating!

Chapter Four

Dinner on Friday—the evening of Lady Cowper's ball—was a trial. Aunt Buxted had invited the Fanton brothers, as well as her godson, Mr Foxley, to dine with them, though Henrietta had complained at length about Mr Foxley's presence.

'I know he is your godson, Mama, and his mother was your old school friend, but he is dull and clumsy and cannot make interesting conversation. And besides, he is only a second son, with no great fortune.'

'Captain Fanton is a second son, but you like *him* well enough.' The quiet Faith, for once, was inspired to challenge her sister.

Bravissima! thought Charlotte. *Good for you, Faith.*

'Yes, though not as well as his brother. The Captain will do well for *you*, Faith, if you can secure him. Besides, he is a *Fanton*. Mr Foxley is a—a nobody.'

Mrs Buxted intervened. 'Yes, my love, but he

is a well-mannered gentleman, and since we have
Charlotte we will need another gentleman to make
up the numbers.'

Henrietta threw Charlotte a resentful look. 'Perhaps Charlotte would prefer to eat something in her
room. After all, she is not even going to the ball.'

Into the silence that followed Charlotte said quietly, 'I would be quite happy to have a meal alone
on Friday, ma'am. I should not wish to cause inconvenience.'

Mrs Buxted turned a page in her fashion journal.

'Mama—' Faith spoke up, distressed. 'You *cannot* send Charlotte to her room. Why, she is a *guest*!'

'I shall do no such thing, Faith. I know my duty
to my guest.' She thought for a moment, then looked
at her elder daughter. 'Henrietta, when you are mistress of Chadcombe there will be times when you
will be forced to entertain unwanted guests, or have
people to stay or to dine against your wishes. You
will at all times conduct yourself with dignity, and
do your duty to your husband and your name.'

'My *husband*!' breathed Henrietta. She considered this. 'As you say, Mama, I will have many such
trials to endure when I am a married lady—a countess. Charlotte may come to dinner.'

Charlotte—with great difficulty—said nothing.
It was becoming daily more challenging to survive
the barbs thrown at her. She knew that Henrietta
would like nothing more than for her to retaliate, as
this would expose Charlotte to Aunt Buxted's wrath.

Behind Henrietta, Faith held her face in her hands, shaking her head. Charlotte, remembering something she needed from her room, excused herself and left. Really, it was becoming harder and harder to bite her tongue.

The invitations were delivered, the acceptances received, and the menu planned. They were to have turtle—a rare delicacy—as well as white soup, partridges with leeks, turbot, a ragout of veal and a selection of blancmanges, fruits and ices. Mrs Buxted spent hours with Cook, planning and organising the finer points, and the housekeeper organised a major cleaning of the dining room. The butler ensured the silver was polished and shining, and the footmen were perfectly presented and well drilled. The staff were well aware that this was a special dinner.

Charlotte, on whom the lack of society was beginning to tell, enjoyed the preparations for the evening. She was not able to go to the ball, but at least she could have her hair dressed and wear one of her evening gowns. Priddy teased and styled her hair so that her Grecian topknot was perfect and her glossy brown curls were perfectly arranged to frame her face. She wore a cornflower-blue gauze dress over a delicate white silk underdress, made for her in Vienna.

She checked herself in the mirror, and was content. Priddy was more than content.

'You'll outshine your cousins tonight, Miss Charlotte, upon my word!'

'Of course I won't, Priddy. They are angels of the highest order, according to their many admirers. Well, so Henrietta tells me.'

'And you are an angel too, Miss Charlotte.'

'But one with *dark* hair, Priddy. I am banished to the lower order of angels, whatever that may be.' She had always accepted that she was pretty, but that other girls could be prettier. She would not allow Henrietta's poison to change that.

Mr Foxley was first to arrive. He was a soberly dressed young gentleman, with a pleasant, open face and a shy smile, and Charlotte warmed to him immediately. Faith, who was looking beautiful in a dress of pale lavender crêpe dotted with clusters of pearl beads blushed and stammered a little when greeting him.

Henrietta and Mrs Buxted acknowledged him politely, if briefly, as their attention was focused on waiting for their remaining guests, while Mr Buxted also seemed distracted, checking the wines Biddle was to serve. Food and drink was of the highest importance to him, and he could talk for extended periods on port, sauces, and the best accompaniments to a squab pie.

Mr Foxley sat with Charlotte and Faith, conversing quietly and sensibly. He showed great interest in Charlotte's life abroad, the war and the diplomatic efforts to support the coalition. He also knew just how to put Faith at ease, with gentle comments and enquiries. He was, Charlotte discovered, a scholar at heart, and he told them he liked nothing more than reading a good book in his library—or outside, if the weather permitted it.

Charlotte agreed. 'I think there is nothing better than to sit in a beautiful place reading. In Vienna, I frequently sat in our garden, among the rose bushes, but my father always knew where to find me. Where do *you* like to read?'

'My parents' house in Kent has a small park— and a walled garden which is wonderful for trapping the sun's rays even in springtime. They have had seats placed there, amid the greenery, and I confess I like nothing better than to sit there with a good text.'

'It sounds pleasant,' said Faith. 'I love to sit in comfort in a beautiful setting, too.'

He smiled warmly at her. 'I do admire beauty.'

Faith smiled shyly and looked down in some confusion, a hint of pink in her cheeks.

Biddle entered, announcing the arrival of the Earl and the Captain. Both were attired in full evening dress, and with their good looks and imposing figures presented an admirable picture. They were both in formal knee breeches, waistcoats and coats of dark superfine. The Earl, who nodded briefly to Charlotte as his eyes swept the room, wore a black coat over a snowy-white silk waistcoat, and his neckcloth was intricately tied in the style known as the Waterfall.

He clearly had an eye for fashion, thought Charlotte, despite his disdain for female shopping. His tailor, though, had the benefit of the Earl's fine muscular figure to work with. No stays, laces or shoulder padding were needed for *this* gentleman. There would no doubt be a great deal of excitement at the ball later, when the two brothers made their entrance. She glanced at Henrietta, whose eyes were fixed with a cool hunger on Lord Shalford. Charlotte looked away. Her spoiled cousin and the Arrogant Earl deserved each other!

The gentlemen bowed and greeted their host and hostess, before acknowledging Mr Foxley and the young ladies. Charlotte curtseyed correctly, and murmured a polite greeting. Henrietta—looking ravishing in a white silk gown trimmed with ruffles and flounces—immediately claimed Lord Shalford, asking him about the ball, exclaiming about how much she was looking forward to it, and hoping it wouldn't be too much of a squeeze.

The Earl, unperturbed, responded calmly, and requested her hand for the first dance—at which she simpered, giggled and accepted.

Mrs Buxted was all graciousness, welcoming them to what she described as 'a little informal dinner'. She patted the Captain's arm. 'For we are all friends now, and you should feel at ease in our humble home.'

The seating arrangements had been carefully worked out. Henrietta was seated between Lord Shalford and Mr Foxley while, opposite, the Captain had Faith on one hand and Charlotte on the other.

'It is important that you have the chance to talk to them during dinner, girls,' Mrs Buxted had pronounced. 'Faith, I have been focusing on Henrietta and the Earl, but I have noticed you are not trying hard enough to fix the Captain. You are a pretty girl, though not as beautiful as Henrietta, and with a little effort I am sure you can secure him. I will be most displeased if I see you sitting silently.'

'Yes, Mama,' Faith had replied, trembling and twisting her handkerchief between her hands.

Conscious of her mother's instructions, Faith was now making careful conversation with the Captain, who was seated on Charlotte's left. Mr Buxted, on Charlotte's right, was focused on his turbot and partridges.

'Delightful! Wonderful seasoning!' he muttered to himself, immersed in the enjoyment of his dinner.

This gave Charlotte the opportunity to observe her fellow diners. The Captain seemed relaxed and comfortable, but he was not having much success in drawing Faith out. She answered his queries politely enough, but there was no animation. If the Captain was bored, he hid it well. Faith, anxious to avoid her mother's displeasure, was tongue-tied, so the conversation remained stilted. It was difficult to watch.

Mr Foxley, who was opposite Charlotte, was also suffering from a lack of conversation. He had the felicity of being seated between Mr Buxted and Henrietta, neither of whom were offering him attention. He ate sparingly and, though he tried to disguise it, his focus kept being drawn to Faith and Captain Fanton.

Mrs Buxted was smiling approvingly as her two daughters held the attention of the Fantons. Charlotte shamelessly listened in on each exchange. Nothing of note was being discussed. Nothing interesting, nothing meaningful. *Nothing.*

She had sat through enough society dinners to know this was usual—even commonplace. Even by those standards, however, the lack of insight and intelligence being displayed by the two Buxted ladies was positively shocking. Perhaps, she thought, girls in England were brought up to be so sheltered and protected it meant they had no opinions to offer—at least in public.

The Captain seemed perfectly comfortable to continue to extract some little conversation from the shy Faith—currently on the topic of how best to get through a long coach journey. On the far side of the table Henrietta was prosing on about correct behaviour for young ladies, and how grateful she was to have a dear mother who had taught her exactly how to go on.

The Earl's eyes were positively glazing over, Charlotte thought, trying to hide her amusement. Her eyes danced with mischief—just as he looked up and caught her gaze. Although discovered, she would not hide, and instead continued to twinkle at him impishly. Surprisingly, he responded with an unthinking, companionable smile of his own before checking himself.

Too late! Henrietta had caught the spontaneous interaction between them. Her eyes blazed.

'For an *English* upbringing,' she said loudly, drawing all eyes to her, 'is infinitely better than a savage youth spent among soldiers and foreigners. Don't you agree, Lord Shalford?'

Chapter Five

Sudden silence surrounded the table as the shock of Henrietta's rude comment was felt. It was clearly directed at Charlotte, though it was not obvious to the other diners what had triggered the attack. The Earl looked confused, as if wondering what was going on between the cousins.

Charlotte, despite what she knew of Henrietta's spoiled behaviour, was stunned—and surprised that her cousin had exposed herself so blatantly. The exchange between herself and the Earl had been a spontaneous, meaningless moment—nothing to threaten Henrietta's position as the Earl's target of interest.

Henrietta was so self-involved—and yet so un-certain of herself. She thought nothing of behaving in an aggressive, unladylike and hurtful fashion. Charlotte, whose own anger had now been roused, was sorely tempted to retort in like manner, but she could not. To respond—even to speak directly across the table—would be ill-mannered and would simply confirm Henrietta's accusations.

As the tension increased Charlotte clenched her cutlery tightly and then, deliberately dropping her gaze, carefully cut a piece of turbot and brought it to her mouth.

As she chewed slowly, tasting nothing, she heard Lord Shalford's response.

'I think,' he said smoothly, 'that it rather depends. I have no doubt there are many people abroad *and* in England who show a lack of refinement—just as there are many who will have been brought up well.'

Henrietta subsided, with a confused expression and bright red angry spots on her cheeks.

Oh, bravo! thought Charlotte. *He speaks so subtly she is not even sure of his meaning.*

The Earl rose a little in her estimation. She raised her eyes to his briefly, trying to communicate her gratitude. He met her gaze, his eyes softening.

Captain Fanton, turning away from Faith, claimed Charlotte's attention. 'I must tell you, Miss Wyncroft, I enjoyed our canter through the park.'

Charlotte smiled gratefully. 'As did I. We will ride again on Tuesday?' Thankfully, her voice was steady, even if her hands—hidden now on her lap—were not.

'Yes, indeed. I will look forward to it!'

Across the table, the Earl once again engaged Henrietta in conversation and the tension slowly eased.

* * *

After dinner, thankfully, there was no time for the ladies to retire to the drawing room, for the carriages were ready. When they rose from the table, as the servants swooped in to clear the remains of the meal and help the Buxted ladies with their boots, gloves and cloaks, Lord Shalford made a point of speaking with Charlotte.

'I do hope,' he said quietly, 'you were not distressed by the conversation earlier.'

About to deny it, she caught the quiet sincerity in his grey eyes and relented. It was good of him to be concerned about her. There was no trace of arrogance about him now.

'I thank you for coming to my rescue. The worst of it is she is right! I wished for nothing more than to give her pepper—even at the dinner table. My temper is not easily aroused in the normal run of things. I have learned I am truly an ill-bred hoyden at times.'

He shook his head. 'I think not. I admit I was a little surprised by your cousin's comment.'

Charlotte did not wish him to think ill of Henrietta. 'She was upset...perhaps thinking we were making fun of her. Her reaction was understandable in the circumstances.'

'You are too considerate, I think.'

'My cousin is young, and not long out. She can be over-sensitive.'

'Now you sound like an elderly matron. Yet you cannot be more than nineteen!'

'I lack only a few weeks until my twenty-first birthday.'

'Then you and Miss Buxted are of an age, for she tells me she will be twenty-one on the first of August.'

'I am a little older than her. That is why my father thought we should be such friends. Unfortunately...' She stopped.

He raised an eyebrow. 'So you and Miss Buxted are not close, then?'

'Well...we are very different people.'

He considered this. 'Yes,' he said slowly. 'I think you are.'

For some reason, this made him frown.

Belatedly, she realised the impropriety of speaking to him so frankly. 'Henrietta has many admirable qualities, and I know I can be extremely irritating.' She laughed lightly. 'Papa allows me no self-delusions. My upbringing and experiences have been so different from Henrietta's it is hardly surprising we do not always see eye to eye.'

He nodded. 'We must also allow that young ladies in general are prone to heightened emotions and to behaviour which would be deplored in a man or an older lady. Debutantes must be forgiven their...'

'Silliness?' she offered tartly, remembering his judgemental comment about her.

He looked startled, but did not disagree. 'What of tonight's ball?' he asked, in an attempt to divert her. 'Do you mind that you do not go?'

'Well, I *thought* I did not mind very much. Though now, when you are all ready to go, elegantly dressed and full of anticipation, I confess I do wish I was going with you. I hope you do not think me ridiculous, but I do like to dance now and again.'

'You are not ridiculous at all,' he said. 'I should have liked to see you dance. I confess it does not sit well with me, leaving you here while we all go out. Is there no way you could have gone?'

'I must be guided by my aunt. She assures me it would not be proper for me to go to a large London ball when I am not yet out. I was too late to be presented at Court this year. I have not lived in England, and I do not know these things myself.'

'I see,' he said, frowning slightly.

'Lord Shalford!' Henrietta's strident tone interrupted their *tête-à-tête*. 'The carriages are ready and we must go, for I should hate to miss the dancing. I *adore* dancing!'

The Earl bowed to Charlotte, smiled a rueful farewell, and took his place by Henrietta's side.

'Charlotte,' said Henrietta sweetly, 'do enjoy your quiet evening. You will be glad to see us gone, I am sure.'

'Such a pity you cannot come to the ball,' offered the Captain, sincere regret in his blue eyes. 'Our party will not be the same without you. Will you be very lonely?'

Mrs Buxted looked displeased.

Charlotte hurriedly denied it, adding, 'I hope

you all enjoy your evening. I shall indeed enjoy the peace and quiet.'

They moved to the hallway, where the men were handed their hats, cloaks and canes. Charlotte stood back, wishing them gone, for this protracted farewell was difficult.

Finally they all moved to the door. At the last, the Earl turned to look at her, and his expression was strangely uncertain.

'Come, Lord Shalford!' Henrietta's tone was imperious. 'You shall travel in *our* carriage, for I must tell you more of my visit to Oxford.'

Then they were gone.

Charlotte hoped they didn't pity her. She imagined them all, travelling to Lady Cowper's townhouse. Henrietta would be enjoying her triumph, while Aunt Buxted would be focused on gaining every possible advantage for her daughters. Mr Buxted would already be thinking of meeting his cronies in the card room, and wondering what would be offered at supper.

Faith, with her kind heart, would not feel fully comfortable with Charlotte's absence, but would be ably distracted by the charming Captain Fanton— and by the gentle Mr Foxley. As for the Earl—no doubt his attention would be fully claimed by the beautiful, wilful Henrietta.

Charlotte went to the library, then to the salon. She was at a loss as to what to do. She felt strangely flat, which surprised her, for she had not thought herself so shallow that the loss of a ball should so affect her. She was not ready to sleep, and reading could not hold her attention. She tried to write a letter to Papa, but the words would not come, and she sat down her pen in frustration.

After almost two hours of achieving nothing, she went to her room.

Priddy helped her prepare for bed, and expressed her opinion on balls and Court presentations and on. 'Old women who have forgotten what it is to be young. Mark my words: she only did it to keep you away from the young gentlemen!'

'Oh, Priddy! You must not say such things. It will make me even more angry, for I fear you are right. But we may be wrong. Why, when Henrietta was angry about my riding with them Aunt Buxted did not support her.'

Priddy snorted. 'She's a clever old bird. She has plans for her daughters and she will not brook opposition.'

'But I am no opposition for her daughters. I have no wish for a husband, and I cannot match my cousins' beauty.'

'I do not understand how you can say you are not beautiful. You are no insipid yellow-haired milkmaid, it is true, but that is just a fashion. You have *countenance*, Miss Charlotte, and your good looks will last longer than Miss Buxted's, mark my words.'

'Oh, Priddy, I know your regard for me deceives you, but I thank you nevertheless.'

Priddy shook her head. 'That's not it. And as for not wanting a husband—it is *every* girl's wish to get a nice husband.' She stared into the distance. 'To have a proper home of your own and little ones.'

'Even you, Priddy?' Charlotte was curious.

'I confess when I was young there was a man.' Her eyes softened. 'We were to be married. But he was carried off by a fever. It was not to be.'

'Oh, Priddy! I'm so sorry.' Impulsively, she hugged the woman who had been the closest thing to a mother to her since she had lost her own mama.

'Now, now,' said Priddy gruffly. 'It was a long time ago. But if you get the chance at happiness you must take it. We none of us know how long we have on this earth.'

Charlotte pondered Priddy's words as she lay wide awake, listening to the sounds of the city at night—carriages rumbling, dogs barking, in the distance, some drunken singing. She knew better than most how easily lives could be snuffed out. Growing up as a war child, she had known many people to die—officers, foot soldiers and their wives—more often from illness and disease than from the heat of battle. She wondered if Captain Fanton, like many of the young men she had known, had felt the trauma of war and of loss.

Her mind moved on from the Captain to his brother. The Earl had been kind tonight. Not arrogant at all. She remembered his cool grey eyes fixing upon hers and felt a strange warmth in her chest. It was altogether confusing, for he held young ladies in disdain, and the squabble between Henrietta and herself would only have strengthened his prejudice.

Yet, surprisingly, her view of him was changing. Where she had seen arrogance and prejudice, she now saw warmth and compassion. Even more strange was this new feeling he had stirred in her. It was something like...*affection*, though there were other, stranger colours in it. It was a good feeling, though somewhat overshadowed by imagining them all at the ball.

She pictured them all, dancing, laughing, talking, and felt...alone.

Chapter Six

Lady Sophia Annesley was in her drawing room when Adam called. As the Earl was a regular visitor, and one who was well known to all of her ladyship's staff, he was shown straight in. Unfortunately when he arrived, Lady Sophia was stretched out on a sofa, gently snoring, a handkerchief over her face to protect her sensitive eyes from the harsh daylight.

Adam coughed discreetly.

She rose with a start, her cap slipping sideways and the comfortable blanket she had spread over her feet falling to the floor.

Retrieving the blanket, the Earl bent to help her into a sitting position and kiss her cheek. 'Good day, Godmama. What a fetching cap!'

'For goodness' sake, Adam, why do you arrive without warning? You should always allow a lady to be ready for a visitor.'

She waved at him to be seated, so he placed himself beside her on the sofa.

Lady Sophia was a lady in her middle years, with a round figure and a pleasant, friendly visage. Her mind was sharp, and she knew everyone in society, keeping track of the latest *on-dits* through her extensive network of friends. She was well-known and popular, though some were wary of her, for she spoke her mind and was scathing of those she termed *'fribbles, fools and imbeciles'*.

Just now, she did not look quite so formidable.

Retying her cap under her left ear, and gathering her thoughts at the same time, Lady Sophia surveyed the Earl. He looked fresh and immaculately groomed. His boots were polished to a high gloss, his neckcloth perfectly tied, and his eyes clear and amused. Yet she knew he—like most of London's elite—had drunk and eaten, danced and talked until the early hours of the morning at Lady Cowper's ball.

'Why are you so awake and so loud at this ungodly hour? I am not long arisen from my bed.'

'But it is almost two o'clock.'

'Yes, but it feels like the middle of the night! I believe there was something wrong with those prawns, you know, though I would never say so to Emily Cowper. I feel distinctly unwell.'

'Well, you look as fresh as a newborn lamb, despite…er…the copious amounts of punch on offer last night.'

She eyed him malevolently. 'Yes, thank you,

Adam, but you really shouldn't be barging in unannounced, you know.'

'Aunt Sophia, *you* summoned me here. I dashed from my bed when I received your message, wondering what desperate crisis had occurred. I came as quickly as I could!'

'Foolish boy! I have no time for your funning today.' She patted his hand warmly, but then spoke intently. 'Something of a most concerning nature has occurred.'

'Do tell, pray.'

'Last night at the ball the Fanton name was being bandied about in a most unpleasant way.'

He frowned. 'Indeed? May I ask what was said?'

'There's the thing. I don't know exactly. But I know the sort of tittle-tattle and gossip…'

'Ah.' He sat back. 'And was this gossip perhaps related to the fact that we were part of the Buxted party at the ball?'

'I cannot like it, Adam. We are *Fantons*. We should not be the subject of demeaning conversation from people with nothing else to do.'

'What are the old tabbies saying? What can they possibly find amiss in our company last night? The Buxteds are a respectable family whose Surrey estate marches with ours. Why, we may have known them for a long time.'

'Yes, but it is known you have never been *intimate* with them. It is drawing attention. It seems Mrs Buxted has been crowing about you visiting their house and having dinner, arranging riding excursions…' She paused. 'There are even rumours that the entire family have been invited to Chadcombe.'

'And what if they have?'

She looked shocked 'But, Adam, you *must* know it is too *particular*… It looks as if you may be planning to offer for one of the Buxted girls. Now, I must say since your father's illness, and this last year, you have surprised all the naysayers who thought you would struggle to manage Chadcombe. I know as few do how things were let slip these last few years, with your mama gone and your father not himself… I also know how you are working hard to repair and improve the estate. You have behaved admirably, my boy. But there is no need to set up your nursery too soon, you know. Better to wait a while for the right girl to come along.'

The Earl remained expressionless.

She took his hand. 'Tell me, Adam, do you think of marriage?'

'Yes—no! I don't know.' He smiled ruefully. 'I had thought it sensible, but unfortunately I am having some difficulty in actually deciding to…well, to cross that particular Rubicon. I have had my fill of debutantes. They giggle and simper and talk too much—or not enough. Or they have no opinions. Or they have ill-informed opinions. Or they are… impudent.'

He rose, trying to shake away the memory of one

particular young lady, and made an absent-minded study of Lady Annesley's ormolu clock on the mantel.

'I must at least consider it, Godmama. It is my duty to marry well. Grandfather almost ruined us, and Papa worried himself into an early grave trying to restore our fortunes. I have made a good start on the estate, but the house has lost some of its warmth since Mama died. It needs a mistress. And Olivia needs female company—someone other than Great-Aunt Clara. Olivia and I argue too much lately. I do not understand what goes on in the mind of a woman!'

'What do you and Olivia argue about?'

'She chafes against the restrictions of Chadcombe. She wishes to come out next season, now we are out of mourning, but in truth I cannot stomach the thought of squiring her to dozens of balls and routs. And as for Almack's—with its orgeat and its gossips—' He grimaced. 'I have been trying hard this season to take my place in the Marriage Mart, but the whole game quite disgusts me!'

'Adam, you have had it your own way for far too long. No, do *not* show me that face. I am not a debutante, to be slain by your wrathful looks. I am your aunt and your godmother and I shall tell you what I think.'

'I am all attention, dear Aunt.'

'You are a good boy, Adam. You work hard with the estate and your interest in politics does you credit. My brother—your poor father—would be proud of you. But you are accustomed to deference, and to having what you want. You have the freedom to go where you will, whenever you wish—to gambling dens, cockfights, boxing matches and other uncouth pursuits if you wish. You have *independence*. Try to remember Olivia does not.'

'Olivia is well cared for. My great-aunt—'

'Clara Langley is too old to be a fitting companion for a young lady. You know I love your mother's elderly aunt, but she does not wish to go out in society and has no understanding of the needs of a young girl like Olivia.'

'Which is why I must marry! My...my wife—' he struggled with the word '—will look after Olivia, help her with her come-out and—'

'But that is not a reason to marry. Why, *I* could take dear Olivia under my wing.'

'Come, come, Aunt Sophia. You would hate it after a week. Like me, you are accustomed to independence. Since my uncle died—and I know you grieve deeply for him—you have built a good life as a widow, have you not?'

'You know me too well. But, Adam, I *will* do it. If you do not find a lady you truly *wish* to marry—a lady you love and wish to share your life with—then I will bring Olivia out next season. *There!*'

He kissed her hand. 'Best of aunts. I thank you—though I still believe you would detest it. How would you survive Almack's every week?'

She struggled to answer.

'Exactly!'

'Wretch! Now, tell me—what of Harry? *His* name is being linked with the Buxted girls too, with speculation that he will also marry.'

The Earl considered this, his forehead creased. 'I cannot say, for Harry no longer confides in me. He enjoys female company, and can flirt and make compliments much easier than I. But I do not know if he thinks of marriage… The wars have changed him, Godmama. Underneath the gaiety, he is still troubled, I think.'

'He is young. Time will help him forget what he has seen. Now we have peace, and will not be murdered in our beds by Frenchmen, he can enjoy his duties without anxiety. You shake your head—do you disagree with me?'

'I cannot be easy about Harry. He hides it well, but… I am being foolish, perhaps. Too much time to think and worry and ponder over things. And now *this* unfortunate mess. I am displeased that my attentions to the Buxted ladies have been noticed—and not just on my own behalf. I should not like to cause distress to any lady—and I should like the freedom to make my choice without an audience watching my every action.'

'Tell me, *have* you invited them to Chadcombe? Just the mother and the daughters?'

'I have—but not just Mrs Buxted and her daughters. The father too. And a relative who is staying with them.'

'And who is your hostess? Clara?'

'Yes, she has agreed to host. I know she struggles to manage the house at times, but she assures me she is happy to host this party.'

'Good. May I advise you?'

'Of course you may. You are, after all, my favourite aunt.'

'I am your *only* aunt. Now, do listen, Adam. Mrs Buxted, from what I know of her, is a vain, silly woman who is ambitious for her daughters. She was Louisa Long before her marriage, and those Longs were always a little... Yes, well, she thinks she has triumphed because of the exclusivity of this invitation to Chadcombe. And, in truth, the exclusivity is what is stirring the gossips. If you have truly *only* invited them—'

'Godmother, I thank you. I shall immediately invite a *dozen* eligible ladies and their families to divert suspicion.'

'No, not a *dozen*. Poor Miss Langley—! Ah, you are jesting with me again, I see. Yes, do invite others to Chadcombe. And it would be wise to be seen escorting other young ladies as well—perhaps take one to the theatre with her family. That way, if you *do* choose to court one in particular, you can do so without giving ammunition to the gossips. But, Adam, listen to me now. Things have changed. In these modern times you do not have to marry out of duty. Better marry for love.'

'*Love?*' He laughed. 'I have no desire to spout poetry and daydream of a lady's fine eyes...'

He paused, then shook his head as if to rid himself of something.

'I just want to find a sensible girl who won't give me any trouble. I must think of the estate. We are in need of money, so I must marry well. The Buxted family owns Monkton Park, which would be a good addition to Chadcombe, and the mother rather clumsily informed me it is dowried on one of the daughters. On the other hand, Miss Etherington has a large dowry, which would boost our funds. And there is another lady—but I do not know what her fortune is.'

'But, Adam, you have done well with the estate since your father died. Don't forget that the woman you marry will be by your side till death parts you. You must think of that when you choose to marry.'

'My problem, Godmama, is that I have never yet met a lady—apart from you, of course—who did not bore me or irritate me within a month of knowing her. And marrying to suit myself is not an option if it causes harm to my family.'

The Earl took his leave shortly afterwards, leaving his aunt in pensive mood. She lay down on her sofa again to think. Adam had had relationships with women of a certain class, she knew—for the *ton* knew everything—but she had never heard of him losing his heart.

He was popular with ladies—the older ones responded to his serious nature, the younger ones liked his handsome face and figure—but he always held a certain reserve. He was used to seeking the company of his friends, and had never, to Sophia's knowledge, engaged in a true friendship with any lady. Adam, like many men, saw ladies as decorative irritations, to be tolerated and enjoyed.

Some young ladies, Sophia acknowledged, did not help matters with their behaviour. And the Marriage Mart itself encouraged young ladies to flirt and be silly to attract attention. She sighed. If Adam was to marry now, one of the simpering misses he so disdained, the marriage would be a disaster.

In this, his sense of duty would work against him. He had been raised with a love of Chadcombe, and the knowledge that when his father was gone the responsibility for the people and the place would pass to him. It had always made him more cautious, more sober—older than his years.

He had not, until now, shown a particular interest in any young lady. That, she guessed, was why the gossips were so fascinated by his attentions towards the Buxteds.

She knew the Buxted family a little, but not well. The mother had managed to engineer a formal introduction last night, so Sophia could now acknowledge them, which would allow her to find out more. Adam had not denied being interested in Miss Buxted, so Sophia needed to meet her—and quickly. She was not at all convinced that the girl she had met last night would make a suitable countess, or that Adam should have Louisa Long for a mother-in-law.

To call on them would be too obvious, drawing exactly the sort of attention she had just warned Adam about. She would have to find another way...

She was still trying to think of how she would manage it when sleep again claimed her.

Charlotte returned to the house after her usual morning walk, wondering if the ladies were still abed.

'Thank you, Sarah,' she said to the housemaid who had accompanied her.

Sarah had informed her that the Buxted ladies had returned late into the night, and that the night footman had reported downstairs that the ladies had been in raptures over their success.

Hearing this, Charlotte had not known whether to be glad or sorry. Of course she wanted her cousins and her aunt to enjoy themselves—and she hoped Henrietta would be easier company today—but some selfish part of her had wanted to hear that the evening had been flat, or dull, or that nobody had danced.

Scolding herself for such uncharitable thoughts,

she went to the breakfast parlour—a small, bright room where she found all three ladies indulging in a light nuncheon of rolls, fruit and cold meat.

'Oh, Charlotte, there you are. Where have you been?' Mrs Buxted looked her usual calm self, but she had a self-satisfied air, sitting upright and smiling benevolently on her daughters.

'Walking, Aunt Buxted. You recall that I ride or walk every morning if I can—though today I was later than usual, as I was waiting for Sarah to accompany me and she was on an errand for Cook.'

Aunt Buxted was only half listening. 'Yes, yes… do not ever go unaccompanied. You are living under my husband's roof, and anything you do reflects on us. Sit here, girl, and pass me the beef.'

'Yes, Aunt. How was your evening?'

'A triumph! My girls were a great success. I declare they hardly sat down all night, for they danced almost every dance. And Lord Shalford and his brother were *most* attentive.'

'Oh, Mama! Did you see Millicent Etherington looking at me when I was dancing with the Earl? She must be so jealous that he accompanied us and not her to the ball. And he only danced with her because he couldn't dance with me *all* night.'

'He danced with Beatrice Ross too.'

'Yes, Faith—which proves what I just said. He danced with *four* different ladies, but he came here for dinner—and they all knew it.'

'Did *you* dance, Faith?'

'Yes, I danced with Mr Foxley, and the Captain, and the Earl.' She smiled shyly. 'I had a wonderful evening. I do feel tired today, though. I am not accustomed to so much dancing.'

Charlotte smiled back at her as she poured herself a cup of coffee.

'Well, you should remember it, Faith,' said her sister, 'for it may not happen for you again. There will be nights when you may have to sit and watch. Of course *I* am rarely short of partners.'

'I was also busy on your behalf, girls,' said Mrs Buxted. 'I was introduced to Lady Annesley last night.'

Her announcement did not have the desired effect. All three young ladies looked at her blankly.

'Who is Lady Annesley, Mama?' asked Henrietta.

'If you had properly studied the copy of Mr Debrett's book I gave you, you would know exactly who she is.'

Henrietta squirmed slightly, while Faith looked anxious.

Mrs Buxted tutted, then told them. 'She is Shalford's aunt—his father's sister. He is, they say, extremely close to her.'

'Yes…?' Henrietta looked confused. 'And why should we be interested in *her*?'

'You are very stupid today, Henrietta. She will *influence* him.' Mrs Buxted applied herself to her beef. 'Why, in my day it was the *families* who decided who would marry whom. None of this non-sense of allowing young people to choose. I hardly knew Mr Buxted when we were wed, but I submitted, as a dutiful daughter must, to my parents' wishes.'

Henrietta snorted. 'But, Mama, we have no need for help from a silly old aunt. If he is in love with me then he will marry me, no matter what she says.'

Charlotte carefully set down her cup, having found herself gripping the delicate handle tightly. For some reason Henrietta's words were particularly grating. The thought of the Earl falling in love with Henrietta shouldn't bother her. But perhaps, now that she was beginning to see him in a better light, she did not want him to be chained to Henrietta for a lifetime.

'Yes, well, that's as may be—but until he approaches your father we can take nothing for granted. We will visit Lady Annesley today.'

'Oh, *no*, Mama,' wailed Henrietta. '*Must* we?'

Mrs Buxted would not be moved, despite Henrietta's pleadings. And two hours later, feeling decidedly uncomfortable, Charlotte found herself in Lady Annesley's hallway. Mrs Buxted, unaware or unconcerned that such a direct approach might be poorly thought of by Lady Annesley, had insisted on this visit to that lady's home, accompanied by all three girls.

Lady Annesley's butler, who was eying them all

assessingly, held Mrs Buxted's card by one corner as she spoke to him.

'Do tell *dear* Lady Annesley that Mrs Buxted is here to see her. We had the pleasure of welcoming her two *charming* nephews to our humble home for dinner last night.'

The butler showed them into an empty drawing room, bowed, and left.

Waiting, the young ladies sat stiffly, listening to Mrs Buxted's last-minute instructions.

'And you, Faith, should not speak much. It is Henrietta who must have priority.'

'But, Mama, what if she should speak to me directly, or ask me a question?'

'Then you should answer, but keep it brief. Foolish girl. Do not try my patience!'

'Lady Sophia Annesley,' intoned the butler.

Lady Annesley swept into the room. If she had heard the conversation between Faith and her mother she affected not to have done so. Charlotte's discomfort increased. They should not be here.

'Mrs Buxted. What an unexpected pleasure. Yes, of course I remember you. We met last night, did we not? A most pleasant evening, though the prawns were a little… Yes, well, it was a crush as always. Emily Cowper will be pleased. May I offer you some ratafia? Tea?'

She waved to the butler, who left to secure the refreshments.

'And these are your daughters?'

Mrs Buxted, all smiles, made the introductions.

Lady Annesley surveyed the Buxted girls critically. 'Yes, both good-looking girls, Mrs Buxted. Accomplished dancers, too—I saw them dance the quadrille last night with my nephews.'

Mrs Buxted looked pleased.

Henrietta fluttered her lashes and tilted her head to one side, saying, 'Thank you, Lady Annesley.'

Lord, thought Charlotte, *she flirts with everyone*. But Henrietta, she noted, had not seen Lady Annesley's wry smile.

'And who is *this* young lady?' Lady Annesley turned her intelligent gaze to Charlotte.

'This is Miss Charlotte Wyncroft. Her mother was my husband's cousin.'

Lady Annesley started, then smiled broadly. 'Then you are Sir Edward's daughter! I did not know you were in England. Is your father with you? How is the old rogue? Is he still breaking hearts in Vienna?'

'He is now breaking hearts in Paris, if I am not mistaken.' Charlotte smiled.

Lady Annesley laughed. 'I do not doubt it. So you are Maria's little daughter, who was born in Portugal. Well, a fine young lady you have become. What an elegant dress. Never say this was made by a *London* modiste.' She studied Charlotte's stylish walking dress—a figured muslin with embroidered trim, complete with matching spencer.

'No, indeed. It was made by Madame Diebolt, an *émigrée* in Vienna. All the ladies compete for her best work—I do declare she has us all under her control.'

'She is clearly a genius. Such stitch-work. Such a cut. And you wear it with style, Miss Wyncroft. How long do you stay in London?'

Mrs Buxted interjected. 'Sir Edward hopes to return for his dear daughter in the next few weeks. We shall miss her.'

Not to be outdone, Henrietta said, 'And we shall *all* visit Chadcombe before that.'

'Indeed? Chadcombe is a wonderful place. I love to stay there when London becomes too much.' Lady Annesley turned back to Charlotte. 'Tell me more of Sir Edward. Does he think of retirement?'

'He does, now that we have peace. Diplomacy must have its day—and rightly so, for every effort must be made to ensure the peace will endure.'

Lady Annesley concurred. 'We need a better way to solve our differences than on the battlefield. Now, if *women* could talk sense into our hot-headed generals and politicians, we would—I am sure—find improvements.'

'I agree,' said Charlotte. 'Though when war is upon us our soldiers—including the generals—do what they must.'

Mrs Buxted spoke again. 'I do not think women should talk of war, or diplomacy, or of any such things. Our role is that of helpmate to our troubled husbands, no more.'

'I believe we can support our husbands and yet

still have an opinion on these matters—though there are many who disagree with me,' said Lady Annesley diplomatically. 'When Lord Annesley was alive we had many conversations about politics and war, and he encouraged my opinions. He also enjoyed our disagreements.'

Her eyes twinkled as she took in Mrs Buxted's shocked look.

The door opened to admit the butler, who brought tea, cakes and pastries. As soon as he had left, Mrs Buxted—intent on her mission—monopolised Lady Annesley's attention with talk of mutual acquaintances until it was time to leave.

As they departed, Lady Annesley thanked the Buxted ladies for calling and wished them an enjoyable stay at Chadcombe. She then turned to Charlotte.

'Miss Wyncroft, it has been an unexpected pleasure to meet you today. You must pass my regards to your father and tell him he is to visit me when he returns. Indeed, I shall expect to see both of you.'

Seated in the carriage a few minutes later, Henrietta spoke up. 'Mama, now we have done our duty and visited Lady Annesley, may we now go for ices at Gunther's? You promised.'

Mrs Buxted, deep in thought, said, 'It was adequate. She focused rather too much on Charlotte, but she is quite eccentric, I think, and Charlotte's strange ideas seemed to find favour with her.'

'Charlotte should not have spoken so much. She was trying to take the attention away from *me*.'

Charlotte could not let this pass. 'Indeed I was not, Henrietta. She knows my father, so it was perfectly natural for her to wish to talk about him.'

'Well, she probably knows *my* father too, but she did not talk about *him*. At least Mama was able to reclaim her attention while we had tea. Anyway, she is old, and quite fat and boring, and I am glad we do not have to visit her again.'

'I thought her charming,' said Charlotte. 'I should be most happy to see her again.'

'Yes, yes, girls... It is done, and I think all in all we achieved success. I am sure she will recommend us to Lord Shalford, which will help your cause, my dear Henrietta,' said Mrs Buxted. 'Tell the coachman to take us to Gunther's.'

Mrs Buxted might not have been quite so triumphant had she seen Lady Annesley's letter to Miss Langley, written a few days later. That elderly lady, already anxious about hosting a party of guests at Chadcombe—though of course she had agreed immediately to dear Adam's request—read Lady Sophia's crossed lines with increasing unease. It seemed, from what she wrote, that she was rather encroaching, and had designs on marrying one of her daughters off to the Earl...

The elder has a beautiful face, with nothing behind it but vanity and self-interest, while the younger is timid and vacuous.

*The one jewel in their midst is their guest,
Miss Wyncroft. A pretty, sensible and amia-
ble girl, she is the daughter of my old friend,
Sir Edward.*

*You will remember my dear friend Maria,
who died abroad? This charming young lady
is her daughter. She is staying with the Buxteds
while awaiting Sir Edward's return.*

*Beware the Buxted mother, though. She is
devilishly ambitious and unintelligent—a dangerous combination. And, unfortunately, one
might describe all the young ladies as having
fine eyes—a most unlucky circumstance!*

Miss Clara Langley set down the letter in some
agitation. While she did not understand Sophia's
fixation with the eyes of the young ladies, she
nevertheless had the impression of complications
and intrigues, and a family that was much too *interesting* for her liking.

She had also had a letter from Adam that morning, informing her that the party was to be larger
than he had first thought. She was to make all the
necessary arrangements, and he hoped it would not
be too much trouble for her.

Nine people—all of them strangers—were
shortly to descend on Chadcombe, and she had not
hosted such a large party by herself before. She
would have to invite a couple of the local gentry to
make up the numbers for some of the dinners, as

there were an inordinate number of ladies among the invited guests.

Miss Langley feverishly referred to her list. As well as the five people—*four* ladies!—in the Buxted party, there was a Mrs Etherington and her two children—one young man, one young lady. There was also a Mr Foxley, who at least was male, thank goodness! Three men and six ladies. She would invite the Squire, his son and the Reverend Sneddon to some dinners, to balance things out.

While Lady Shalford had been alive, Miss Langley had given her assistance on many occasions, and with much larger parties, but now, lost in anxieties over pillows and candles and how many extra maids to hire, she realised just how competent her niece had been.

She did not think Adam understood how much had to be done, or how complicated it all was. But then, men never did, did they?

Chapter Seven

As promised, Lord Shalford and the Captain called on the following Tuesday to take the young ladies riding. They all walked their horses sedately through the park and back again, while Henrietta flirted outrageously with Captain Fanton in an apparent attempt to arouse jealousy in the Earl.

Henrietta was wearing her new and exceedingly fashionable riding habit, which had military epaulettes and a matching shako, like Charlotte's. It had been delivered just this morning, and Henrietta's glee at her dashing appearance had made her light-headed with confidence.

Adam was unmoved by her tactics. It reinforced his opinion about the empty-headed, self-seeking behaviour that he was used to seeing from young ladies. Henrietta was no better and no worse than the other young ladies he'd encountered. He decided, instead, to get to know Miss Wyncroft, for he had a vague suspicion that she might be different.

* * *

Charlotte watched, bemused, as her cousin tried out various tricks with the Captain—looking into his eyes intently, leaning across to tell him something no one else could hear, and laughing loudly at his comments. To any observer it would seem as though she was enamoured of the Captain. She ignored Lord Shalford completely.

The Earl rode alongside Charlotte, all politeness, and it seemed to Charlotte that he did not notice Henrietta's behaviour. He probed Charlotte about her reading habits, and they discovered similar tastes in books. Intrigued by her recent appreciation of him, Charlotte was quite enjoying the conversation—until a chance remark about his admiration of people who enjoyed reading recalled her to the present. It was Henrietta he should be complimenting. Henrietta he truly admired.

Charlotte lapsed into silence. She felt deeply uncomfortable, knowing that he was only making conversation with her because Henrietta was unavailable. She wondered if he was feeling hurt or angry with Henrietta. Either way, the last thing he probably wanted was to be conversing with *her*.

Remember his arrogance! she told herself. *Just because he was nice to you at dinner, it doesn't mean he's changed. He and Henrietta will make a perfect match. I just wish I wasn't stuck between them while Henrietta plays her games.*

'You are quiet, Miss Wyncroft,' he said, smiling slightly. 'Does my conversation bore you?'

'I am quiet,' she said pertly. 'What of it? Can a person not be silent at times?' She bit her lip. Perhaps she could have phrased that more courteously. 'Indeed—I am often criticised for being the quiet one.'

In front of them Henrietta laughed shrilly at some witticism from the Captain. Charlotte closed her eyes briefly.

'Quite.'

She looked at the Earl, unsure what he had meant. He looked only amused.

They all agreed to meet again the following Tuesday, though the Earl promised to call on them during the week, to see how they did.

Charlotte was happy to hear this, but confused as to why. She really must stop thinking about him! They had shared a companionable hour together on horseback, and his arrogance had given way to kindness, but she had met dozens of attractive men in her life. There was nothing special about him, she told herself. Nothing at all.

As they left Half-Moon Street, Adam reflected on the outing. Although the Beauty had been focused on Harry, he acknowledged that he himself had been quite content conversing with Miss Wyncroft. Her character was much more appealing to him than Miss Buxted's. He had enjoyed her hu-

mour and been impressed by her intelligence. Nor
had he failed to notice how attractive she looked in
that dashing riding habit. She had style!

He chuckled at the memory of her accompanying
a witty barb with a mischievous sidelong glance,
then pushed the thought away. Determined not to
confuse the issue with too much emotional analy-
sis, he refused to dwell on the unexpected feelings
swirling around in his chest. He would proceed with
logic, for he needed to keep a clear head.

Two days later, Mrs Buxted brought some news
to the young ladies. She had been on a shopping ex-
pedition, and on her return hurried into the yellow
salon, where they were seated.

Charlotte was writing a letter, Faith was embroi-
dering a pillowcase, and Henrietta was perusing
La Belle Assemblée and expressing her opinions
on the fashion plates displayed in its pages. When
her mother entered the room, Henrietta immediately jumped up.

'Oh, Mama, just see this beautiful gown. I should
so like to have one like it. I will need more new
gowns for Chadcombe, for Lord Shalford has seen
all my gowns except for the blue silk, and that is
old-fashioned and I do not like it any more.'

'Hush, now, child, for something terrible has happened.'

Mrs Buxted did indeed look distressed. Her
cheeks were bright, her breathing laboured, and she

seemed to be suffering under the burden of some terrible shock. The young ladies immediately rushed to her aid, imploring her to sit—no, to lie down on the couch. Charlotte placed an embroidered cushion under her aunt's head, while Faith searched for smelling salts in the drawer of the side table. Henrietta held her mother's hand and made soothing noises.

After the smelling salts had revived her, Mrs Buxted insisted on sitting up.

'I have heard terrible news—which affects *you*, my dear Henrietta.'

Henrietta gasped. 'What is it, Mama?'

'I had the misfortune to meet that loathsome Mrs Etherington at Grafton House. She took pleasure in informing me that she—and her odious son and *Millicent*—are also invited to Chadcombe.'

'Millicent Etherington? To Chadcombe? *Noooo!*' Henrietta shrieked. 'For her to crow over me and try and win him! And flirt with him with her ugly red hair and her boring brown eyes and her horrid three thousand pounds!'

She burst into noisy tears.

Charlotte was dumbfounded. *This* was a crisis? Another family was to join the Chadcombe party? The Etheringtons were, she knew, a perfectly respectable family, and she had understood they were friends of the Buxteds, for Millicent and Henrietta visited each other's houses regularly and often went shopping together.

'But Henrietta,' she offered, 'Lord Shalford did not say we were to be the *only* guests.'

Henrietta, through her noisy sobs, said, 'He *did*. Well, he *meant* it to be so. I *know* he did.' Her breathing was becoming dangerously fast as she worked herself up into a full tantrum.

Mrs Buxted, having recovered from her own fainting fit, said, 'Charlotte, do not speak to her. She is upset. Call my abigail—she will know what to do for her. Faith—the smelling salts. Quickly!'

Mrs Buxted tried to administer the smelling salts but Henrietta was now lying down on the expensive carpet, drumming her feet on the floor. She was also becoming louder in her cries.

Charlotte had never seen a display quite like it. Her own heartbeat was increased, but her agitation stemmed more from indignation than pity. Why should Henrietta behave like this, just because her wishes were thwarted?

Mrs Buxted's abigail—a stern maid called Miss Flint—entered and immediately took charge. Faith was instructed to hold Henrietta's feet as Flint tried to hold a burning feather under Henrietta's nose.

Mrs Buxted cried noisily on the sofa, repeating 'Oh, my poor Henrietta. My poor, poor girl.'

The door opened again—this time to admit a young footman. Shocked at the sight before him, he reddened and immediately turned to face the wall. Addressing a large portrait of Henrietta's great-grandfather which was hung there, he said, 'Lord

Shalford is below, madam. I...er...should I bring him up?'

'Of *course* not!' shrieked Mrs Buxted. 'Tell him—tell him—put him in Mr Buxted's library.'

The footman made a hasty exit.

'Charlotte—go down to him and tell him we are unwell—we are unavailable. I shall join you as soon as I may. Leave the library door open!'

'Of course, Aunt.'

Glad to escape from the unnecessary drama, Charlotte retreated downstairs.

Unfortunately the sounds of Henrietta's distress were clearly audible all over the house. Charlotte passed a flustered Mrs Walker in the hall, bustling towards the stairs with what looked like laudanum.

'Oh, dear, miss,' she said as she passed. 'Miss Henrietta hasn't had a do like this in a long time. She was a sensitive child—had tantrums regularly. Every time it happened, poor Mr Buxted was so distressed he would leave the house.'

Charlotte felt sympathy for Mr Buxted.

Squaring her shoulders, Charlotte entered the library—leaving the door open, as instructed, as she had no chaperon.

The Earl turned from his perusal of the books on the left-hand bookcase to greet her. 'Ah! Good day, Miss Wyncroft.'

She curtseyed. 'Good afternoon, Lord Shalford. Are you well?'

Both ignored the sounds from upstairs. 'I am well, thank you.'

Charlotte took a deep breath. 'And is your brother well?'

A gleam of humour lit his eyes. 'He was indeed well when I saw him last. Around an hour ago.'

They sat—Charlotte on a settee upholstered in red satin, the Earl on a winged leather chair. Neither spoke. Charlotte looked at him helplessly.

'We are having good weather this week, Miss Wyncroft, are we not?'

The drumming on the ceiling—coming from the yellow salon above—became louder.

'Er...yes, it is becoming quite warm. It is exceedingly pleasant.'

'After the harsh winter we deserve some mild weather, don't you think?'

'Yes, indeed, Lord Shalford.'

Sarah entered, bringing tea and pastries. Charlotte dismissed her, then politely offered the Earl refreshment. He thanked her, and they sipped their tea in silence.

Loud shrieks were now sounding through the open doorway, the ceiling, the very *walls* of Buxted House.

Charlotte raised her voice a little. 'The warm weather will surely help your crops at Chadcombe.'

He raised an eyebrow. 'Miss Wyncroft, how much do you know of farming?'

'Nothing—oh, you wretch!' She set her teacup

down and collapsed into laughter, mirth finally overcoming her.

The Earl laughed with her as the noises above finally began to subside.

'Tell me,' he said, 'what on earth is happening upstairs?'

Not wanting to expose her cousin—though he must surely suspect Henrietta was the source of the demonic wails—Charlotte hesitated.

'You *should* tell me, you know,' he said. 'I will find out somehow.'

Charlotte was saved from answering by the arrival of Mrs Buxted.

She bustled in, all energy and noise. 'Dear me, Charlotte, why did you not tell me that we have a guest? You will really have to work harder at learning good manners, you know. I do apologise for keeping you waiting, Lord Shalford. Such a pity my daughters are unavailable at this precise moment.'

'Indeed? Are your daughters out, Mrs Buxted?'

'Er…well, they are at home, but they are…indisposed. Yes, indisposed.' She thought for a moment. 'You see, the second housemaid has the toothache, and has been weeping and wailing like the souls of the ungodly. You may have heard some of her carrying-on when you first arrived. But Mrs Walker has given her laudanum now, so she will sleep.'

'I see. I sincerely pity anyone plagued with the toothache. A most intense sensation.' He paused. 'Do your daughters also have the toothache?'

From the red settee a sound suspiciously like a snort emerged from Charlotte.

'No, no! For toothache is not *catching*. At least, I have never *heard* that it is. And I—and my poor dear children—have had a great many toothaches over the years.'

He waited.

'You see, they are so *sensitive*—yes, both my daughters are so sensitive—that they cannot *bear* to see poor Sarah in pain, and they have become so distressed they would not be good company today.'

'Sarah? Ah, it is your housemaid *Sarah* who has the toothache?'

Mrs Buxted confirmed it.

He sent a wicked smile to Charlotte, who raised a hand to her forehead. Why must Aunt Buxted have chosen *Sarah*?

'You must be wishing me gone. I shall leave you.'

'Oh, no! But, yes—well, it would be better for you to see the girls at another time.'

They all rose.

'Miss Wyncroft—I do hope you will not also have the toothache, or become distressed like the other young ladies.'

Oh, he was a wretch!

'Oh, but Charlotte was raised in the *Army*, Lord Shalford. You must know she has a heart of stone from all the terrible sights she has witnessed.'

Charlotte would not let this pass. 'Indeed, Aunt,

I am *not* hard-hearted, and I must suffer when I see anyone in genuine distress.'

Mrs Buxted ignored this. 'I shall, of course, tell Henrietta—tell *both* girls—you called to see them and had to go away disappointed.'

'Oh, please do not—for I am not at all disappointed.'

He made his bow to both ladies, and left.

Mrs Buxted waited until the door had closed behind him, then sank into the nearest chair.

'Lord, give me strength…' She sighed. 'Why must he visit *now*, of all times? But, Charlotte, I must tell you—' her tone was serious '—it is true what I said about the Etheringtons. They *are* invited to Chadcombe.'

Her shoulders were slumped and she looked quite defeated. Charlotte was moved by pity. Her aunt, misguided as she was, believed she was acting in her daughters' best interests.

Charlotte spent a few minutes reassuring her that as Miss Etherington was not yet actually engaged to Lord Shalford nothing was lost. She then tactfully tried to suggest that perhaps Henrietta could be a little more composed, a little less demanding, in Lord Shalford's company—but this was not acceptable to Mrs Buxted.

'No and no and *no*!' she said. 'Henrietta is a sensitive child—she always has been—and she cannot change now. Nor would I wish her to. You mean well, but you have not been reared to be truly female. Gentlemen understand that we females are emotional creatures and need to be cared for. If she arouses his caring instincts it will be a *good* thing.'

Charlotte was dubious, but did not argue. She had a lot to think about. Her newfound charity with Lord Shalford was quite confusing. He had not been at all arrogant today—in fact she had enjoyed their moments of shared humour and understanding. Why should he suffer a lifetime of Henrietta's tantrums? Perhaps, she thought soberly, he shouldn't marry Henrietta after all.

Something about the thought disturbed her, so she pushed it away.

Adam, walking to his club, was having similar doubts. He could not know for sure which of the Misses Buxted was responsible for the appalling tantrum he had heard, but he hoped it was not Henrietta. He enjoyed his quiet life, disliked histrionics and instinctively shied away from drama. Perhaps Aunt Sophia was right—the *character* of his wife might be as important as her dowry.

His thoughts turned to Charlotte, and he chuckled at the memory of her discomfort in the library. He smiled then, remembering their shared laughter, and a feeling of warmth pervaded his chest.

He shook it away.

No! Laughter is all very well, but I will not make my grandfather's mistakes. He married for love—a penniless woman of good birth—then spent his life wasting his inheritance and running the estate down almost to the point of ruin. My father married an heiress whom he learned to love. He knew his duty.

He squared his shoulders, his expression grim.

Our fortunes are not yet secure. I must live up to my responsibilities—whatever the consequences for myself.

Yet a small, hopeful thought persisted. Perhaps Miss Wyncroft would turn out to be wealthy?

Now, why did that make him squirm? What was wrong with wishing she was well-dowried? He liked her, didn't he? More, perhaps, than he liked any of the others. More than he had expected. That was surprising to him.

Logic forced him to consider her dowry. If she was eligible, then he could pursue her. Emotionally, something in him recoiled from such thoughts. He did not like the thought of selecting Miss Wyncroft on the basis of whatever money she could offer. It belittled her.

You are thinking too much, he told himself. *Do what you must.*

Chapter Eight

The distance to Chadcombe was around forty miles, so they had decided to make the trip in a single day, with two stops to break the journey. Yet it seemed to Charlotte that time had slowed down, and the day was in fact a week pretending to be a day.

Perhaps it was because she was in the backward-facing seat of the carriage, with Faith by her side, while Mrs Buxted and Henrietta had, of course, taken the more comfortable forward-facing seats.

Yet that could not be the only explanation, for Charlotte had travelled much longer journeys, backward-facing at times, on worse roads and in carriages much less comfortable than the Buxteds' well-sprung travelling chaise.

Nor was it the scenery, for the Portsmouth road, and now the leafy lanes of Surrey, allowed fine views of the verdant countryside, which was now in full summer bloom—though the cool summer had not lived up to the warmth promised in spring.

Charlotte had heard many tales of the bitter winter that had just passed—how the Thames had frozen over in February, and how a Frost Fair had been staged on the frozen river, with printing presses and roast oxen on a spit. An elephant had even been walked on the ice near Blackfriars Bridge.

When the snow had stopped and spring had arrived, everyone had talked of a warm summer to come. April had been deceitful, with false promises of warm days. May, June, and now early July had been mainly dull and grey, with rainy days outnumbering sunny ones.

Charlotte, used to the intense summer heat of Austria, Italy and Spain, could only be grateful for the mildness of the English summer. And she quite liked the rain, which had made England lush and beautiful, with the earthy smell of farms, rich soil and flowering hedges.

Reluctantly, Charlotte conceded that the journey was being made difficult by her companions. She had never yet spent a trip in the company of an opinionated middle-aged lady and two quarrelling misses, and from the moment they had left Half-Moon Street the Buxted ladies had maintained an incessant flow of noisy emptiness. Even Faith, whom Charlotte had come to love dearly, was displaying her least attractive side, complaining about the backward-facing seat at least once every half-hour, and refusing to ignore some of her sister's selfish barbs. Faith was developing the habit of defending herself, which Charlotte applauded, but she was feeling its full effects today.

Oh, how she missed Papa's easy companionship. Normally when she travelled, Papa—along with Priddy—would accompany her, and now she was without both of them. Papa had written to say he had some final duties to complete, but that he would be home for the Peace Celebrations. Charlotte had to admit she would be glad, for the company of the Buxteds—and her lack of freedom—was now chafing badly. London had not been the pleasant adventure she had hoped for.

Unbidden, an image of the Earl came into her mind. Her heart missed a beat. If not for him, she reluctantly admitted, London would have been hard indeed.

She enjoyed his company. Despite her initial reactions to his arrogance, she now knew him to be warm, intelligent and humorous. She refused to read anything more into her reaction. Spending her days with the Buxteds, it was hardly surprising that she reacted warmly to the only congenial person in her orbit. If Papa had been here she would not, of course, have hungered for the Earl's company, for Papa would have given her all the stimulating conversation and wit that she craved. Yes, that was surely the reason why she was so focused on Lord Shalford.

And Priddy had been left in London with Joseph, for the Buxted party were bringing only three servants to Chadcombe—a groom to look after the carriage horses, Mr Buxted's valet and Mrs Buxted's abigail. The abigail would dress Miss Henrietta.

'You will understand,' Mrs Buxted had explained, 'that the needs of my firstborn are of the utmost importance. This visit is to ensure that Henrietta secures the Earl.'

Oh, Charlotte understood. They talked of little else.

The Earl had been busy these past weeks, and they had only seen him four times at Buxted House. He and his brother had ridden with them every Tuesday, and Henrietta had ensured she was always present for the rides. The Earl usually managed to speak with Charlotte on each occasion, and she had come to enjoy their easy discourse.

They had also heard he had escorted a theatre party that had included the Etheringtons. Charlotte had kept to her room that day, until Henrietta's storm of weeping and wailing had died down.

June had passed in an orgy of shopping, packing, and visits to dressmakers, with the result that all of them—including Faith—had an entire wardrobe of new dresses, cloaks, hats and spencers.

Charlotte herself had even become a little caught up in the excitement, and had been unable to resist ordering two new dresses—one a pale green day dress with long sleeves, a lace trim and a row of tiny seed pearls, the other a stunning evening gown in the new French satin. She hoped she would have the opportunity to wear it at Chadcombe, as it was a private house and there could be no objection to her taking a full part in any parties organised by their host. This extravagance meant she would have to be careful with her remaining money until Papa arrived back, but she was confident she would manage.

Mr Buxted was to join them in two days, for he needed to complete some business in London. Charlotte strongly suspected his 'business' was to avoid travelling with the ladies, and envied his ability to make that choice.

For the past two miles they had been following a stone wall on their right, and now to Charlotte's relief they stopped briefly at a gatehouse before entering what must be the Chadcombe estate. Charlotte noticed the gateman had mounted a horse and was riding ahead of them up the drive.

The drive passed through a pretty wooded area, where a few bluebells still remained. The clouds were breaking up for the first time since they had left London, and long fingers of sunlight pointed to the secret beauties of the woods.

The trees widened out to reveal a large deer park, and then suddenly Mrs Buxted and Henrietta simultaneously emitted sounds of awe. Faith jumped up and looked out of the window to see what they were exclaiming at.

'Faith. Sit down this instant!'

'Is that the house? It looks like a *palace*!'

'Yes, Faith, but they will *see* you—hanging out of the carriage like an urchin. Be seated, or I will box your ears.'

Faith jumped back as if stung, while Henrietta and Mrs Buxted spent the next few minutes exclaiming on the merits and beauties of the house, estimating the number of windows and speculating on how much it had cost to build.

Finally the coach came to a halt. Charlotte was last to descend, and she took a moment to absorb the scene.

Chadcombe was a large, elegant house built in the Palladian style. It was built of Portland stone, with stucco ornamentation and Venetian windows over the portico. The symmetrical wings contained long, elegant windows which would ensure a great deal of light in the public rooms. It was truly beautiful.

The gardens, from what Charlotte could see, contained topiary, trees and flowers, and gave way gradually to the natural splendour of the deer park. She could see a lake glistening, diamond-like, in the distance to her left, and could hear the tinkling splash of garden fountains.

While Charlotte had been looking around, the front door had opened and her aunt and cousins were now mounting the steps. She hurried to catch up, and entered the house just behind the others. She was struck by the impressive hall they entered. It was large and airy, with a chequered floor and an impressive wide staircase. The ceiling was adorned with plasterwork in the style of the Adam brothers, including classical paintings in the cartouches.

The Earl was there to welcome them, looking handsome and solemn. He wore a well-cut olive-green coat with biscuit-coloured inexpressibles and polished Hessians. Charlotte curtseyed with the others, while Mrs Buxted expressed her gratitude in the most animated terms. The Captain, whom Charlotte had initially failed to notice, assured Mrs Buxted of their welcome. The Earl then introduced his sister, Lady Olivia, and his Great-Aunt Clara—Miss Langley.

Olivia smiled shyly at them. She, too, had inherited the Fanton good looks and was extremely pretty, with dark hair and grey eyes like the Earl. She was dressed demurely in a high-necked figured muslin gown, with long pointed sleeves and a mauve satin ribbon. Charlotte smiled at her, recognising that the girl was a little nervous.

Miss Langley was an elderly lady, with white hair confined under a lace cap. She was wiry, wrinkled, and talkative, and greeted them warmly.

'So glad to meet you. Adam and Harry have told me you are all good friends. Yes, you will have a lovely time at Chadcombe—and I have allocated you rooms near each other so you may be comfortable. You must have had a terrible journey—I hate to travel now, though of course when I was younger...'

Henrietta moved her reticule from one hand to the other, then adjusted her left glove.

'But here I am, rabbiting on—you must wish me at Jericho! Our housekeeper will show you to your rooms, then I hope you will all join me for tea in the morning room. Well, it is *called* the morning room, though I do not know why. Of course, we use it in the morning, but also in the afternoon, so why it should be called a *morning* room… The Etheringtons have arrived too—not half an hour before you—and Mr Foxley is expected later today—'

The housekeeper, a kindly-looking woman wearing a starched white apron over a grey dress, smiled courteously at them all, then led them upstairs. The keys she wore at her waist, which proclaimed her profession, jingled as she walked.

As she mounted the stairs, Charlotte couldn't resist looking back. The Captain was leading Miss Langley and Olivia off through a doorway to Charlotte's right, while the Earl stood watching them ascend, his gaze flicking from her to Henrietta and back again. His expression was unreadable, and Charlotte felt a little disturbed. What was he thinking?

She raised her eyebrows quizzically. Noticing, he turned abruptly on his heel and left.

Charlotte did not know what to make of this. Gone was the light-hearted gentleman who had laughed with her in the library. Just now he had seemed more serious, more intense. This visit was all to do with Henrietta. She knew it—knew the only reason they were all there was to allow him to get to know Henrietta better and decide if they should suit. A budding friendship with his soon-to-be-betrothed's cousin was not his priority. Charlotte understood that.

Millicent Etherington was part of the picture too. Mrs Buxted was sure that she was another candidate for the Earl's hand, and had cautioned Henrietta to be wary. The whole thing, thought Charlotte, was sordid beyond belief. They were all part of it—the Earl, the young ladies, and the matchmaking mamas. And *she* would be forced to watch. She shuddered inwardly.

Adam watched them ascend. He was having so many doubts about this house party. It had seemed logical to invite the three ladies—Henrietta, Millicent and Charlotte—to his home, so that he could choose between them. He had not anticipated having such misgivings.

It offended his sense of honour.

He laughed quietly at his own pride. Honour would not pay the bills to restore the east wing, or pay his servants, or develop his farms. He needed to be rational.

He wondered again—for the thousandth time—about the state of Charlotte's fortune. Despite discreet enquiries, he had been unable to discover how things stood with her father because he lived abroad. Adam frowned. Distasteful as he found the idea, an early conversation with Mr Buxted was needed.

Things were clearer with the other two. He knew their dowries and in both cases he sensed that they—*and* their parents—would support a match with him. Mrs Etherington, like Mrs Buxted, had made it plain. Clumsily so, in Mrs Buxted's case.

He supposed all three ladies had been trained in the skills needed to run a house like Chadcombe. As a man, his role was focused more on the estate and its financing—the mysteries of household management were beyond him. It would also be important, he thought, that his bride should get on well with his sister and his great-aunt. The last thing he needed was friction at home.

Conscious that he was building a list in his head, he was again struck by discomfort. A wife was not a horse, to be selected on the basis of looks and performance. Yet he must not be clouded by personal preference.

As Henrietta and Charlotte climbed the stairs together he couldn't help but compare them. Henrietta, angelically fair—but so young and emotional. Charlotte, darkly pretty and much more sensible—though with disconcerting flashes of spirit at times. In terms of whose company he favoured, Charlotte was infinitely preferable. He enjoyed her intelligence, wit and demeanour. There was just something about her that denoted Quality. But he must not be too hasty. He would now have plenty of opportunity to discover more about each of them.

Turning sharply on his heel, he called for his steward.

Chapter Nine

Faith and Charlotte descended the stairs together for dinner. This was their third day at Chadcombe, and already they knew their way around the beautiful light-filled house. Their bright, comfortable rooms were on the second floor. Charlotte's room was at the front, and she had a stunning view of the lawns, the deer park and the home wood.

Chadcombe had a large staff, who ensured that all the guests' needs were looked after. The female workforce, led by Cook and the housekeeper, Mrs Gordon, and directed by Miss Langley, prepared the food, kept the house clean and ensured that the beds were made, the guests had warm water for washing and fires were lit on the cooler days. The butler, Merrion, presided over the menservants, managed the Earl's cellar, and served the finest wines, port and—in the case of the ladies—ratafia. He had been with the family over forty years, starting as a second footman, and knew every inch of the house.

As the lady of the house—until such time as the Earl should marry—Miss Langley oversaw all household matters, and she had told Charlotte that she met with the housekeeper and butler daily. Something in her demeanour had made Charlotte wonder if the elderly lady found the responsibility a strain.

Their party was now complete, and fourteen would sit down to dinner tonight. Charlotte, wearing an elegant blue crêpe dress, and with her hair dressed loosely *à la Grecque*, was looking forward to it. She and Faith had helped each other prepare, and dressed each other's hair. Faith had said she was enjoying her first 'grown-up house party', which had made Charlotte feel quite old.

Most of the guests had already assembled in the main drawing room. Mrs Etherington—a thin, pale widow who suffered from an impressive number of ailments—was seated on a settee, listing today's symptoms to Captain Fanton, who was giving the impression that he was listening intently. Henrietta was looking mutinous near the middle window, and was clearly complaining to Mrs Buxted about something.

Charlotte instinctively sought out the Earl, and then realised why Henrietta appeared unhappy. He was enjoying a conversation with Millicent Etherington beside the grand pianoforte. They were standing close together, and as they spoke, she briefly laid a hand on his arm to emphasise a point. Millicent was a spirited young lady, with a lively manner. Her hair was an unusual shade of auburn, and combined with creamy skin and hazel eyes, it had made her the focus of many a gentleman's attention this season, when she'd made her come-out.

Mr Buxted, who had arrived that afternoon, was seated with Mr Foxley and Miss Langley.

Mr Foxley, who had been watching the door, promptly rose to welcome Faith and Charlotte. Faith responded to this kindness by greeting him with a warm smile, which made him blush. Charlotte felt even older.

Lady Olivia, looking pretty in pale yellow muslin, was seated near the fireplace. She looked at ease— unlike the Reverend Sneddon, who was standing alone nearby, looking as though he wished to join one of the conversations but was unsure how.

Charlotte accepted a glass of wine from Merrion, who moved unobtrusively among the guests. Half listening to Faith and Mr Foxley's conversation, she continued to observe with amusement the interplay between Henrietta, Millicent and the Earl. The girls were transparent in their feelings and intentions, whereas Lord Shalford was much more difficult to read. Since they'd arrived she had seen him engage both ladies, seeming to favour first one, then the other. This was a gauntlet thrown down to the former friends, who were using every trick they could think of to win his attention.

He had maintained a courteous equanimity with

Charlotte, keeping his conversation general, though coincidentally he had often ended up near her. They had twice been paired for cards, and had had fun trouncing Faith and Mr Foxley on the previous evening, but he did not toy with her as he did with Henrietta and Millicent.

But then, she thought ruefully, *I cannot be coquettish.*

Mrs Buxted remained anxious about Henrietta's prospects, and continually advised her daughter on how to flirt 'properly'—complete with stories of her own successes as a debutante.

If Charlotte were to guess, she would say the Earl's heart was not engaged with either young lady. But the choice of marriage partner among the *ton* was usually more about land and money than affection—even now, in these more enlightened times. She shivered, unsure why the thought disturbed her so.

'Are you cold, Miss Wyncroft? May I send a servant for a shawl? This evening is most inclement.'

Reverend Sneddon, all solicitousness, was at her elbow.

'I am not cold, thank you.'

'May I then fetch you a drink? Ah, I see you have one.'

'I have.'

'Would you like to sit down? You see…this chaise is free. We could sit here and have a little chat and you would be comfortable.' He indicated a nearby settee.

Charlotte, helpless to rebuff him any further, sat. He joined her, flicking out his long coat-tails with a practised movement.

Reverend Sneddon was an old soul in a young man's skin, with a wet mouth, an eager manner and a slowness of thought which meant he missed some of Charlotte's attempts at humour. Unfortunately, he had begun to single her out for particular attention.

'I wish to ask you, Miss Wyncroft, what you think of our Surrey countryside. It has not the grandeur of the Alps, but it has its own beauty, do you agree?'

'Surrey is exceptionally beautiful. Its beauty is typically English, I think.'

Reverend Sneddon nodded approvingly. *"'The hills gird themselves with joy, the meadows clothe themselves with flocks."* You are correct, Miss Wyncroft, and the acuity of your observation does you great credit.'

'Er...thank you,' said Charlotte dubiously.

The Reverend, like Mrs Buxted, liked to quote obscure verses from the Bible, and was always pleased when he thought of a suitable verse.

As the Reverend droned on, Charlotte found her attention drifting to the conversation between the Captain and the Earl, who were standing nearby.

'Dash it, Adam, where did you find such a prosy fellow?'

'He is a temporary incumbent in the parish—just

for a couple of months, thankfully. He has quite a way with words, does he not?'

'We should rescue poor Miss Wyncroft.'

'She stands in no need of rescue, Harry. Besides, it is quite an entertaining spectacle.'

Charlotte, glancing up and seeing the amusement in his eyes, flashed him a challenging look. He raised his glass and gave her a wicked smile.

The Fanton brothers made a striking tableau, thought Charlotte, both so tall and handsome. The Captain said something which amused his brother. Charlotte couldn't help watching the Earl laugh. She liked him like this...relaxed.

In fact, she simply *liked* him. Seeing him here, at home, she had been pleased to discover more of the warmer, more human side to him—the one she had seen glimpses of in London. He was affectionate towards his great-aunt and his young sister, who clearly looked up to him despite hints of occasional differences in opinion. Lady Olivia was delighted to have such a large party at Chadcombe, and was warm and friendly towards them all.

The Earl was also resolute in putting his heritage—Chadcombe and the family—above all else. He took his duties seriously, meeting daily with his steward. Charlotte had concluded that her father would approve of him. *Officer material*, he'd say. He was always on the lookout for men of all classes who deserved promotion.

The Earl was not a soldier, and had no need of

patronage or promotion, yet Charlotte recognised in him the qualities of intelligence, leadership and vitality so valued by Papa. She wondered what the Earl would think of her father, and tried to imagine the two of them meeting. It gave her a strange but good feeling to imagine them together.

Charlotte made her excuses to the Reverend and joined Olivia. She immediately felt more comfortable.

It was nearly time for dinner, and almost everyone was there. Charlotte counted. Who was missing? Then she realised. Millicent's brother, Mr Hubert Etherington, who had arrived the day before, had yet to make his entrance.

Chapter Ten

Charlotte watched as Hubert paused in the doorway before mincing into the room, taking small, careful steps because the heels of his evening shoes were so high. They were made of shiny black leather and were adorned with large silver buckles which had been bevelled so as to catch the light as he walked.

Charlotte had endured a full half-hour with him earlier, hearing about his clothing.

His thin legs were encased in white silk stockings, embroidered at the ankles with golden birds. Charlotte knew all about those stockings. He had asked the seamstress for eagles, but she had never seen an eagle and so had given him matching crows. Golden crows. After he had recovered from his initial frustration, he had come to understand that there was something exceedingly noble about golden crows.

His small-clothes were of a yellow so bright it was almost shocking to the eye, while his evening coat was white and gold squares, interspersed with dark blue lines. He had told her that tying his neck-cloth normally took at least six attempts before he was satisfied, as each layer had to be folded and re-folded until his chin was forced to remain high. His shirt had points so high that he could turn his head neither to the left nor right, but instead had to turn his whole body. His waistcoat was double-breasted, with a wide shawl collar, and was patterned with intricate swirls of red, yellow, gold and white.

Charlotte glanced around, enjoying everyone's reaction. Mr Buxted, who had never before encoun-tered Mr Etherington, lifted a quizzing glass to his eye, uttering, *'Good God!'* in an animated tone. Miss Langley had her mouth open in shock. Lady Olivia moved her hand to her forehead, while Lord Shalford shook his head slowly.

His eyes instinctively sought Charlotte's, and they shared their amusement at Hubert's ridiculousness.

Hubert made his way carefully to the central win-dow embrasure, where Henrietta and her mother stood. He bowed equally carefully—but with great grace.

'Ladies, you look beautiful tonight. Demeter and Persephone personified.'

Mrs Buxted was unsure how to interpret this. Henrietta had no such reservations. Seeing only the admiration in his eyes, and still smarting over Mil-licent's outrageous flirting with the Earl, she gave Hubert an encouraging smile.

'Thank you, Mr Etherington. I must say your waistcoat is most impressive.'

Mrs Buxted eyed it suspiciously. 'I believe these colours are quite the thing among you young men. Fashions have certainly changed since *I* was a young girl.'

'Oh, but, Mrs Buxted, you are still a very young lady. Why, if I didn't know you had a grown-up daughter, I should not believe it.'

Mrs Buxted responded well to this sally, while across the room Mr Buxted guffawed loudly. By the time Hubert—hampered by his shirt-points—turned to view him, he seemed engrossed in conversation with Miss Langley.

The Earl and Harry had joined Charlotte and Olivia, and the men shared their opinions of Hubert's attire.

'Thank God I was never fashionable,' Harry said with feeling.

'Oho! I do recall,' said the Earl, 'a certain hat that you thought was *extremely* fashionable.'

Harry looked outraged. 'Well, if you are talking of the smart beaver that I wore when I was fifteen, then I shall tell you that you are off the mark. And furthermore you are a blackguard and a scoundrel, Adam, for you know that I would not stoop so low as to make *you* embarrassed in front of the ladies.' He winked at Charlotte and Olivia. 'I shall not even *mention* the incident with the raft.'

'Oh, do tell,' said Charlotte, 'for I should love to see Lord Shalford embarrassed.'

The Earl held up his hands. 'I take it back, Harry. The hat was perfectly fine and stylish, and it suited you perfectly. And nothing happened with any raft.'

'Of course not. You certainly *didn't* challenge me to a race on the lake with home-made rafts, and your raft certainly *didn't* sink within yards of the start.'

'No!' Charlotte clapped her hands together with glee, then directed a sympathetic look at the Earl. 'Were you *very* humiliated?'

'Completely mortified,' said the Earl, shaking his head mournfully.

'Oh, you poor thing!' Charlotte laughed insincerely.

She noticed that Harry and Olivia were staring at her and the Earl, transfixed.

'What?'

Harry nudged his sister forcefully. 'Nothing... nothing. Oh, look—I think it is time to eat.'

He was right, for Merrion was just announcing dinner.

Charlotte, moving with the others to the dining room, wondered briefly what they had been staring at, then put it out of her thoughts.

Charlotte sat at the pianoforte, concentrating on her music. She loved to play and sing and—unlike her cousins—took pleasure in practising until she was content. She had found a kindred spirit in Olivia, who had shared some new pieces with her, and they had successfully performed a duet for the guests last night.

Just now, Charlotte was practising a beautiful aria by Mr Handel that she had never learned before. She thought she had the piano part mastered, but was still working on the vocal performance. *Lascia ch'io pianga* were the words—*Let me weep*. Ironic that she was singing a lament, and yet she could hardly recall a happier time.

She finished the piece and looked up—to find the Earl standing in the doorway, watching her.

'Beautiful,' he said softly, then turned and left, leaving her blushing and more than a little bewildered.

It was difficult to understand the effect that he had on her. Each time he entered a room her heart beat a little faster, and she was ever conscious of where he sat or stood. Her ear had attuned itself to his voice, and she could hear it even now, when he was not near.

Why? *Why* did she react to him so particularly? Was she simply becoming caught up in Henrietta and Millicent's games? She frowned. She must be true to herself. Empty flirtation and the competitive games of the Marriage Mart did not become her. If she married it would be based on a genuine bond with a man she loved, not on his wealth and rank. Although, she conceded ruefully, she was unlikely to marry outside her own class.

Perhaps I am just as shallow and vapid as the rest of the ton.

Completely confused, and no nearer to seeing her own heart clearly, she returned to her music.

Adam strode towards the stables, desperately trying to shake the feelings that had swamped him just now, as he'd listened to Charlotte's beautiful clear voice. He had enjoyed watching her, her face intent and focused, knowing that he was unobserved. He had had the strongest and most unexpected urge to kiss her.

Where had *that* come from?

It would not do.

Finally he had had a discreet conversation with Mr Buxted. Charlotte, it seemed, was no heiress. Mr Buxted had explained that Charlotte, though of excellent family, had inherited the consequences of a spendthrift grandfather—just like his own. Charlotte's father was in the military—not an occupation associated with creating great wealth. It was likely that Charlotte's dowry would be no better than respectable.

Adam had listened in dismay. In truth, the strength of his disappointment had surprised him. It seemed that he had entertained strong hopes—unrecognised even by himself—that Charlotte would prove to be eligible. And after his conversation with Mr Buxted last night he had dreamed of her—of holding her hand as they walked together.

When he had awoken, the sense of loss he'd felt had reminded him of the pain he had felt when each of his parents had died.

Yet when he had heard the beautiful music Charlotte was making he had been unable to resist opening the door softly, just to watch her for a moment. And now here he was, with tumultuous thoughts and feelings battling in his head, his chest and his stomach. Somehow she had penetrated his defences, and he was well on the way to being beguiled by her.

Now that he knew he could not marry her, to dwell on his own feelings and preferences was an indulgence he could not afford. That way led only to pain. He must overcome it. He could be her friend, but nothing more.

'Saddle my horse!' he snapped to the stable-boy.

'Yes, my lord.' The boy moved quickly, wondering what had put his normally even-tempered master into such foul humour.

They had now been at Chadcombe for two happy weeks, and the guests had all developed their own routines. While many of the party slept late, still accustomed to London hours, the early risers—Charlotte among them—often met for breakfast. The Earl regularly ate with them, before disappearing to meet with his steward.

Mr Foxley and Mr Buxted had formed an unlikely friendship, forged over a mutual love of fishing. Most mornings they fished together in the trout stream, usually returning empty-handed but occasionally with a fish or two, which they bore triumphantly to Cook with all the eagerness of schoolboys.

By late morning, when Charlotte had visited Miss Langley and finished her music, Faith had usually appeared. She and Charlotte had developed the habit of walking in the gardens, and the Earl—surprisingly—often accompanied them. They had explored all the gardens around the house, discovering such delights as a grotto, an avenue of fountains and a rose garden. Even the kitchen garden was of great interest to Charlotte, who loved its neat lines and delicious scents. And while they walked, they talked—of books, family and gardening, among other things.

Charlotte looked forward to this part of the day with much more intensity than she should. She and the Earl were becoming fast friends, and Charlotte was revelling in his company. She had succeeded in subduing many of the tumultuous feelings he aroused in her—partly because he was now unfailingly polite towards her, with no hint of the warmer emotions she had been surprised to see in his eyes before. She had convinced herself that she had imagined it. He sometimes seemed tired, and distracted, as if struggling with some hidden emotion, but always she had a feeling of warmth in his company.

Faith, too, was blossoming at Chadcombe, and

took a full part in the three-way conversations—though some of the lively teasing between Charlotte and the Earl passed her by.

They had once seen what looked like a Greek temple in the distance, on the edge of the woods, and the Earl had promised to escort them to it. After two days of showers today was dry, with the promise of sunshine, and so they were to walk out. Charlotte donned kid half-boots and a pretty straw bonnet with a blue satin ribbon, and brought her cloak in case it should turn out to be cool. When she reached the hall Faith and the Earl were waiting, along with Mr Foxley, who had just returned from his fishing trip.

'Oh, Charlotte, what a pretty bonnet,' said Faith enthusiastically.

Charlotte smiled. Faith was so much kinder than her sister.

Mr Foxley gallantly agreed, and the Earl, who rarely complimented any of the ladies on their looks or fashions, said, 'It becomes you.'

Charlotte, gratified, felt her cheeks go a little pink, then chided herself for reacting.

They meandered companionably through the deer park up to the temple—which, the Earl explained, had been erected in his grandfather's day as a place from which to enjoy views of the house. He turned back, indicating the scene.

They all turned—and collectively caught their breath. From this position, the view was stunning.

The green sward of the deer park, dotted with mature oaks and elms, swept like a verdant carpet down from the temple, then gently up again to the gardens, and from this angle the lines seemed to converge perfectly to frame the house. Beyond, the Surrey hills provided the perfect backdrop.

The whole scene was a perfectly balanced vista of solid grey stone melding perfectly with the green-brown hues of nature.

Charlotte was singularly hopeless at art, but she had never more wished for artistic talent so that she might paint Chadcombe and keep its perfection alive in her memory.

'My goodness,' said Mr Foxley.

'It *is* beautiful,' agreed Faith.

She accompanied Mr Foxley to the right side of the temple, to explore the view from there. Charlotte remained immobile.

The Earl stayed, watching her. 'Miss Wyncroft…?' he prompted gently.

'It is flawless,' she said simply. 'I think I have not seen a house more perfectly suited to its surroundings.'

'Thank you,' he said gruffly.

He looked directly at her, and her heart melted. 'Your grandfather made something wonderful.'

'He did. He also left us with debts and mortgages, which my father worked hard to pay down. He had not the money to build grand things, but this beauty belongs as much to him as to my grandfather, for he paid for it with hard work.'

'It belongs to you, too.'

'It's my turn,' he said. 'They each did something great in their own way. Now it is for me to add my contribution. I know that you understand that.'

He offered her his arm as they stepped through the back of the temple, where stone steps led to an uneven winding path through the woods. Mr Foxley and Faith joined them, and Mr Foxley, taking his lead from the Earl, awkwardly offered his arm to Faith. Blushing, she placed her gloved hand on his arm.

'This path through the woods will take us to the main drive, and we can walk from there to the house,' said the Earl.

By unspoken agreement they stayed in their pairs as they walked. Mr Foxley and Faith walked a little ahead, close together, while Charlotte and the Earl dropped behind a little.

The path wound its way through a pretty wilderness. The twists and turns of the trail meant Mr Foxley and Faith, though only a little ahead, were frequently out of view. It seemed to Charlotte that there was no one else in the world save her and the Earl. On their right the woods were dark and mysterious, while to their left they caught occasional glimpses of the deer park and the house as they walked.

In one part the trees were young and small, and the Earl stopped to point them out to Charlotte.

'My father planted these oaks when I was a child. Look, some are starting to produce acorns this year.' He indicated the small half-formed pods on the lower branches. 'It takes great vision to plant an oak.'

She understood. 'He planted these knowing he would never see them fully grown, never sit in their shade.'

'Yes.' His voice broke a little. 'His illness… He should not have been taken away so soon.'

'You still miss him.' She spoke softly.

'Every day.' He looked into her eyes. 'How is it that you understand me so well?'

They stood, not speaking, while the silence of the woods surrounded them. Her hand was still on his arm. She could feel his warmth through the fabric of his coat. Her pulse was beating so fast she feared her heart would explode.

'You know, that bonnet *is* extremely fetching.'

His voice was low and his eyes held hers. She could not look away.

'You are remarkably pretty.'

He lifted his hand and gently touched her face. His fingertips left a trail of fire on her skin. She didn't move, afraid to break the moment.

Tilting her chin up, he bent his head and kissed her.

His lips were warm, intense and delicious. Charlotte's heart was beating so loudly it seemed the whole world moved to its rhythm. For a timeless moment they kissed. It was the sweetest, most beautiful moment she had ever known.

Chapter Eleven

The Earl stepped back in agitation.

'Ch—Miss Wyncroft, I apologise! You are a guest in my home and I have taken advantage of you. I should not have— I mean, I have never—'

He raked his fingers through his hair. His expression was one of self-disgust.

'And your father is far away. You have no protectors. I am a wretch, Miss Wyncroft! I have no excuse, though you are simply— But I must not speak. Do please say you will forgive me?'

Charlotte, who felt greatly confused, could only mumble stupidly.

'Oh, no! Of course!'

Her face must be a fiery red, and she wondered what he must think of her. Did he know how she liked him? Did he think that she, like Henrietta and Millicent, was on the catch for him? Did he think her *forward*? Was that why he had kissed her?

Her mortification knew no bounds.

Adjusting her bonnet, which was decidedly askew, Charlotte began walking, her eyes on the path ahead, hurrying a little to get away from him—away from the moment.

They quickly caught up with Faith and Mr Foxley.

Mr Foxley, seemingly unaware of any tension, said cheerfully, 'Shalford, tell me—how many tenants do you support?'

The Earl answered steadily, and he and Mr Foxley began to speak of farm workers and livestock, and the best crops for different types of soil. Mr Foxley had developed an interest in agriculture, and he and the Earl spoke easily on such topics as yields and cattle breeds until they were back at the house.

Faith and Charlotte dropped back a little, allowing the gentlemen an opportunity to talk. Thankfully, Faith did not try to engage Charlotte in conversation, and was content to follow the gentlemen, a dreamy half-smile playing on her lips.

Charlotte was surprised by the Earl's air of calm so soon afterwards. It was as though, for him, the kiss had never happened. She knew that men often took such things lightly, and hoped this meant he would forget the incident. She felt incredibly shaken by the kiss—probably because she had not been kissed very often.

In fact this was only her third ever kiss. She had enjoyed a brief flirtation with a young officer in Vienna last year, and two years previously had been kissed by a rather good-looking Italian count, who had professed undying love for her. Charlotte had been impressed by his fervour, but unmoved.

Neither kiss had stirred her like this one. She was unsure why. Something about the man and this place, their conversation, perhaps. Certainly when he had spoken of his father and Chadcombe she had felt a strong affinity, a sense of connection to him.

She pushed the thought away, strangely reluctant to dwell on it.

The Earl was indifferent to the kiss, it seemed, and was feeling guilty because she was his guest. Remembering his agitation, the words he had used, and most of all his regretful tone, she felt flooded with mortification and hurt. It clearly had meant nothing to him—which meant that *she* meant nothing to him. She needed to get as far away from him as she possibly could.

As they mounted the steps to the house, the gentlemen stepped back to allow her and Faith to enter first. Charlotte could feel the Earl's eyes on her. Staring fixedly ahead, she went inside and continued straight to her room.

There she paced in some agitation for quite ten minutes, before removing her bonnet, cloak and muddy boots. Her skirt hem was muddy too, and without Priddy she would have to deal with it herself. She was reluctant to call on Mrs Buxted's dresser or a housemaid just now.

After brushing the mud from the dress as best she could, she let down her overdress, tidied her hair and prepared to face the others again. Her pulse was less tumultuous, though each time she remembered the kiss she suffered renewed discomfiture.

Thankfully, her reflection in the mirror showed no sign of her distress.

'Be calm,' she told herself. 'All is well.'

With her own reassurances ringing in her ears, she ventured downstairs.

Approaching the drawing room, she heard the hum of voices—male voices as well as female ones. What if he was in there? With her hand on the door, she felt her courage suddenly fail her, and she walked on, away from the room, to visit Miss Langley.

She failed to notice the Earl, watching her as he walked along the landing above.

Adam watched her, knowing she was still distressed. Internally, he berated himself again for having taken advantage of her. He who prided himself on his self-control, his calm good sense and judgement! He had actually kissed a young, innocent lady who was a guest in his home! He imagined the cold, angry eyes of her father upon him. *Any* father would be justifiably outraged. If someone had behaved so towards Olivia…!

He could not account for it. Why had he behaved so rashly—especially since he already knew he could not marry her? He was not one to trifle with women. Yet each time he remembered how she had looked at him, her beautiful face framed perfectly by that damned bonnet…

She haunted him. He could not sleep, and some nights he had taken to drinking or reading in the library until he was exhausted, for to retire too soon meant hours of restless wakefulness.

He would resist this. He must.

Miss Langley's parlour was a small, comfortable room, with a fireplace and a lady's desk, and Miss Langley had used it as her own since Lady Shalford's death. Charlotte had formed the habit of visiting each day after her hostess's meeting with the housekeeper, to see how she did. The elderly lady seemed to value Charlotte's support, which appeared to soothe her worries about household matters. Charlotte was careful not to overstep her role as guest, but listened sympathetically to poor Miss Langley's daily trials.

Today, Miss Langley was walking around the room with a long piece of paper in her hand, muttering.

'Dear Miss Wyncroft, I am *so* pleased to see you. What a to-do!'

The paper—which looked like a list—was rather crumpled, and her voice was tremulous.

Charlotte took the elderly lady's hand and spoke in a calming tone. 'Miss Langley, let me assist you. Let us sit, and you can tell me what has happened.'

'Oh, dear… Well, the new oven is not working,

and Cook says it will not do, for the third footman and Philip the groom have both tried to mend it, and she says she never *wanted* a new-fangled oven, and how is she supposed to cook for so many people on a modern contraption she says is quite *useless*? And the night footman tells me Mrs Cotter in the gatehouse is ill, and so is her baby, and I need to visit them—and Mrs Gordon says the young ladies are too demanding, and she will need two extra housemaids, but *where* I am supposed to find more housemaids I do not know!'

Miss Langley wept quietly into a lace-edged handkerchief. Charlotte's heart melted for her. She held the dear lady's hand and made soothing, reassuring noises, while all the time her mind was working on solutions to the day's difficulties, none of which seemed to be insurmountable. It was a good distraction from her own troubles.

When Miss Langley seemed ready to talk again, Charlotte said tentatively, 'Tell me…do you know who installed the oven?'

'No, I cannot remember the name…' Miss Langley thought for a second, her aged face crinkled with concentration. 'But, wait—yes! It was Mr Price, from Farnham. He is an ironmonger, but now he sells new stoves.'

'Could someone fetch Mr Price to repair the oven?'

'Yes, of *course*. One of the grooms could go. But what if he cannot come? Or what if he cannot mend it today? What shall we *do*?'

'Is there also a stove? Have you any other means of cooking?'

'Well, yes, the top stove is still functioning, and we have the bread oven, which is in the third kitchen…' She thought for a moment. 'And we could use the fire griddle in the back chimney if we need to… But what of the pies and the roasted meats?'

'Is it possible to review the menu with Cook, so she can avoid dishes normally finished in the oven? Just until Mr Price can restore it?'

'Of course! I shall call her directly.' Miss Langley moved to the bell-pull with renewed vigour.

Cook appeared quickly, with a harassed expression. Miss Langley, with great authority, told her of the plan. Cook, relieved, undertook to carry it out immediately. She and Miss Langley then had a discussion about a revised menu, which was soon agreed. Cook flashed a grateful look towards Charlotte as she left, though Charlotte had not spoken.

'And now,' said Charlotte, 'tell me of the housemaids, and of the unreasonable demands that I and the other ladies are making.'

'Oh, *no*, Miss Wyncroft! I should never suggest that *you*— Why, when you are so helpful, and so undemanding, and—' She twisted the handkerchief between her hands. 'No, never *you*, Miss Wyncroft. But the Etheringtons have brought only one maid, and of course, although dear Miss Faith has such an unassuming nature—'

'She is a dear girl, is she not?'

'Indeed she is. And not in the least like— But it is of no matter. We need two extra housemaids, and I do not know where we shall get them, for all of the village girls are already working in the kitchens, and none would be fit to attend the ladies above stairs.'

'Could you perhaps use an agency? I know that in Vienna my father and his man of business always found staff to hire—except for my abigail and groom, who have been with us since before I was born.'

'An agency? Perhaps… We have not entertained much in years. We normally hire extra staff from among the servants' families, or from the village if we need to, but it is many years since we had such a large party at Chadcombe. Perhaps dear Adam *would* agree to an agency…'

'Might Lord Shalford's steward be of assistance?'

'Indeed, yes—Grove will know how to do it. A capital idea! I shall seek him this instant. Thank you, my dear. Now, will he be in his office…? Or perhaps not—he was to meet with the thatcher today. Perhaps he… But no…'

She left in a flurry of trailing shawls and half-sentences, but Charlotte thought she was less anxious than she had been.

After lunch, the ladies, as well as Mr Foxley, Captain Fanton and Hubert, gathered in the drawing room. To Charlotte's relief the Earl had left immediately, muttering about matters of business. She needed time to think. Was he playing with her? The hurt she had felt at first was now giving way to anger.

She had no great dowry. She was not eligible. So by kissing her, she could only conclude that he was trifling with her. Perhaps her first negative impression of him had been correct. Yet, she was finding it hard to think ill of him. Something in her wanted to find a way of reconciling things. What was he— honourable or dishonourable? And what of Millicent and Henrietta?

She stole a glance at her cousin. Henrietta was flirting with Hubert again. He paid her outrageous compliments and was unwavering in his attentions. They were bemoaning the fact that since their arrival at Chadcombe there had been no opportunities to dance.

'Charlotte will play for us,' Henrietta pronounced, 'and you and I shall dance, Mr Etherington. Or perhaps Captain Fanton would like to dance with me?'

Charlotte's heart sank. How was she to concentrate on music when her mind was awhirl? Before she could respond, however, Henrietta paused— changeable as quicksilver—frowning in concentration.

'I have just had the most wonderful idea, Olivia,' she said in a trilling voice.

Henrietta moved to sit with Lady Olivia, who had been quietly sewing a shirt. Olivia was surprised at Miss Buxted addressing her directly, for after the first couple of days Henrietta had not given much attention to any of the other ladies.

'We have only a week left at Chadcombe. Should we not have a ball before we all part?'

'Oh, how wonderful that would be!' Olivia's eyes lit up. 'But Adam may not like it.'

'Nonsense—we will persuade him. Would you not like to have a ball?'

'Of course!'

'We talked of going on a carriage ride tomorrow, if the dry weather should hold. We shall ask him then, and you and I can prepare all our arguments.'

Harry, who was just leaving, smiled mischievously at Charlotte. He was clearly enjoying Henrietta's machinations. Charlotte sighed.

Adam was busy in conversation with his steward, Grove, when Harry found him. One of the estate cottages had suffered a small fire earlier in the day, and Grove had organised for the family to stay with relatives until repairs could be made to their home. It was the perfect distraction for Adam's troubled mind.

'Listen, Adam—you are to be assailed by the ladies.' Harry's eyes were dancing.

'Indeed? What's amiss?'

'Miss Buxted has taken it into her head that you should hold a ball before they all leave. She's got Olivia by the ear and the two of them are plotting to ask you.'

'A ball? There hasn't been a ball here for years. Remember when we were children, how we would hide on the landing and watch the guests arrive?'

'Yes, and when we'd been put to bed Mama would come in to say goodnight, all satin and perfume and jewels!'

They grinned at each other.

'So, what do you think?'

Adam shook his head slowly. 'I'm not sure. It would be a lot of extra work for the servants, and for Great-Aunt Clara. I'm impressed that she has coped with our guests so well...'

Grove coughed delicately. 'If I might be permitted, my lord—?'

'Yes, Grove?'

'Miss Langley has spoken to me about hiring two additional housemaids. If I make that four, and add two manservants, then I expect we will manage any extra work.' He paused. 'It would be good to see the ballroom in use again.'

Harry agreed. 'Indeed it would. And Olivia would love it.'

The Earl considered this. 'It might be good for Olivia to test her wings here at Chadcombe before she debuts in London next year... But still, I am conscious of the burden Great-Aunt Clara carries in being hostess. She assures me all is well, but to ask her to organise a ball on top of her existing duties...'

Grove intervened again. 'I am aware, my lord,

that Miss Langley is receiving assistance already. From one of the guests.'

Harry and Adam both looked surprised. 'One of the guests?' asked Harry. 'Who?'

'Miss Wyncroft, I believe, has been advising and supporting her. The staff all speak highly of her. A most excellent female, I understand.'

'Miss Wyncroft!' The Earl stood, lost in thought for a moment. 'A ball here…away from London…a *private* ball… There should be no objection to *all* of the guests taking part…'

Here was the perfect opportunity to do something for Charlotte. He could not forget how she had been left out of all the London parties by her hard-hearted aunt.

He grinned. 'Very well. Let's do it. We *shall* hold a ball—my first Chadcombe ball.'

'Capital!' said Harry. 'I shall leave you to make the arrangements.'

'Harry!' called the Earl, as his brother turned to go.

'Yes?'

'Say nothing of this. I shall enjoy Olivia and Miss Buxted's campaign to…er…*persuade* me.'

The next day dawned bright and dry, with hints of blue sky amid fluffy clouds. Miss Buxted was in high alt, and was driving everyone to distraction. No fewer than five dresses were rejected before she finally settled on a half-dress of jonquil and white striped percale, with gathered Mameluke sleeves and a high poke bonnet.

Flint had already attended Mrs Buxted, who had gone downstairs, leaving the three young ladies to finish their preparations in Henrietta's room. The housemaid now returned with hot water and curling irons. The irons had had to be heated in the kitchen fire, as the oven was to be mended today.

'Now, miss,' said Flint, 'let me do your side curls.'

'Make them *perfect*, Flint,' said Henrietta. 'If I am in an open carriage I should not wish for the wind to blow my curls out.'

'Do you travel in an open carriage today?' asked Flint. 'I understand the closed coach will also be used.'

'There will be three carriages,' said Henrietta. 'I wonder which one I should choose. In the closed coach I can avoid the sun and the wind, but I shall be stuck with only the dull people to talk to—for I believe some of the gentlemen are to ride alongside us.'

'What about the open carriage?'

'Well, I would if I was sure my hair would not be ruined, for I could converse more naturally with Lord—with the gentlemen. I will travel in the curricle, because at least that is more exciting than a boring landau. Captain Fanton will drive the curricle.'

Charlotte had noted Henrietta's reference to the Earl. She was clearly planning to reignite his interest in her. She dreaded having to spend the day watching them.

'The day promises sunshine,' said Flint, 'so you may need a parasol. It will also protect you from the wind.'

'An excellent notion! Faith, I shall take *your* parasol, for it will match this dress perfectly.'

Faith looked mutinous, but said nothing.

'Where do you travel today? Where is your destination?'

'Oh, I don't know. Some old ruins, I think. Do stop, Flint! That is enough.'

Faith was helping Charlotte with the sleeve buttons on a handsome day-dress of pale green muslin. Faith was already dressed, in a pale blue figured muslin with a neat flounce. Both ladies were ready, and in no need of Flint's assistance. They donned light spencers, rather than pelisses, as the weather looked so promising.

Charlotte forgot her reticule, and had to return to her own room for it, so was last to arrive downstairs.

Outside was a scene of glorious chaos, with three carriages and a number of riding horses taking up space in front of the house. A groom in full livery was assisting Miss Langley into the coach, where Mrs Etherington was already seated.

Millicent was sitting primly in a dashing raised curricle, twirling a pretty pink parasol, with Captain Fanton beside her. She looked decidedly smug, and was clearly enjoying her perch—in the carriage that Henrietta had wanted to travel in. Millicent had won *that* particular battle, having taken less time over her toilette and gotten there first.

Lady Olivia, the Earl and Mr Foxley were mounted on fine horses. The Earl, Charlotte noticed, was on the same stallion he'd had in London. His attire of buckskins, gleaming hessians and a well-fitted brown redingote showed off his fine figure to advantage. And his horse was magnificent. Charlotte felt a pang, wishing she could ride her beloved Andalusia today. But Lusy was in London, so she must sit sedately in a carriage.

Of the other gentlemen, Mr Buxted was not to travel—preferring a more sedentary day filled with reading and sleeping and enjoying a home-cooked nuncheon—and Mr Etherington—looking dazzling in puce pantaloons with a salmon waistcoat and his usual high starched collar—had had the sense to wear outdoor boots with a low heel. They gleamed with a glossy shine and had golden tassels which swung as he walked. He and Reverend Sneddon would join the ladies in travelling by carriage, neither being comfortable on horseback.

Seats in the carriages were filling up. Reverend Sneddon looked hopefully at Charlotte as he entered the closed coach. Charlotte—reminded of a mournful puppy—studiously ignored him, and the final seat was taken by Mrs Buxted.

Henrietta was being handed into the landau, muttering under her breath. Hubert and Faith were already seated on the large front-facing bench. Instead of sitting between them, Henrietta stood, looking steadily at Hubert. Belatedly realising his error, Hubert jumped out of the seat as if shot.

'My dear Miss Buxted! *You* shall have this seat and I shall sit here.'

He moved to sit in the single rear-facing seat, telling her he preferred it since it allowed him the pleasure of gazing at her angelic face. That seemed to be what he was trying to say, anyway. The words did not emerge with any sequence or fluency. Flustered, he stopped halfway through, realising his angel was not listening.

Henrietta was trying to open her parasol in the limited space. She spoke curtly to her sister, who was beside her.

'Faith! *Do* move to the corner so I can use my parasol.'

With a cross look, Faith moved as far as she could into the corner. The sun broke through for the first time just as Henrietta succeeded in opening her parasol.

After a quick scan of all the carriages, Charlotte approached to join her cousins. The other carriages were now full, and there was easily space for her to sit between Henrietta and Faith.

Henrietta disagreed. 'Charlotte, you must sit in one of the other carriages—for there is no room left in this one, as you can see.'

'The other carriages are full, Henrietta. This is the only space left.'

'But you will crumple my dress. And I need to keep my parasol opened, for this sunshine might ruin my complexion.' Her chin set mutinously.

Charlotte stood, uncertain. If she persisted Henrietta might make a scene. Yet there were no other seats free. Perhaps she should stay at the house with Mr Buxted…

'Miss Wyncroft!' The Earl approached on his tall stallion. 'Might I make a suggestion?'

Charlotte looked up at him, her heart suddenly pounding. She had managed to avoid conversation with him since the incident in the woods yesterday; this was the first time they had spoken directly since then. She squirmed uncomfortably, overwhelmed by a combination of anger, hurt and sheer mortification.

'If you have brought your habit, you may ride. My sister Olivia has a second horse which you might find to your liking. I am sure she would not mind.'

'I certainly would not mind!' confirmed Olivia, who had overheard this exchange. 'Indeed I would be most grateful to you, Miss Wyncroft, for she has not been exercised in days.'

Faced with the smiling generosity of Lady Olivia, her sudden thrill at the thought of riding again, and the need to escape from the Earl's keen gaze, Charlotte agreed. 'Give me ten minutes to change. I shall return directly.'

She was true to her word. When she returned a little less than ten minutes later, in her blue velvet riding habit, a groom was leading out a beautiful grey mare.

'Oh, you are *so* pretty,' she said to the mare, stroking her soft face.

The groom helped her mount and the party set off.

Charlotte's heart was still beating unaccountably fast. Riding with Mr Foxley, Olivia and the Earl meant she could no longer avoid *him* without making her discomfort obvious. She hoped that she would survive the encounter without revealing that the kiss they had shared was consuming her thoughts.

She still did not know how to interpret it. When she remembered his tenderness, the way he had touched her face, she felt sure that he had not been playing with her. Yet they both knew he could not marry her. She had shed hot tears into her pillow last night, mixing sadness with anger and frustration, but right now all she wanted was to avoid revealing to him just how much he had affected her.

She resolved to stay by Olivia's side.

Chapter Twelve

Charlotte gradually relaxed. Lady Olivia's mare was a joy to ride, the weather was perfect, and she was enjoying the trek through leafy lanes and by-roads. The ladies rode side by side, talking and commenting on the views around them, and Mr Foxley rode alongside the landau when the road was wide enough, so he could converse with Mr Etherington, Henrietta and Faith. He had a good seat, and showed himself to great advantage on the tall gelding provided for him by his host.

The Earl led the party, but as their pace was determined by the trundling coach, progress was slow. He dropped back to speak to Olivia, Mr Foxley and Charlotte.

'I am thinking we might leave the road here and ride through the countryside, where we can let the horses have their heads. We can take a longer route and meet the carriages at Waverley.'

'Oh, yes, Adam,' said Olivia. 'Let's do that.'

Mr Foxley declined, indicating that he would stay with the carriages. When the plan was divulged to the others, Mrs Etherington welcomed Mr Foxley's decision.

'Oh, thank goodness Mr Foxley will stay with us.' she said. 'For what if we should be set upon by thieves or highwaymen?'

The Earl looked concerned. 'If you do not like it, ma'am, we will all stay with you.'

'Oh, no,' she said faintly, 'for we will also have Reverend Sneddon and my dear Hubert to protect us.'

Reverend Sneddon looked quite startled at having been placed in the role of protector, while Hubert— from the landau—announced dramatically, 'Fear not! I will protect these lovely ladies with my life if needed!'

Henrietta looked impressed.

They continued together on the Farnham Road as far as Elstead, then the Earl, Charlotte and Olivia left the carriages and turned up a side lane. The Fantons were familiar with the country around Waverley for, Olivia told Charlotte, it was one of their favourite rides.

The next hour was delightful. At times they picked their way carefully through fields and farmland, but they also cantered through two wide meadows. Olivia rode protectively beside Charlotte at first, until the Earl realised what she was doing.

'You need not worry about Miss Wyncroft,' he said. 'She has as good a seat as any lady in England.'

'Praise indeed,' replied his sister.

Charlotte's face flushed, but she could only be pleased. Really, it was all just too confusing.

Finally, they slowed to ford the River Wey. Olivia went first, and then Charlotte, with the Earl beside her, entered the river. They moved together across the shallow watercourse. Olivia went ahead, urging her mount up the shallow riverbank. Charlotte and the Earl paused for a moment and let the horses dip their heads for a drink. The summer sunshine sparkled on the water, which looked clear and clean. Charlotte could feel the comforting warmth of the sun on her back.

'Did you enjoy that?'

'Oh, I did!' she said, with passion. 'It was wonderful.'

'Good. I like to see you happy.'

He looked intently at her, and her heart beat faster. His mouth opened and closed, as if he wished to say something. She waited, unsure.

Finally words burst from him. 'You look glorious with colour in your cheeks and your eyes bright.'

Her colour deepened. 'Thank you.'

They continued to look at each other, neither speaking. As his eyes fixed hers, Charlotte felt a warm happiness surround her such as she had never known. How long the moment lasted she could not afterwards remember. Her confusion, hurt and anger disappeared, melted by the sunshine, the diamond-sparkling water and the warm intensity in his gaze.

'Here we are!' called Olivia, indicating some grey stone ruins ahead.

She spurred her mount to a trot, and the Earl and Charlotte followed.

Charlotte felt as though she was under a spell. So quickly he had charmed her into forgetting how he had hurt her. Was she so weak that she should succumb so easily? Yet the delicious warmth inside could not be denied. If he had tried to kiss her again…what would she have done?

Set among summer greenery, the ruins looked as if they had simply grown into the landscape, like silvery stone hedgerows. Two walls of a long building remained, with another beyond. Charlotte could clearly see the arched window spaces, and could imagine it complete. All around were interesting lumps and bumps, covered in grass and ivy, with hints of further treasures beneath. The whole scene was bathed in sunlight, and was verdant, serene and beautiful.

Olivia disappeared among the dappled ruins, while Charlotte and the Earl paused again.

'Monks lived in this building,' said the Earl. 'It is thought the other was for visitors and lay people. It's said King John stayed here.'

'How old is it?' Charlotte was fascinated. She had visited historical sites in Europe, but she was finally *home*, in England, and its history called to her in a different way.

'I don't think it is known for sure. After the Conqueror—possibly twelfth-century. It was destroyed in Henry VIII's dissolution.'

Charlotte drank in the atmosphere. 'It's so peaceful here today. It's hard to imagine the pain and trouble of that time.'

He nodded, and their eyes met. A slow smile lit his face and she could only smile back, again lost in the moment. Oh, this man. How he affected her!

He nudged his horse closer to hers and bent towards her. Charlotte's pulse was racing. She took in every detail of him—his handsome face, the intense grey gaze, those lips… She held her breath—

'Aaaaaargh!'

The silence was shattered by a shriek from their left. They turned to see the rest of their party walking across the grass. Two grooms followed, staggering under the weight of a huge picnic basket.

The shriek, it seemed, had come from Henrietta. Blushing at the thought of what had just *nearly* happened—and in full view!—Charlotte nudged her horse towards the group. Henrietta was flushed and distressed, Mrs Buxted was patting her hand ineffectively, while the others looked on. No one, it seemed, had noticed that near-kiss on horseback.

'It was a rat, I tell you! A *huge* one! It ran across my foot!'

The Captain flashed his brother a wry smile, while Millicent looked decidedly sceptical.

Faith looked towards Charlotte and the Earl and mouthed the word *mouse*. She then indicated with her finger and thumb the size of the now absent rodent.

Fieldmouse, Charlotte guessed.

'Oh, you poor thing,' said Mrs Buxted. 'A rat, you say?'

Mr Etherington, hopping from foot to foot in agitation, made comforting sympathetic noises—then distracted himself by noticing a spot of mud on one of his glossy boots. Tutting in exasperation, he produced a large handkerchief from his pocket and began wiping furiously at the offending stain.

'Did you see it, Mama?'

'I did,' said her parent, perjuring herself without a blink. 'Nasty, horrid thing. My poor girl. You should sit down. Why is there nothing to sit on?'

'We shall have our picnic here,' said Lord Shalford, his expression unreadable.

The grooms unburdened themselves of the basket and began to unpack it. Cloths were quickly found and Henrietta, pleased with all the attention, sat carefully, spreading the skirt of her overdress until she was satisfied. The rodent forgotten, she twirled her parasol and smiled benignly at those around her.

The riders dismounted and handed their reins to the grooms. They all found places to sit, and enjoyed an excellent lunch of meats, cheeses, preserves, breads and fruit, with a choice of wines and lemonade to drink.

Henrietta took the opportunity to scold the Earl for abandoning them on the road, which he took in good spirit. He was remarkably patient with Henrietta, Charlotte noted. Why did that anger her so much? Was he playing games with all of them?

Millicent, thrilled with her curricle ride, was today focusing on flirting with the Captain. She was sitting on the edge of one of the picnic blankets, sharing a bunch of grapes with him. The Captain looked as if he was enjoying the light dalliance.

Henrietta looked at them, then shrugged. Coquettishly, ignoring Hubert completely, she asked the Earl if he might show her the ruins. He complied with alacrity, offering his hand to help her rise. As she stood up Henrietta stumbled slightly, and he instinctively put out an arm to steady her. Charlotte, watching, felt pain stab through her. Henrietta leaned into him briefly, until he stepped back, offering his arm to her.

Hubert was not amused, while Mrs Buxted looked pleased and Millicent pursed her lips.

Seeing his arm around Henrietta, even momentarily, caused a wave of agony to swell in Charlotte's chest. Only minutes ago he had been flirting with *her*! When she'd first met him he had not seemed like a rake, or someone who would play with dalliance without thought for others. Yet here was the evidence of her own eyes. She was so angry she felt that she actually hated him in that moment.

He must not know! No one must know how vulnerable she was.

Determined not to watch them as they walked away, arm in arm, she asked, 'Are there any more strawberries?' of no one in particular. Her voice was remarkably steady.

Reverend Sneddon, attentive as always, secured some berries for her, then spoke for quite five minutes about how he could not eat strawberries as they gave him hives. Charlotte could hardly bear it.

Mrs Etherington, always keen to learn more of interesting afflictions and conditions, was fascinated, and she engaged the Reverend in a discourse about the foods that did not agree with her. The two found an affinity in their distrust of tomatoes, and both felt liver was most efficacious in curing a bilious habit.

Charlotte tried hard to listen, tried not to think about Henrietta and Adam walking alone together.

They returned some ten minutes later, with Henrietta in high spirits. 'Well,' she said, 'I have never been more disappointed. For it is only a couple of old walls, as you see, and they look like a thousand other church walls. The river was pretty, though. If it were not for the excellent company—' she flashed a sidelong glance at the Earl '—I should have been *bored*!'

Had Adam looked at Henrietta the way he had looked at her? Had he even, perhaps, kissed her cousin just now? Men, she had often been told, liked to steal kisses at every opportunity. She felt hurt that he could have used her so, and was almost overcome by the unexpected urge to hit him, and then pull her cousin's hair, just to remove the smirk from her beautiful face.

'Do you enjoy walking, Miss Buxted?' asked Lady Olivia politely.

'Normally, no,' admitted Henrietta. 'But on a lovely day, and with good company, I do.'

'I should be happy to accompany you on a walk, if you wish,' said Hubert forlornly.

Henrietta, enjoying her power, smiled condescendingly at him.

Charlotte concentrated on breathing in, then out. She unclenched her fists.

'Of *course* I shall walk with you as well, Mr Etherington. But not today.'

'Then tomorrow?' asked Hubert hopefully. 'I understand Lord Shalford—' he inclined his head coldly to his host '—accompanied some of the young ladies on a tour of the woods yesterday.'

Henrietta glanced sharply at the Earl.

Oh, no, thought Charlotte. *I had hoped she wouldn't find out about that walk. I hope she doesn't make a scene. I don't think I could cope with a Henrietta scene right now.*

'Indeed?' asked Henrietta, with a raised eyebrow. 'And why was *I* not invited on this *cosy* walk?'

'It was quite a spontaneous outing,' said Mr Foxley in a soothing tone. 'We visited the temple at the far end of the deer park, and then walked through the woods to the main drive.'

'Hmmph,' said Henrietta. 'I shall go on this walk tomorrow, if someone will accompany me.'

Hubert immediately confirmed that he would, and Lady Olivia also offered to walk with her.

'I shall go too,' pronounced Millicent—to Henrietta's clear displeasure.

The Earl had turned to speak quietly to one of the grooms, and so missed the opportunity to commit to the outing. Henrietta frowned.

'Hubert!' said Mrs Etherington. 'You must be careful if you walk in the woods. I hope tomorrow will not be damp. He had a bronchial condition when he was a child, you know,' she confided in Miss Langley.

During the ensuing litany, in which Hubert's devoted mama recollected the various conditions that had characterised his childhood, Charlotte noticed that Faith was looking flushed and uncomfortable, and kept closing her eyes tightly. Mr Foxley had also noticed, and took the opportunity to speak to Faith quietly. She looked at him gratefully and answered in a low voice. Mr Foxley stood, and assisted Faith to rise.

Charlotte also stood, and made her way to the pair. 'Faith,' she said quietly, 'what is it?'

'Oh, it's nothing,' said Faith. 'It is just—I have the headache.'

'I think perhaps Miss Faith has had too much sun,' said Mr Foxley solicitously.

Charlotte glanced around. The sun was now directly overhead, and there was very little shade to be seen.

'Perhaps…the coach?' suggested Mr Foxley.

'Of course!' said Charlotte. 'Mr Foxley, could you bring some lemonade for Faith?'

He agreed immediately, and Charlotte accompanied Faith to the closed carriage. It was stifling and airless inside, but offered Faith blessed relief from the bright sun.

Faith was suffering greatly, with her fair complexion offering her no protection from the noonday heat. Unlike Henrietta and Millicent, she had no parasol, and had been exposed to the full force of the sun during the journey to Waverley.

Once inside the coach, she pressed her hands to her head and began rocking gently back and forth. Charlotte, upset by poor Faith's obvious distress, spoke calmly to her, and deployed a chicken-skin fan which she found behind the squabs. She was relieved to have something to divert her attention from her own troubles.

Mr Foxley soon arrived, with a large jug of lemonade and a drinking cup. Charlotte thanked him, and held the cup while he filled it.

'Here, Faith,' she said. 'Drink this.'

'I feel sick,' said Faith.

'It is the heat,' said Charlotte. 'Take small sips, so it does not upset your stomach.'

The Earl arrived, and joined Mr Foxley at the door of the carriage. 'What is amiss?' he asked quietly.

'She has a headache,' said Charlotte. 'We need to get her indoors.'

'We could take her to an inn,' said the Earl. 'There is one only a few miles away…'

'No, no,' said Faith. 'Please—I should like to go back to Chadcombe.'

'But the journey…' said Mr Foxley. 'Are you sure?'

She looked at him plaintively. 'Please,' she said, 'take me back.'

'Of course, my little love,' he said softly.

Charlotte stood. 'Mr Foxley, can you take my place here for a few minutes?'

The Earl handed her out of the coach, and Mr Foxley entered to sit by Faith's side.

By unspoken agreement Charlotte and the Earl moved a few feet away, allowing the couple a brief moment of privacy.

'Does Mrs Buxted know?' asked the Earl, indicating the couple in the coach.

'I do not believe so,' said Charlotte. 'Faith and Mr Foxley have kept their feelings well-hidden before this. And my aunt does not focus much on Faith.'

'I shall ask the grooms to fetch water from the river, so we might dampen some cloths for Miss Faith. It may give her some relief.'

'Thank you,' said Charlotte gratefully. 'Will the party split, or shall we all go home?'

He looked at her, an arrested expression on his face.

'Home? Yes, home…' he said cryptically.

'Lord Shalford?' said Charlotte.

'Do you…*like* Chadcombe?'

'Very much. It is a special place.'

'I am glad.' He smiled.

'Adam! What's amiss?' Harry was approaching the carriages, with Lady Olivia and Henrietta.

The Earl turned to face the newcomers. 'Miss Faith is unwell. She wishes to return to Chadcombe.'

Henrietta spoke sharply. 'Nonsense! Faith is *never* unwell. Why, Mama will tell you *I* am the one who becomes ill. I have a frail disposition.'

They all looked at her. She was the picture of health, and a vision of beauty—apart from the petulant expression she wore.

'We *cannot* go home yet. Why, we have only just finished our picnic.'

Charlotte felt compelled to intervene. 'Faith is indeed unwell. She has heatstroke, which I have seen before.'

'She is only trying to be *interesting*, and to take everyone's attention for herself.'

Lady Olivia looked shocked at Henrietta's words. Her brothers, who had had more contact with Miss Buxted, merely looked disgusted.

Charlotte, anxious for Henrietta not to damage

herself further, appealed to the Earl. 'Cold water from the river would be *most* helpful.'

He bowed ironically at her imperious tone. 'Yes, ma'am.' He hailed a groom and passed on the instruction.

The rest of the party had reached them and were now gathering around, expressing loud sympathy for the stricken Faith.

Mrs Buxted, loath to miss any drama, proclaimed, 'I must go to my child,' and replaced Mr Foxley in the coach.

Reverend Sneddon agreed that he would of course give way, and would travel back to Chadcombe in the landau. Miss Langley asked one of the grooms to tear up a white tablecloth used for their picnic.

Everyone was ignoring Henrietta. Too late, Charlotte recognised the danger signs.

'Lord Shalford!' Henrietta's tone was sharp.

Everyone had started climbing into the carriages, and the Earl was speaking intently to the coachman.

'There is something I particularly wished to ask you. That is, Lady Olivia and I wished to ask you—' She signalled frantically to Lady Olivia, who looked confused.

'One moment, Miss Buxted,' said the Earl, continuing to give instructions to the coachman.

Henrietta looked outraged.

Charlotte spoke to her quietly, attempting to soothe her. 'Henrietta, as you see Lord Shalford is busy. Perhaps later…'

'No! *Not* later! And he is not busy with anything important. Why, he is talking to the coachman. How *dare* he ignore me in favour of a servant?'

Adam approached, behaving as though he had not heard Henrietta's last statement. 'Now, what is it you wish to say to me?' He looked pained.

Henrietta employed her most winsome smile. 'Lord Shalford, we are leaving next week, and we have all had a lovely time at Chadcombe. Lady Olivia and I were talking yesterday—'

She threw an impatient glance at Olivia, who shook her head urgently.

With a disgusted look at her accomplice, Henrietta continued. 'Do you not think it would be a splendid idea if we were to have a ball at Chadcombe?'

'Excellent idea,' he said curtly. 'Let me help you into the landau, Miss Buxted. There—now you shall be comfortable.'

Abandoning Henrietta with relief to the prosy vicar and the empty-headed coxcomb, Adam walked away. Today was fast becoming a nightmare. He had even been deprived of his chance to tease his sister about the possibility of a ball by Henrietta's inappropriate timing.

He shook his head, trying to deny the unwanted thoughts that threatened to overpower him again. The contrast between Henrietta and Charlotte had been particularly noticeable today.

It had seemed so right, so natural, when Charlotte had referred to Chadcombe as 'home'. He knew that she would love it, and already understood what a special place it was. He had barely tolerated the walk with Henrietta, who was irritating him more and more. All the while he had made polite conversation, and deflected Henrietta's obvious attempts at flirtation, he had been keen to get back to Charlotte's company again. He had felt lost.

Adam's groom gave him a leg-up—the others were mounted already—then the party moved off.

Mr Foxley stayed beside the coach, watching as his beloved's head was bathed with wet cloths by Miss Langley, for Mrs Buxted was too distressed to minister to her. His anxiety was high, for he could see Faith was in much pain.

If the journey home had seemed long to Adam and Charlotte, for Faith it had been interminable. She told Charlotte afterwards how her head had pounded as though it was a drum and someone was beating her with huge drumsticks—from the inside! She had kept sipping lemonade, and managed not to be sick, and the cool cloths and soft hands of Miss Langley had helped immeasurably.

But, she confided through her pain, inside she had felt happier than she had ever been. He had called her his little love! He *had*! Surely Charlotte had heard him!

Sitting by her cousin's bedside, Charlotte quickly

reassured her. Yes, Mr Foxley had said exactly those words.

Faith smiled weakly. Charlotte felt like crying—and she didn't know why.

Chapter Thirteen

Colonel Sir Edward Wyncroft was tired. Tired of war, tired of France, tired of a nomadic lifestyle. Now that retirement was so close he realised how much he wanted to go home. The days could not pass quickly enough.

He had led his men through France, where most had boarded ships to England. A few had remained in France and others, once they'd had their prize money, had left to explore parts of Europe before returning home.

After Paris he'd been part of the British group accompanying Napoleon through France to the ship which had taken the former Emperor to his exile in Elba.

In each town they'd passed through, the reactions had been varied. At first, when Napoleon had been accompanied by his own Imperial Guard, the cry had been, *'Vive l'Empereur!'* but later, when the royalist Allies had formed his escort, the French people had called out, *'Vive le Roi!'* The angry crowds had become more intense as the journey had progressed, and the erstwhile Emperor had been a trembling idiot by the end, fearful of his shadow and agonising over how he should disguise his identity in order to escape the mob.

After watching Napoleon board the frigate *Undaunted* at St Tropez, Sir Edward had made the laborious journey to his base in Vienna, where he'd dealt with matters of business and arranged for a coachful of luggage to be sent to his barracks in London. Now—finally—he was on his way home.

He was looking forward to seeing Charlotte again. He missed his daughter's lively opinions and insightful warmth. Her letters were full of vivid description, but they reminded him of how much he missed her. She seemed happy enough in England, and was always respectful when speaking of the Buxteds, but Sir Edward had a fairly clear notion of how things stood.

Her tales of the young men she had met intrigued him. These Fantons seemed to feature in many of Charlotte's letters. He'd spoken to Captain Fanton's commander, who had had nothing but praise for the young officer. And Charlotte was grown up now— he supposed she would leave him one of these days to make a home of her own.

Feeling suddenly old, Sir Edward came back to his surroundings and surveyed the road ahead. Something was not quite right. At first glance all looked well. They had left Reims a few hours earlier, and the next major town was Laon. It was now close to sunset, so they were looking for somewhere to stop for the night.

Travelling with Sir Edward was Captain Foden of the Fifteenth, and a couple of Light Dragoons—Mercer and Hewitson. Their destination was Calais, where they would find a ship to take them across the Channel.

Dressed in their uniforms, they had been immune from attack so far. The usual bandits who preyed on travellers tended to avoid any group of armed soldiers on horseback.

Sir Edward's attention was drawn to a copse ahead on their left. Was someone there? He thought he detected movement... At the point at which an attack would surely come he tensed, but nothing happened. After they passed, Sir Edward saw a dark figure slink off through the trees, but said nothing. Whoever the lurker was, he had thought better of attacking them. Some less fortunate traveller might not be so lucky.

Twenty minutes later, with the light fading, a dilapidated hamlet came into view. There were two inns, the larger bearing a metallic sign with a faded image of a red-haired child and the legend 'Charlotte de Valois'.

Taking this as an omen, Sir Edward indicated the inn. 'Let us try this one first.'

They dismounted easily, well used to life in the

saddle. Mercer and Hewitson remained with the horses while Sir Edward and Captain Foden went inside. They emerged after a few minutes with good news.

'Well, boys, they have a room for us. Flea-ridden, possibly, but we'll have a roof over our heads tonight.' Sir Edward took his horse's reins from Mercer. 'And they have promised to kill a couple of chickens and a piglet for our dinner.'

All took heart from the promise of a cooked meal, for they had been travelling most of the day, keeping a steady pace so as to spare the horses. They saw their animals rubbed down and fed in the stables, before entering the inn with their saddle-packs.

In darkness, the inn looked much cosier. A small fire was lit in the huge fireplace, though the night was warm, and a group of farm workers were drinking ale in the taproom.

The four soldiers chose a table in the corner, which allowed them to keep a watchful eye on the rest of the room. It was hard to forget that until a few short weeks ago they had been at war with the French. The landlord came with foaming beer for all of them, setting it down without speaking. Ignoring him, they sat quietly, enjoying the light of the fire, the cool beer, and the fact they were not on horseback.

A scrawny old man with tattered clothing eyed them intently, listening to their conversation. *'Anglais?'* he asked, in strongly accented *paysan* French.

They confirmed this, at which point he launched into a tirade of vitriol against foreigners, Englishmen, murderers and thieves. Ignoring the sentiments, they shooed him away, but paid the landlord for a drink for him. He continued to mutter malevolently in their direction—although he still accepted the drink.

The landlord had warmed to them slightly, helped by evidence that they were not short of funds and would happily pay for a generous dinner. He was almost affable as he served them a surprisingly tasty meal of chicken, pork and potatoes, with haricots and peas. He asked them where they were bound, and seemed unsurprised when they told him they were heading to Calais.

'Ah,' he said. 'Then you will need the west road after Corbeny, for the main road is hard to pass outside the village. Look for the Chemin des Dames, near the *abbaye*. Turn right after a few miles to get back to the Route de Laon.'

Thanking him for the local knowledge, they retired to their room. It was a large attic with low timbers and two tiny windows. It was of no matter. There were four fairly clean straw pallets which they sank onto gratefully. With the benefit of long practice, they were all asleep within minutes.

Charlotte had hoped for a quiet breakfast, but both Millicent and Henrietta rose early. Of the Earl, there was no sign.

Henrietta helped herself to chocolate and rolls, wondering aloud where everyone else was.

'Faith is still a little unwell,' said Charlotte. 'Though she is much better than yesterday. She will keep to her room for most of today, I should think.' She glanced at Henrietta, then said casually, 'Mr Etherington will no doubt be up early too, as he said last night he is looking forward to your walk around the estate today.'

Henrietta frowned. 'I had forgotten about that. Still, it is a good opportunity to see how large the Earl's holdings are.'

Millicent looked up sharply.

'I mean…to see the beauties of the woods.'

'The woods are indeed beautiful,' said Charlotte, trying *not* to think about the delightful kiss she had had there.

Trying, and failing.

It was seared into her memory, and it played over and over in her mind. And had he really been about to kiss her again yesterday? She was more than half-way to believing she had imagined his intent. Walking in the woods with him again today would be difficult, but so far she had failed to find a reason to avoid it.

'Now we are to have a ball, should we not go shopping in Farnham or Godalming? I may need some trinkets, and I do believe Lady Olivia has no ball-gown—imagine that!'

'The local dressmaker will come later today to

meet with Lady Olivia,' said Millicent. 'She will have no difficulty in making a ball-gown for Olivia this week.'

'Oh. But I *still* want to go shopping!'

Henrietta's petulant tone recalled Charlotte to the present. 'Well,' said Charlotte soothingly, 'perhaps we may go to Godalming another day.'

'Good morning,' announced Hubert from the doorway. 'Aha! My luck is in—three fair ladies.'

He made an extravagant leg—an impressive achievement, given the limitations of his high starched collar, his satin waistcoat, embroidered with what looked like peacocks, a tight-fitting military-style jacket, complete with gold braid and frogging, and close fitting small-clothes in a virulent shade of pink.

Charlotte wondered idly how the Earl would react to today's blinding attire. A few days ago they'd have shared the humour of it. Now she was unsure how things stood.

Behind Hubert, wearing a sober black suit and a scowl, was the Reverend Sneddon. Because Hubert was filling the doorway, the clergyman was having some difficulty entering the room. As Charlotte watched, Reverend Sneddon raised himself on the tips of his toes to view the ladies over Hubert's shoulder, then gave a sickly smile.

Charlotte, overcome, made a choking sound and quickly sought her handkerchief to cover it. Oh, why could the Earl not have been here to witness this? How amused he would have been!

Realising he was no longer the sole focus of the ladies' attention, Hubert turned stiffly. 'Ah! Reverend Sneddon! Why are you standing there? Do come in!'

The Reverend, outraged, pushed past him, brushing against the sleeve of Hubert's coat. Hubert manfully resisted releasing the expletive that was on the tip of his tongue, and instead subjected his sleeve to a rigorous inspection. Thankfully there seemed to be no damage done, so he calmly took a seat at the table.

Reverend Sneddon, who seemed to be carefully not looking at the abomination that was Hubert's waistcoat, addressed the ladies. 'What an exciting day we had yesterday. A bucolic idyll, followed by a dash home to assist the wounded and infirm. For we must give succour to those in need—it is our duty on all occasions. How is dear Miss Faith today?'

Not certain Faith would appreciate being described as 'wounded and infirm', Charlotte replied calmly. 'She is much recovered, but is inclined to rest today.'

'A wise decision. I am sure her mother must be tending to her with great care and compassion.'

'Er…yes.' Mrs Buxted, as far as Charlotte knew, was sleeping still.

'Miss Buxted!' Hubert was not to be outdone. 'I believe the weather will hold today, so we can have our walk in the woods. I have taken the time to stand outside the front door for a full five minutes, so as to test the weather. I can tell you the day is cloudy, and has the coolness we are used to. Yesterday's sun has gone; I am sure you will be delighted to hear it.'

Henrietta did not look particularly delighted. 'I did not mind the sun, for I had a parasol to protect my complexion. I have no freckles,' she said proudly.

'No, indeed,' said Hubert, 'for a freckle would not dare to mar your beauty.'

'I shall wear my new bonnet,' announced Millicent. 'I have brought it down to show you all.' She picked up an extremely fetching bonnet from a side table, and they all dutifully exclaimed over it. 'I do hope the Earl can join us,' she said wistfully. 'I should like him to see me in my new bonnet.'

Henrietta looked balefully at Millicent.

Oh, dear, thought Charlotte. *Henrietta is definitely back to wanting the Earl again.* Her heart sank.

'For our walk today,' said Hubert, 'I shall wear my new country coat, which I designed for just this opportunity. My tailor understands my genius.'

What a remark! Laughter was bubbling up and Charlotte did not dare let it out. Instead, she said quickly, 'Excuse me—I must go to Miss Langley,' and left, maintaining her composure until she was in the hallway.

'What amuses you, Miss Wyncroft?'

The Earl was descending the wide staircase, looking elegant in buckskins, a blue coat which fitted him perfectly, and a snowy white neckcloth. If one were to judge only by appearances, as Hubert might, then he would do well. He was the perfect foil to the Reverend's ecclesiastical dowdiness and to Hubert's flamboyance.

If men were horses, she thought, rather randomly, *Hubert would be a showy-looking prancer, all gloss and no substance. The Reverend Sneddon would be a plough-horse. And the Earl, of course—*

'Miss Wyncroft?'

Charlotte composed herself with some difficulty. Lord Shalford waited patiently, a crooked smile and the light in his eyes telling her he was enjoying her amusement. Her heart skipped a beat.

Stop acting like a silly schoolgirl, she told herself. *You are a mature young lady of twenty and should behave as such. And, besides, you are angry with him!*

'I am sorry, but I could not stay a moment longer in there without laughing.'

'Should I guess who is in there?'

'Yes, do! I think you will guess correctly.'

He considered for a second. 'I imagine it is perhaps one of our gentleman guests? I am debating between Mr Etherington and Reverend Sneddon.'

'You are right—*and* wrong!'

'A riddle!' He was quick to see the solution. 'It is both of them, then.'

'Yes, *and* Henrietta and Millicent.'

'Good God! I thank you for the warning, for I was about to enter. I shall instead seek refuge with my horses. I hope to see you later to walk in the woods.'

His voice deepened, as did Charlotte's blush.

He bowed gallantly, then impulsively lifted her hand and kissed it. A shiver went through her. She watched helplessly as, whistling, he disappeared outside—perhaps to ride his magnificent stallion...

Once outside, Adam paused. Why did he continually fail in his resolve to be distant with her? He knew it was what he *should* do, yet when he was in her company all self-control was lost. Seeing her laughing helplessly, he had been overwhelmed by feelings of warmth towards her. He had kissed her hand before he'd even known what he had done.

He had barely slept last night. His path ahead was unclear and he had no one who could advise him.

Letting her breath out slowly, Charlotte went the other way—to Miss Langley's parlour. The events of yesterday—particularly the way the Earl had looked at her—had kept her awake late into the night. She could not deny the warmth she felt for him. Indeed, he was becoming rather an obsession with her.

If someone had told her he was equally obsessed, she would not have believed them. Nothing had changed, she told herself. Though he spoke to her as an equal—as a friend, even—he dallied lightly with Henrietta and Millicent. Yet there were times when both girls clearly irritated him.

It was altogether confusing, and she was unsure why it even bothered her. She had known from the start that he was not for her. She should not feel the things she felt. She should have been able to avoid this. All she could see ahead was hurt.

At least events yesterday—especially their shared concern for Faith—had finally eased the awkwardness she had felt when he'd kissed her. No, that was not quite right. The awkwardness had been *afterwards*. The kiss itself had not been awkward at all.

She chided herself for letting her thoughts wander again. There was work to do. Though she was embarrassed by Henrietta's outrageous lobbying yesterday—and at such a moment—she had to admit to feeling a certain excitement about the ball. She had missed out in London, but even a high stickler like Mrs Buxted would find no reason to stop her from attending an event in the house where she was staying.

This time, she told herself, *I* shall *go to the ball after all.*

She found Miss Langley sitting quietly in her favourite chair, sipping a dish of tea. The elderly lady seemed calm, but when Charlotte asked how she was, she confessed she had not slept well.

'The oven is mended, thank goodness, and Grove

is hiring extra servants—but I am not sure how to start organising a ball. I have never done it before, you see.'

'You know,' Charlotte offered gently, 'my papa loves balls and routs, and all kinds of social gatherings. Our house in Vienna was always busy when he was on leave. Once we had one hundred and fifty people at a garden party.'

'One hundred and fifty! My goodness!' Miss Langley seemed horrified at the idea.

'But Papa has no interest in domestic matters. He is, I believe, a most excellent soldier, and an able commander in war. At home, though, he expects everything will just happen—as if a magician had waved a wand.'

'A magician…? Yes. I wish we had a magician—for this ball.'

'Or a fairy godmother?'

'Fairy…? Oh, I see, yes—*Cinderella*.'

'Papa fails to understand the amount of work involved. Or perhaps he understands but thinks it is nothing to do with him.'

'Yes, men *do* see things differently. Who organised your parties in Vienna?'

'I did. Including a Grand Ball once.' She smiled impishly. 'I confess I enjoyed it—thinking about the guests, the food, the musicians, and feeling a sense of achievement on the night.'

Miss Langley shook her head slowly. 'I cannot believe anyone would *enjoy* such an ordeal. My only wish is to sit with the other chaperons and enjoy watching the young people dance.'

Charlotte spoke carefully. 'I am honoured to be a guest here at Chadcombe, and I am happy to assist you in whatever way I can—though I should not wish to intrude.'

'Oh, Miss Wyncroft, indeed I should *welcome* your assistance and I thank you most *warmly* for your kindness. I have been sitting here this hour, afraid to *move*, for I cannot imagine how to start.'

'Well, you know, the staff will do most of it. Shall we make a list?'

Miss Langley, relief written all over her kind face, assented.

She and Charlotte discussed invitations, staff, food, music, and the need to organise a deep cleaning of the ballroom and the supper room. Mrs Gordon, Merrion and Grove were called upon, and together they agreed what was to be done.

Miss Langley was to make a list of those to be invited, and Charlotte would help her write the invitations. The elderly lady seemed surprised and relieved to find she had little else to do.

'Miss Wyncroft, are you *sure* you do not mind doing this work?' she kept asking.

Charlotte, laughing, assured her she was happy to do it.

Miss Langley could only exclaim, and admire, and be grateful.

Lady Olivia entered at this point, and claimed

Charlotte. 'Ah, there you are. Great-Aunt Clara, I *must* take Charlotte, for we are to walk in the woods now and I need her to be my second.'

Charlotte laughed. 'It is not so bad, surely?'

Olivia shook her head. 'It is much worse. Mr Etherington is worried about getting mud on his boots, if it should rain, but is determined to walk regardless, for Miss Buxted's sake. It could be a disaster, and we need your calmness and that way you have of smoothing things over.'

Charlotte laughed lightly. 'Well, I am sure I do not know what you mean.'

Not more than a half-hour later, Charlotte finished buttoning her boots, took one last look in the mirror, then descended to the hall. While she waited she could not help daydreaming of another kiss from the Earl. He probably wouldn't want to kiss her again, and with a larger party walking today there might be no opportunity anyway. But his eyes yesterday…his voice earlier…his warm lips on her hand…

Stop! she scolded herself. *Stop thinking about him.*

'Ready to go?'

It was the Earl. Charlotte's heart leapt when she saw him, and she could feel herself flushing.

He raised a quizzical eyebrow at her. 'Is something amiss?'

'N-no—no. Of course not!' she stammered.

He frowned and spoke quietly. 'I do wish you would—'

Crash! The door of the breakfast room slammed loudly against the wall. They turned, alarmed.

Millicent emerged, clearly upset, clutching her bonnet. A flattened, broken bonnet.

'Someone has destroyed my new bonnet!' She burst into noisy tears. 'My beautiful bonnet.'

'Oh, dear,' said Charlotte. 'How terrible!'

'I forgot to take it with me after breakfast. And now it is *ruined*!'

Hubert, Olivia and Henrietta had come to join them.

'Steady on, Millie,' said Hubert, comfortingly. 'It's only a bonnet.'

'*Only* a bonnet! You, who care only for your clothes, should understand. Oh, who would *do* such a thing? How has this *happened*?' Millicent was genuinely distressed.

Charlotte went to her. 'Oh, you poor thing.' She took the distressed girl's hand.

The Earl nodded approvingly at Charlotte.

Seeing it, Henrietta's chin went up. 'Charlotte, why were you in the breakfast room just now?'

'What? I—' Charlotte suddenly noticed that all eyes were on her. 'I went to fetch my reticule. I forgot it again. I need it for our walk.'

'Did you see Millicent's bonnet?'

'No—I don't recall seeing it.'

Henrietta's eyes narrowed. No one spoke.

Charlotte flushed again, this time in anger. Did they—did *he*—think she had destroyed Millicent's bonnet? She glanced his way. He looked grave, his mouth a hard line.

'I came to inform you all,' said the Earl, 'that I am unfortunately unable to accompany you today. I have pressing matters of business to attend to.'

Nodding curtly, he spun on his heel and marched off, tension clearly visible in his gait.

Charlotte stiffened. He clearly thought *she* had destroyed Millicent's bonnet.

Is this his opinion of me? How dare he think me capable of such a petty act?

She felt so angry. All those moments when she had thought he understood her, their hours spent walking and talking together, and yet he thought she had done this? He really did have a low opinion of her. Which meant that his behaviour towards her was just empty flirtation.

'Well, we shall still go, regardless,' said Henrietta, tossing her head defiantly.

'Of course we shall,' said Hubert. 'Millicent, why don't you go to Mama?'

'Yes, I don't want to walk now anyway.' She marched off to share her troubles with her sympathetic parent.

They set off—a small party of four in the end, just Charlotte and Olivia, Hubert and Henrietta.

Charlotte wondered if any of them really wanted to be there. She herself would have preferred to hide in her room for a while. She was so angry at the Earl's reaction. Angry and hurt. She couldn't help but contrast his cold, angry face just now with the warm light in his eyes just moments earlier.

She dug her fingernails into her palms and tried to look calm.

Hubert and Henrietta enjoyed the first part of the walk, towards the temple, and exclaimed over its prettiness. Hubert likened Henrietta to a Greek goddess—though he was not exactly sure which one—which seemed to please her immensely.

Charlotte was glad to be walking slightly ahead with Olivia. They chatted lightly about the upcoming ball—which was understandably occupying the younger girl's thoughts. The day was cool, but dry, and the ground underfoot was firm. They progressed at a measured pace, keen to return to the house. Charlotte was enjoying talking to Olivia, who told her how delighted she was to have house guests.

Unexpectedly, as they rounded a bend in the woods, they were faced with a most shocking sight. Three ragged men, approaching from the other direction, noticed them in the same instant and stopped abruptly. The middle one was tall, gaunt and dirty, and carried a musket over his shoulder. The others were smaller and wiry, but just as filthy. One had a grubby bandage on his hand.

'Well, well, well,' said the tall one. 'Pretty ladies! What a treat!'

Chapter Fourteen

At the French inn, the night passed without incident and the morning dawned clear and sunny. After a hearty breakfast Sir Edward and his comrades paid the landlord. He wished them a safe journey as he pocketed their payment.

Remembering the man's advice, they looked out for the blocked road. Sure enough, after they'd passed through the village of Corbeny, the main route was piled high with rubble, where a large building had succumbed to the damage caused by the recent fighting. Reluctant to cut across fields when they did not know the country, they bore left and followed the road their landlord had suggested.

After about two miles they passed a poorly kept cottage on their left. Outside, a familiar-looking scrawny old man was alighting from a cart.

'Is that our friend from last night?' asked Hewitson.

'Looks like it,' said Captain Foden. He raised his hand in ironic greeting as they passed.

The little man pointed at them and laughed hysterically.

'Lost his mind,' commented Mercer.

'Many have in these times,' said Foden.

Sir Edward hushed them. His instincts had been awakened again. The road on both sides was now lined with tall trees, and to their right the woodland was dark and dense. Years of campaigning had left him with the ability to sense danger—or at least the possibility of danger. It was what had kept him alive for so long.

'There,' he said. 'To the right. Somebody in the trees.'

Remembering the dark figure from yesterday, he wondered if this possible assailant would slink away too on seeing the soldiers. He shifted his weight slightly, briefly touched his sword handle to reassure himself it was there, then drew his pistol.

Slowly into danger, and quickly out of it.

Remembering the words of his first commander, Sir Edward slowed his pace to a walk. The others copied.

Mercer's horse whinnied. An answering whinny came from the trees on the right. Horses! Then a second noise, this time on the left. Sir Edward raised his hand and they all stopped. A concealed horse whinnied again.

'Ambush!' he said. *'Turn!'*

All four wheeled their mounts around with a practised movement. A single highwayman would not cause them much trouble, but there were at least three horsemen concealed in the woods, and Sir Edward did not want to take unnecessary risks. Better to regroup in a place where their odds were better.

As they turned they heard shouts of dismay from the woods, followed by a barked French order to attack.

Sir Edward spurred his horse into a gallop.

Charlotte immediately stopped and reached for Olivia's hand. The younger girl had let out a little gasp of shock, but did not speak. Henrietta and Hubert had now rounded the bend.

One of the ragged men went into a half-crouch, drawing a knife, then straightened as he realised they were facing three ladies and a startled gentleman in a yellow coat.

'Good God!' said Hubert, stopping.

Henrietta, unusually, did not scream and carry on. Instead, genuinely frightened, she instinctively leaned towards Hubert. He put a protective arm about her.

'Lovebirds too!' cackled the man on the right, also drawing a knife from among his rags.

'I reckon this lot'll have plenty of blunt, Corny. Nice li'l jewels for us.'

'Best bit o' luck we've had since we left Newhaven,' said Corny—the short one on the left.

'You're right there, Corny.'

'Now, then, ladies,' said the tall one. 'You are a fine sight on this fine day, but we will thank you for your money and jewels—you too, sir—then we'll be on our way, all nice and friendly-like.'

'And if we refuse?' Charlotte had found her voice.

'Oh, well—then we will have to *take* what we want.' His eyes gleamed as they swept over Charlotte.

Her head snapped up and her spine stiffened. How dared he look at her like that?

'Now, then,' said Hubert. 'This is private property and you should not be here.'

'Private property, is it?' sneered Corny. 'You hear that, Davis?'

Davis—the tall one—smirked openly. 'That's as may be, but they won't begrudge some ex-soldiers a few rabbits or a deer, will they?'

'Poachers!' said Hubert loathingly.

'Yes—except now we've snared ourselves some better game.'

'A few game pullets, maybe.'

'One each!'

'And a pigeon in a cockerel's plumage.'

They all laughed heartily.

'We have no money, for we are just out for a walk. And you shall not have my jewels!' said Henrietta assertively.

'Oh, it's not just your *jewels* we want, my beauty,' said Corny menacingly, taking a step forward.

Henrietta shrieked.

It made no difference. The three bandits moved forward, towards their prey.

Sir Edward, riding as fast as his horse could travel, turned his head to look at their attackers. They had burst onto the road and were following at full tilt.

'Five mounted—six or seven more on foot!' he shouted to his comrades.

They outran their assailants for a few hundred yards, but their horses were tired and the mounted attackers were gaining on them.

'To the woods!' Sir Edward ordered, veering to the left. They would have more chance of evading attack there.

The light changed as they entered the forest. It held a green tinge, coloured by the sunlight filtering down through the lush canopy. Another time Sir Edward might have stopped to enjoy the beauty of the woods, its lines and colours, sounds and smells. Not now. His only thought was to flee.

The smell of fear, a familiar tang, filled his nostrils. The sounds enveloping him were of his horse's hooves, the jingle of the harness rings, the beating of his heart. He strained to hear the sounds of pursuit, but wasn't sure if the horses he heard were friends or foe.

Suddenly the light changed and he burst through the edge of the woods. Fields and farmland opened

up before him. Spotting the ruins of an old building to his left, he swerved in that direction. Mercer's
horse outstripped his and reached the ruins first.
Foden and Hewitson caught up and they all turned
together to face the foe.

Four horseman against five. The men on foot
were a good distance behind. They needed to defeat the cavalrymen before the runners reinforced
them. From behind a broken wall Sir Edward aimed
and fired his pistol, seeing one of the riders drop.
He reloaded and fired again, but missed. No time
for a third shot, so he drew his sword.

His comrades had reacted swiftly too, firing their
weapons as the attackers closed on them. Another
assailant was hit, though he rode on, blood flowing from his arm.

As they moved in, Sir Edward shouted orders.
'Mercer! With me—to the left! Foden, you and
Hewitson take the right!'

Their horses, well-trained, obeyed the commands
of reins and spurs, and the four soldiers moved in
unison to bring the fight to the remaining assailants,
swinging their swords low as they jousted past, then
turning and attacking again.

The attackers had the upper hand. Sir Edward
knew they had to cut them down before the foot soldiers appeared, while the French just had to delay
and survive. Each attack Sir Edward mounted
melted away as the French horsemen took evasive
action, holding out for their colleagues to arrive.

The number of options was dwindling. The horses were spent, and would not manage another retreat. Their guns had been fired, with no chance to reload. There were no reinforcements to come to their aid. And now the foot soldiers were upon them, slashing and cutting.

These assailants had battled cavalry before, Sir Edward realised. They knew how to sidestep at the right time, evading the horses' hooves, and they were trying to cut the animals with their weapons—military knives and short swords.

Still Sir Edward fought, with Foden, Mercer and Hewitson. They moved close together, with the wall at their back, giving their attackers less room to manoeuvre.

Sir Edward took a hit on his left arm—thankfully with the flat of a French blade. Pain flooded through him, and his arm went quite numb, but he managed to hang on to the reins. One foot soldier was trampled by Mercer's horse, while Foden seriously injured another. They were suffering hits themselves, though. Mercer's shirt-front showed a slowly growing red stain, and then Captain Foden missed a thrust and was pulled from his horse by the men below.

Foden's leg was caught in one of the stirrups, so he could not right himself in order to fight back. A tall man dealt the killer blow, stabbing Foden directly in the heart. His horse, maddened with fear by Foden's body hanging strangely to one side, reared, catching Hewitson on the side of the head with one of its hooves. As Hewitson, too, slumped in his saddle, their attackers gleefully moved in for the kill.

Sir Edward knew they were lost. His death was moments away.

As he twisted and turned, slashed and cut, he knew he was a dead man. This was it. War was over, he was retired, and yet he was to die in a quiet French field, cut down by renegades. As his fighting arm began to tire and his breathing became more laboured his thoughts turned to Charlotte. His beloved daughter, so far away.

He wished her farewell.

The Earl trotted back into the stable yard. He had enjoyed his long ride—had needed the time to think. From a distance he had seen Hubert and Olivia with Miss Wyncroft and Miss Buxted, entering the temple, but did not regret his decision to avoid the walk. He'd needed some solitude.

He was no closer to a solution than before, and could not see his future clearly. Henrietta Buxted and Millicent Etherington were typical of the young ladies of the *ton*—vain, selfish and heedless. That was part of the reason why he had been glad to delay Olivia's come-out—he feared she would change from the gentle, thoughtful girl he knew into something sillier, harder. Like the two misses who were vying to become Mistress of Chadcombe.

The incident with the bonnet earlier had crystallised his impression of them. He suspected that

Henrietta had destroyed Millicent's bonnet, and the way she had tried to blame Charlotte had quite disgusted him.

Neither Henrietta nor Millicent had feelings for him, he knew, but he did not expect them to. He supposed either would make someone a suitable wife—though *he* was struggling to spend more than an hour at a time with them. But perhaps that was not a requirement for married couples—once an heir was secured both parties were free to live separate lives, as long as they were discreet in their *affaires*. Ladies of the *ton* knew the rules.

He was sure there were many men out there who would happily shackle themselves either to Henrietta or Millicent. So why was he so hesitant? His thoughts wandered—as they often did—to Charlotte. He frowned. *Again Charlotte!* He had to stop thinking about her. His decision should be based on logic. His responsibilities demanded it.

He knew that the younger generation wanted to marry for love, not alliance, but that was not what he expected for himself. His parents—who had barely known each other when they were married—had enjoyed a close, loving relationship, but that had been luck. As head of the family he knew his duty—to marry well despite his godmother's romantic notions.

Henrietta Buxted was the obvious choice. Monkton Park would add nicely to his estate and the girl was of good family—and a beauty. On the other hand, Millicent Etherington's large dowry was attractive—an injection of cash would allow him to speed up the improvements he was making to his lands.

Again and again he rehearsed the same arguments. Yet somehow he could not bring himself up to scratch and actually offer for one of them.

He despised the weakness making him dither and delay. He should not be shirking this duty. And his attraction for Miss Wyncroft was not helping matters. She offered no incentive save herself and a 'modest' dowry, as Mr Buxted had described it. His feelings towards her were growing daily, but the attraction was making him irrational, causing him to act against his better judgement.

Impulse had blindsided him twice already—once when he'd kissed her in the woods, and the second time in the sunshine, when he'd nearly done it again. She was so good, and so beautiful. He saw how she cared for others, how she quietly and competently solved problems, noticed how people were feeling, helped. He admired her intelligence, her humour and her insight. He desired her body with a madness he had never before experienced. Yet duty prevented him from marrying her.

He did not know what to do. He—

Martin, his chief groom, approached at a run.

Suddenly alert, the Earl sat up straighter in the saddle. 'What is it, Martin?'

'Armed poachers in the home wood, m'lord! Cotter's boy saw them and ran all the way to tell me!'

'Good God! That is where they are walking!' He wheeled his horse around, shouting, 'Follow me up there! Bring a shotgun!' and then left the yard at a gallop.

The next few minutes were the longest in his life. His horse, though surprised at this second outing, showed his class by flying swiftly along the road towards the woods.

Adam's logical musings of just moments before were meaningless now. Charlotte was in danger. Olivia too! Suddenly everything was clear. No longer could he deny his feelings. He loved Charlotte. How stupid he had been. Stupid and blind and arrogant. He loved her. Loved her kindness, her wit and intelligence, her face and form—her very self. And he knew not what danger she was in! If he lost her now… Oh, *why* had he not walked with them? They had only Hubert—and he was worse than useless.

Adam urged his horse to speed faster. He left the road and plunged into the forest path. Through the trees he caught sight of flashes of colour ahead. There they were!

He thundered towards them—then pulled up at the strange scene. Two groups—one grubby and unkempt, the other in brightly coloured muslin and superfine. They were all alive—they seemed unharmed. His heart still pounding hard, Adam tried to make sense of what he was seeing. They were all immobile, as if in a tableau.

One of the poachers glanced at him briefly. The other two didn't move, continuing to focus on Hubert and the ladies.

Henrietta was clinging tightly to Hubert's arm. Olivia and Charlotte stood immobile. A musket was lying on the ground, off to the side, along with assorted knives—the Earl counted four. What was this? The poachers had been disarmed? He was all confusion.

Charlotte spoke calmly, keeping her eyes on the intruders. 'Are you sure you have no further weapons? Perhaps in your boots?'

The tall man elbowed one of his accomplices, who cursed.

'All right, all right—I'll get it!' The rogue spoke to Charlotte. 'Ah, you're a downy one!' he said admiringly. 'As corky a lass as I ever see'd!' Reaching into his boot, he extracted a tiny knife and threw it onto the pile to his right.

'Anything else?' Charlotte's tone was steady. She looked calm and unafraid.

'I give you my word, milady.' said the tall man.

'Why should I trust your word? You are a disgrace to your regiment.'

'Ah, now, miss!' One of the short men spoke. 'We was only trying to survive. Not much work around for the likes of us now Boney's beat.' He shuffled forward slightly.

'*Stop*!' Charlotte's imperious tone halted him immediately.

Adam was at a loss to understand what was going on...why they were obeying her. But for now he would trust her to continue what she was doing. He carefully nudged his horse past the intruders.

Charlotte continued to command them. 'Now, all of you take three steps back.'

The poachers muttered, then did as she said.

As the space opened up between them the Earl saw the reason for the outlaws' compliance. With a steady hand Charlotte was holding a tiny, lethal-looking silver pistol. The workmanship, from what the Earl could see, was exquisite. It was like no other pistol he had ever seen, and had clearly been designed specifically to fit the smaller hand of a lady.

'Thank you. I told you all would be well if you did what I said.'

'Ah, miss! We meant no 'arm! We was just having a jest with you!'

Charlotte was unmoved. 'I want no Banbury stories, if you please. Hubert, can you please remove the weapons?'

Hubert shakily complied, gathering them all up into his arms and muttering about the damage they would do to his country coat.

Adam dismounted.

'My lord!' said Charlotte steadily, without raising her eyes. 'What would you like to do with these ruffians?'

The Earl handed his reins to Olivia, who took them with a wavering smile. He pressed a hand to her shoulder, then went to Hubert.

He checked the musket was unloaded, then took a knife. He felt safer now he was armed.

'First I think they need to visit my stables, until we can decide what to do with them.' Addressing the rogues directly, he spoke in cool, authoritative tones. 'Turn around! Now, start walking slowly. We are going to the road.'

They complied, and Adam followed them with Charlotte by his side. He threw a quizzical look at her, but she seemed as calm as before. Oh, but she was a diamond.

His heart still racing, he felt a hundred things at once. Fear, still—though it was swiftly being replaced by relief and pride. She truly was a woman in a million. His heart swelled with love for her. He wanted to take her in his arms and declare it, though he knew he couldn't. Not yet, leastways.

What a strange procession! thought Charlotte.

Three ragged outlaws, grumbling and muttering as they proceeded along the path, followed by an earl with a knife and a lady with a pistol. Behind them were Henrietta and Hubert—the latter struggling to carry the musket and the knives and protect his coat. Henrietta was—thankfully—still silent. Then, to the rear, Lady Olivia was leading the tall black stallion.

Why, it is better than a harlequinade!

A gurgle of laughter bubbled up. The Earl caught her eye, an answering gleam of humour in his. He shook his head admiringly and Charlotte's smile broadened. Now that the danger had passed she felt quite exhilarated.

As they reached the road they heard the sound of hoofbeats. Reinforcements had arrived from the stables: two grooms on horseback, carrying shotguns and ropes, and a little behind them the aged former king of the stables—Old Harold—driving a rumbling farm cart.

Harold subjected the outlaws to a venomous tirade which, far from cowing them, made them open their eyes wide in admiration. They allowed their hands to be securely tied, marvelling that one so old and decrepit could swear so well and so colourfully.

'I never heard the like of it,' said one of the short ones to the other. 'Why, he's better than our old sergeant when he was in his cups!'

Safely installed in the back of the cart, and eyeing the alert grooms with resignation, they fell silent. Henrietta and Olivia climbed into the front of the cart beside Harold, who told them to keep their skirts away from the floor.

'Er…might I perhaps join you?' asked Hubert, with an earnest, pleading look.

'Hmmph! You may—if you keep an eye on the stock in the rear,' said Harold.

Charlotte watched in bemusement as Hubert

walked to the back of the cart. Taking out his hand-kerchief with a flourish, he dusted a small area of the floor of the cart. After inspecting his handiwork he spread out the kerchief, ensuring it was perfectly aligned with the side of the cart. Finally he carefully arranged himself on it, ensuring that his coattails would not be crushed.

The bandits watched too, with rapt attention and open mouths, before declaring it as good as a trip to Vauxhall.

Henrietta and Olivia, now feeling safe, began talking of their shock and fear at the unexpected events—their tones displayed thrilling excitement rather than fear, which was reassuring to Charlotte.

The cart lumbered off, with an armed groom riding on each side, while the Earl and Charlotte followed on foot, leading the Earl's horse.

Charlotte put her weapon away.

'Miss Wyncroft, allow me to say you are a most unusual female.'

He looked at her with that same glow of admiration in his eyes. Charlotte felt herself blush.

She looked up at him shyly. 'Oh, no! Papa insisted I must have my gun in my reticule at all times—it is quite a habit with me. I am quite a good shot, too.'

'Really? Somehow that does not surprise me.'

'I also had lessons in how to defend myself from attack—one of Papa's colleagues had trained in the Far East. He had interesting techniques, whereby even a frail woman might escape from a taller, heavier man—though it did not come to that today.'

'You were managing the situation incredibly well.'

'Have you not realised I am a "managing" female?'

He laughed. 'The thought had occurred to me. But, tell me, were you not afraid?'

'Completely terrified!'

'Then how did you manage to appear so composed?'

'Calmness of mind, Papa says, and the ability to think while frightened is a soldier's skill.'

'Do you see yourself as a soldier, then?'

'We are all soldiers when we have to be. And, besides, I was the only one with a gun to hand. That gave me a certain advantage.'

'May I inspect it?'

Fishing it from her reticule, she handed it to him. He felt it in his hand. It was nicely balanced, and was the smallest pistol he had ever handled. The workmanship was excellent.

Then he made a discovery. 'It is loaded!'

'Well, of course it is! How can I shoot if it is not loaded?'

'And would you really have shot someone?'

'I believe so, yes. But I could only have shot one of them, so I needed to keep them all guessing as to who it would be until they were disarmed. I could see the musket was not ready to fire, so they just had their knives.'

'What did they want? Jewels?'

'Yes—and they may have…harmed us. They certainly threatened it.'

His jaw tightened.

'I am not wearing any jewels, apart from this amber cross which was my mother's. I should hate to lose it.'

'Olivia does not wear expensive jewels yet. What of Miss Buxted and Mr Etherington?'

'Henrietta is wearing a silver necklace today, and Mr Etherington has a signet ring—and his snuff box looks expensive. I do believe, though, that his main concern was for his coat!'

He lifted an eyebrow.

'Oh, dear, now you have made me say something indiscreet.'

'Not at all—for I agree with you.'

Something strange and surprising then occurred. Charlotte was suddenly, unexpectedly, assailed by delayed fear. A warm rush of reaction flooded her stomach, her leg muscles felt weak and she began to shake violently. She faltered in her steps.

'Charlotte! You are not well! Please—let me assist you.'

Adam took her hand in his large, warm one and placed his arm around her waist to steady her. He led her to a nearby tree stump, where she sat with relief.

'I am so sorry. I do not know what has come over me. I am not normally a weakling.'

He crouched down beside her. 'It is a natural reaction to what has happened. I confess I feel a little the same. I was fearful of what I might find, and now I am greatly relieved. I think my mind has yet to catch up with my beating heart.'

She looked at him curiously. 'How did you know? Or was it by coincidence that you came to the woods?'

He told her, and they talked of the incident again.

He planned to send the poachers to Godalming, for the attention of the authorities, with the grooms acting as armed guards. The magistrate might wish to speak to Charlotte and the others before deciding their fate. Prison—possibly transportation—awaited the trio.

Charlotte understood that she would not encounter them again, for which she was profoundly grateful.

Neither commented on the fact that her hand, somehow, remained resting in his, and his arm still encircled her tenderly. Charlotte felt safe with him. She wanted nothing more than for him to take her fully into his arms, though she knew he could not.

'They are former soldiers, you know. I did not wish to ask them their regiment as they do their comrades no credit.'

'Yes, I heard them say so. There are many like them in England these past weeks, looking for work.'

'They should have their prize money.'

'I suspect for some the prize money does not last

long. The taverns and gambling dens of the port towns have been busy since the army started arriving back.'

And the whorehouses, he thought, though he refrained from mentioning this.

Silence fell. The cart was out of sight.

'I declare I do feel much better. Shall we walk on?' asked Charlotte.

'You are still dreadfully pale. I shall take you up before me.'

Despite her protests—which, indeed, were half-hearted, for she was relieved not to have to walk—he lifted her onto his horse. Using the tree stump as a mounting block, he climbed up behind her.

Charlotte was seated awkwardly, on one corner of the saddle and facing to the left. His left arm was around her waist and, although he did nothing improper, she was conscious of the closeness of their bodies. She could feel his warmth burning through her and could smell his scent—a mix of soap, the outdoors and something else…something uniquely, wonderfully him. This close, she was struck by how large he seemed. She was a little less than average height for a lady, but he made her feel tiny. She relaxed into him.

He walked them towards the house slowly—very slowly—perhaps because his horse was tired. The poor animal did not protest at the extra weight, but ambled easily along the road. Charlotte wished the house a hundred miles away, for she could have sat like this, in bliss, for ever.

It was not to be.

Grateful that no one was around when they arrived, she slid off, allowing him to continue to the stable-yard. She murmured a word of thanks while avoiding his eyes, then mounted the steps to the house.

She entered to a scene of chaos. The hallway was thronged with servants and the door to the drawing room was busy with comings and goings. She could hear loud wailing in the drawing room and hurried there, although she suspected she knew what she would find.

The room was full of people. Henrietta, as expected, was the focus of attention. She was lying on a sofa, howling and crying, as her mother held her hand and Flint applied hartshorn. The house guests were ranged around her, expressing shock and sympathy.

Ignoring the tragedy being enacted, Charlotte crossed the room to sit with Olivia, who was sipping tea in the corner. She looked pale, and her hands shook slightly. They talked quietly, Charlotte telling her how she too had been affected by aftershock, that it was to be expected. Olivia confessed to feeling unwell—partly because she was distressed to see Henrietta in such a state.

'Well, you know Henrietta becomes distressed

like this from time to time. It is her way of reacting to things. And we have all suffered a shock today.'

'It is only now, when I reflect on it, that I remember how frightened I was, and how those men looked. You were so brave, Charlotte.'

'Indeed, I was quaking in my boots. But I think we were *all* brave, for we all maintained self-control. You were my adjutant—strong and quiet by my side. Even Henrietta did not panic at the time.'

Olivia liked this. 'We rescued ourselves, did we not? Though I was glad to see Adam arrive.'

'As was I! I wasn't sure I could keep all three of them under control for much longer.'

Miss Langley brought Charlotte some tea, declaring how shocked she was. 'This is all most dreadful. And poor Miss Buxted is so distressed. I must go to her…see if anything more can be done for her.'

The Earl entered the drawing room at this moment, having come directly from the stable-yard. His eyes swept the room, alighting first on the drama featuring Henrietta, then seeking…

His gaze found Charlotte and Olivia in the corner, talking quietly, their heads close together. As he watched Charlotte set down her teacup and took Olivia's hand. The Earl's gaze softened.

Harry, observing this, smiled knowingly.

He called his brother's attention. 'Adam, what's all this about you going off after poachers without me? And riding into goodness knows what without even stopping for a gun.'

'I knew you would scold me for that, Harry.'

'Where are the villains now? I understand the grooms have them trussed and helpless?'

'Yes. They have just left for Godalming, accompanied by Old Harold and two grooms. I have sent Martin to ride ahead and alert the magistrate.'

Henrietta's wails began to subside as she became interested in the conversation.

'What a shame,' said Hubert. 'For I wished to have words with them about the amount of dirt and grime on their weapons. It is truly shocking! Have you seen this mark on my sleeve? Rust! My coat will never recover, I fear.'

'My dear, brave son,' said Mrs Etherington affectingly, raising a handkerchief delicately to dab at the corner of her eye. 'I am sure you protected the ladies exceedingly well.'

'I did my best, Mama. But, you know, they really shouldn't allow such scoundrels to wander through the countryside.'

Henrietta, from her sofa, murmured faintly, 'If not for Mr Etherington I do not know *how* we should have managed. He steadied me when I should have fainted, and he took the weapons from those dastardly rogues.'

Remembering anew, she burst into noisy tears. Millicent, who had remained in the background, shook her head and pursed her lips.

Miss Langley, Mrs Buxted and Flint renewed their care of Henrietta, rubbing her feet and hands and applying cold cloths to her forehead. They were joined by Mrs Etherington, who had been inspired by Henrietta's sympathetic portrayal of Hubert.

On the far side of the room, Charlotte only just managed to prevent an outraged Lady Olivia from challenging Henrietta's version of events.

'But, Charlotte, it was *you* who rescued us! Mr Etherington just stood there, making stupid comments about his clothes.'

'Hush, now. Henrietta is upset, and Mr Etherington did indeed support her. And he did pick up the weapons.'

Charlotte said what she knew she ought, though inside she agreed completely with Olivia.

'Only because *you* asked him. And he grumbled about it the whole time. Why, he is still grumbling. He is *not* the hero. Charlotte, *you* are the hero, and I shall always remember it.'

Reverend Sneddon sidled up to them. 'Dear Miss Wyncroft… Lady Olivia. I was never so shocked in my life. To think this could happen here, at Chadcombe. And I might have been with you, only I was not feeling well today.'

'That was a lucky circumstance.'

'Indeed it was, Miss Wyncroft. But I was decidedly colicky all night. I had no sleep whatsoever, and providentially fell into a light doze this morning.'

'And are you now recovered, Reverend Sneddon?'

'I do not say "recovered", for I expect it will take at least two days to fully defeat this. But I have always been stoical about sickness. It is one of my strengths, I think.'

Nearby, Adam and Harry were listening.

Fuming, Adam muttered to his brother, 'We need to rid ourselves of this little man. Prating on about his colic instead of asking how Olivia and Miss Wyncroft do!'

'You are right,' said Harry, 'for anyone can see they are both pale.'

'They were extremely brave. Miss Wyncroft held all three rogues up, you know.'

'What? I had not heard this!'

Adam explained.

Harry was most impressed, asserting that Miss Wyncroft had risen even more in his estimation. 'Intrepid as well as beautiful. And kind with it. An excellent young lady.'

'She is unique,' said the Earl simply, looking towards her.

Chapter Fifteen

The day of the ball dawned cool and cloudy. It had rained during the night, and the scent of fresh-cut grass seeped through Charlotte's window, which she had left ajar. The scythe men had been busy for three days, cutting the lawns in front of the house, and had finished the job last evening.

Charlotte had requested to be woken early, as she would be busy all day. She had also insisted that Miss Langley should not be woken earlier than her usual hour, for she wished the old lady to have as little as possible to do today. Miss Langley, grateful, had agreed.

One of the new housemaids helped Charlotte don a pretty morning dress of figured muslin, and made her hair into a simple topknot. Flint had hung up Charlotte's ball-gown in preparation, and seeing it gave Charlotte a girlish thrill. The day had finally come.

Her excitement was tinged with sadness, for tomorrow would be their last full day at Chadcombe.

The thought of returning to Buxted House was strangely oppressive, though it would be good to see Papa again. She had not heard from him in the last ten days, but there might be a letter today, giving details of his arrival.

On her side table was a carefully drafted list of her tasks for the morning. Casting an eye over it, she left her room and headed straight for the kitchens.

A cheerful cacophony greeted her as she hurried along the narrow corridor—clanging, chopping, sizzling, and the babble of voices. She opened the door. The kitchen was filled with steam, servants and the smell of food.

Cook, though harassed, had everything well in hand. Charlotte was relieved to find the ovens were all functioning perfectly, and that the preparation of supper dishes was on schedule. An extravagant dinner was also to be served, for they would have a number of dinner guests from among the local gentry. The majority, though, would arrive after dinner, leaving their homes in the early evening and returning by the light of lanterns hung on their carriages.

Leaving the kitchens, Charlotte mounted the back stairs to Merrion's room, near the main door. The butler had been polishing the silver all week, since the ball had been announced, and now had only a few pieces yet to complete. Later he would mix the punch—a delicate operation which would conceal powerful alcohol beneath a sweet fruity taste.

In the hallway she encountered Grove, who invited her to accompany him to the ballroom.

The ballroom looked magnificent. It was a large room, elaborately decorated in the rococo style. Gilded cherubs adorned the mirrors and picture cartouches. Classical scenes had been painted directly on the walls, while the ceiling featured a large painting of Dionysus and his Maenads.

Along the sides were ornate chairs and side tables, as well as a few sofas, all in an exuberant style that matched the room. These were arranged so as to give a good view of the dancers for the chaperones and those who were not dancing.

The floor was of Italian marble, and featured a herringbone pattern around the edges. Two large chandeliers had been imported from France before the wars, and these had been lowered for cleaning earlier in the week. They still rested on soft cloths on the floor, and two housemaids were inserting dozens of long candles into each of their lights. They were beautiful, delicate pieces of bronze *doré*, with myriad pieces of cut glass to reflect the light and make it dance. Charlotte was excited at the thought of the effect tonight, when the darkness would be banished beautifully by crystal candlelight.

New candles had also been placed in various sconces and candelabra around the room, and would ensure the ball was brightly lit. Three hundred beeswax candles had been ordered for the ball, at a shocking cost of fifteen pounds—more than Priddy's annual salary. They were to be used throughout the public rooms, the hallways and the privy rooms. A hundred would light the ballroom itself.

The new housemaids—hired from London— were busy cleaning mirrors, walls and tables, and the floors would be washed in the afternoon, when the other tasks were completed.

There were three sets of double doors along the left side of the room, which opened onto a terrace near the rose garden, and they would be opened tonight if the ballroom became too hot. To the right was the card room, where Mr Buxted and others of a like mind would retire to play piquet, whist and *vingt-et-un*.

At the far end of the ballroom, next to the dais where the musicians would sit, was a door to the large supper room. Here they found Mrs Gordon.

'Oh, good morning, Miss Wyncroft... Mr Grove,' she said, curtseying to Charlotte. 'I should like your advice, for we must decide about the supper tables. We can lay them across the room or along it, in two long lines.'

They debated the options for a few moments, finally agreeing that with the numbers expected the long tables were the better option. Relieved that everything was under control, Charlotte left them to it and went to the gardens.

As arranged, she met Fradgely, the head gardener, who provided her with a chestnut and willow trug and a stout pair of metal shears. Grove had ordered

large numbers of flowers from a trader in Farnham,
who was travelling to the Covent Garden market
for fresh blooms that morning. He would not be expected to arrive until mid-afternoon, but the vases
were ready. Charlotte's task was to cut a selection
of flowers from Chadcombe's own gardens for the
large display that was to adorn the ballroom dais.

Satisfied that the staff had everything under control, Charlotte enjoyed an hour meandering among
the sights and scents of the gardens, gradually filling her basket with Sweet William, honesty, gera-
niums, hollyhocks and a variety of roses. The day
was still cool, cloudy and dry, and Fradgely believed
there would be no rain until the morrow.

Lost in thought, and humming to herself, she
failed to notice the Earl until he was right in front
of her.

'Oh! Lord Shalford.' She made her curtsey and
could not prevent a smile spreading over her face
on seeing him.

For the Earl's part, it seemed the sun had just
come out.

Adam was wearing his favoured buckskins,
which clung tightly to the muscles of his legs. His
coat of grey superfine looked as if it was moulded
to him, and accentuated his broad shoulders. Charlotte could not recall being so conscious of a man's
figure before. It was disconcerting, to say the least.

Since the incident with the poachers, and their
ride home, Charlotte had been aware of him in this

new way. Her heart leapt whenever she saw him, she had a strange warmth in the pit of her stomach, and she liked to imagine he had a partiality for her that he did not have for anyone else. Yet she could never forget that her lack of dowry meant that there was no future for her in his life. Which still left the possibility that he was trifling with her.

She had been spending more time in his company, for she still liked to walk every morning. Now, though, he insisted in accompanying her—and whoever else was walking that day. It was her favourite part of the day, and she hated the thought that it would all end when they left Chadcombe in two days' time.

'Are you well today, Miss Wyncroft?'

Unexpectedly he lifted her hand, bent over it, and kissed it. Charlotte was acutely conscious of the sensation of his lips on her bare hand, and the fact that her heart was beating rapidly.

'I am well, my lord,' she said, trying to keep her voice steady. 'As you see, I am cutting some of your flowers. Are they not beautiful?'

Still holding her hand, he looked intently up at her. 'Beautiful.'

Charlotte could feel her colour rising. She was not imagining things—he was still flirting with her. Reminding herself yet again that he could not possibly be serious in his intentions—she might not know the exact state of her dowry, but she knew she was no heiress—she withdrew her hand from his.

'I must go to my cousins, for they will surely be up and preparing for the ball.'

He allowed her to go, smiling inwardly at her agitation. Soon, he thought, her father would be home and he could petition him to support his suit. Then he would woo her properly. All worries about her lack of dowry were gone. His path was clear. He loved Charlotte and would marry her.

It meant that he could do very little to improve the estate in his lifetime, but with Charlotte by his side they would hold Chadcombe well. The family and the tenants would be cared for by a master and mistress who had a true love for Chadcombe.

He was sure his father would have understood. In fact, he did not care about what his father would have thought—which the old man would have liked!

Charlotte, knowing nothing of his plans, was all confusion. She *did* know she was in severe danger of losing her heart to him, and then, when he married Millicent—or Henrietta—she would be broken.

They had only two days left in Chadcombe. She would enjoy the ball, make the most of her time here, and then she would go away, far away, with Papa, to recover.

She increased her speed, seeking the safety of the house.

* * *

Charlotte gazed at her reflection, thrilled. She had known from the start that this ball-gown was special. It was a stunning white gauze evening gown, worn over an under-dress of midnight-blue French satin. It had little puffed sleeves and a demi-train, and was embroidered with tiny silver rosebuds.

She had loved the dress from the moment she had tried it on, and had looked forward to wearing it. Now, with the addition of long evening gloves and matching satin dancing slippers, her preparations were complete. Biting her lip in excitement, she acknowledged she had rarely looked better. Her eyes were dark blue and sparkling with anticipation, her cheeks had a rosy blush, and her dark hair had been expertly arranged by Flint, with pretty side-curls framing her delicate face. Her only jewels were a simple string of pearls which had belonged to her mother.

She was unaware that she was also glowing with happiness, giving her an inner light that was almost ethereal in its radiance.

Tonight she was going to enjoy every moment. She was going to stand up for as many dances as she could, and make up for all those evenings spent sitting in her room in Buxted House, trying not to think about what she was missing.

This staircase was surely designed with ball-gowns in mind, she thought whimsically as she walked carefully downstairs. She imagined the huge panniers of fifty years ago, and was glad current fashions were so much more elegant.

The Earl and Miss Langley had already taken up their positions in the hallway, ready to greet their guests. Some sixth sense made the Earl turn as Charlotte was about halfway down. On seeing her, his eyes widened and he smiled warmly. The look in his eyes was one of admiration, and Charlotte's heart beat faster. He—like all the gentlemen—was in full evening-wear: the knee breeches and plain black coat much favoured by that leader of fashion, Mr Brummell.

'Miss Wyncroft.' His voice was a little husky. 'You look stunning.'

Miss Langley turned. 'Oh, Miss Wyncroft, what a beautiful dress! You look charming, my dear.'

A dimple peeped out in Charlotte's cheek. 'As do you, Miss Langley. What an elegant headdress.'

Why, thought Adam, *have I never noticed that dimple before?*

With his inner turmoil resolved, he was looking forward to the freedom of being in her company again. Tonight she looked dazzlingly beautiful. He wished he could partner her to the ball, and his mind raced ahead to envisage her as his wife, standing with him in this very spot, waiting to receive their guests jointly.

Miss Langley was explaining to Charlotte that dear Olivia had persuaded her about the headdress, though she had thought to wear her usual cap. But now she had done it she thought perhaps feathers were not so outlandish.

Charlotte reassured her.

The Earl picked something up from a side table. 'A gift for you, from myself and Miss Langley. There is one for all the lady guests.'

She took it. It was a beautiful, delicate fan, decorated with swirling colours and patterns.

'Thank you, my lord. I shall treasure it.'

There was a little ribbon on the bottom of the fan, so she hung it over her arm. Now she was truly ready for the ball.

Four hours later, Charlotte left the supper room to return to the ballroom, knowing that Lord Shalford's ball was a great success. All those invited had attended, and the public rooms were thronged with guests—some of whom had travelled many miles to be there. Already they were saying that this July night was the biggest event of the year. The music, the food and the dancing were excellent, and all agreed that the new Earl certainly knew how to entertain.

Charlotte had been conscious of keeping an eye on the staff, for fear some disaster might occur, but she need not have worried. Everything had gone smoothly—a credit to the large team of servants that most of the guests would barely notice.

She had been surprised to find herself in much

demand as a dancing partner. Thankfully Reverend Sneddon would not dance, and nor did he approve of dancing—though he conceded he could not single-handedly change society's preoccupation with balls.

'The Lord,' he had pronounced, 'hast pleasure in uprightness, not pleasure in pleasure.'

He was so pleased with this witticism that he shared it with as many people as he could find, with disappointing results. No one, it seemed, appreciated his genius.

Charlotte had danced with Harry, with Mr Foxley, and with two of the local young men, who had flirted with her and complimented her in a most enjoyable manner. She had also danced a cotillion with the Earl, which she had particularly enjoyed. He was a good dancer, moving with an easy grace that had belied the complexities of the dance.

Henrietta, Faith and Millicent had also been in demand, and Olivia was thrilled to be enjoying her first 'proper' dances—albeit with young men she had known all her life. She had told Charlotte, shyly, that in this new setting she looked at some of them in quite a new manner.

Faith had been careful not to spend too much time with Mr Foxley, although Charlotte suspected they were both deeply in love. She wondered when the diffident Mr Foxley would have the courage to speak to her aunt and uncle.

Henrietta was in alt, having attracted a new throng of beaux. Poor Hubert had been reduced to hanging around, muttering about country bumpkins who knew nothing of fashion.

Indeed, many of the young gentlemen were impressed by Hubert's elegance. Not for him the rigidity of Mr Brummel—*his* palette, he said, was wider than that! For tonight he had chosen a coat of ruby-red brocade with gold frogging, which reminded Charlotte of a dressing gown. Wearing it with an impressive mustard waistcoat and high, starched shirt points, he certainly stood out amid the boring black, blue and grey evening coats of the other men.

This circumstance, plus his air of distance, had caused many of the younger guests to look at him admiringly—the ladies wished to flirt with him and the young gentlemen tried to take in every detail of his costume. For here, surely, was a Pink of the *ton*.

Henrietta's new admirers were clearly awestruck. Charlotte, watching, could only wish Henrietta had not worn so much jewellery, for it made her look quite vulgar. Diamonds dripped from her earlobes, hung around her neck and glistened on her wrist. She flirted expertly with her new fan, which was similar to Charlotte's.

Millicent, too, was enjoying the ball, and had danced every dance. She also had collected a swarm of local swains, interested to know her name and her opinions, and to offer their services should she need some punch.

The older guests were either in the card room or seated along the right-hand side of the room, watching the young people dance. Mrs Buxted's enormous purple turban dominated the huddle of chaperons, most of whom had spent the evening reminiscing about their own dancing days.

Olivia sidled up to Charlotte. 'Great-Aunt Clara has just given an instruction to the musicians to play a waltz. It is *so* exciting. I only wish I had learned to waltz, for I will need to know how to dance it before my come-out. But at least I shall get to *see* it.'

'Well, Olivia.'

It was the Earl.

'Are you enjoying yourself, chit?'

'Oh, I am. And you are a wonderful brother.'

She dashed off before he could reply, hoping to get a good spot from where to watch the waltzing.

The Earl looked a little startled, but pleased. Recovering, he bowed to Charlotte. 'Would you do me the pleasure of dancing the waltz with me?'

Charlotte's happiness was complete. 'I should be delighted, my lord.'

There was a murmur of excitement as the couples took the floor. Belatedly Charlotte realised that Henrietta was glowering at her. *Oh, no!* Henrietta had probably expected the Earl to offer her *the* waltz.

'My lord, I think Henrietta wishes to dance the waltz with you. And I feel a little unwell, so—'

'Oh, no! You shall not sacrifice yourself for her this time. You are not unwell, for I never saw you in greater looks, and it is *you* I wish to dance with—not your cousin. Let her find a partner from among her admirers.'

Shocked, but secretly pleased, Charlotte let it go. In truth, this *was* her wish. Right now she wanted to enjoy *this* dance, with *this* man, in *this* ballroom and wearing *this* dress.

The music began.

Whirling around the ballroom, Charlotte felt as if she were in a dream. The room and the people were blurred with movement. In the golden light of a hundred candles the only thing in focus was his face. His eyes were fixed on hers. She could feel his arm around her, steadying her as they swept around the floor. The music lifted them, swelling and flowing with emotion and grace.

They moved effortlessly together, and drew many admiring glances from around the room.

Too quickly for Charlotte's liking the waltz came to an end. She and the Earl, very properly, took a step back from each other and she curtseyed as he bowed.

'Did you enjoy that?' he asked as they walked towards the large table near the doors, where two liveried footmen were serving punch.

'Oh, I did! It has been so long since I have danced the waltz.'

'You should dance it every day, if you wish, for you dance especially well.'

'Oh, well, it was expected in Vienna. We had

many hours of lessons in my school with the dancing master. I can actually dance the man's part, too, for my friend Juliana and I would practise together.'

He handed her a glass of punch. 'Indeed? I can imagine it easily, for you are a masterful lady. Where is your friend now?'

'Still in Vienna—but she will come to England this year. I shall be happy to see her again.'

She sipped the sweet punch, glad of the cooling liquid in her throat as the room was so warm. She glanced around. Many eyes were on her and the Earl. Some people were chatting behind fans; others were simply eyeing them speculatively. Mrs Buxted was glaring at them.

'Oh, my goodness!' She spoke aloud without thinking.

'What is it? Something ails you?' He was all concern.

'They are all looking at us. It is *horrible*.' A flush rose in her cheeks.

He had already noticed the gawking, but tried to soothe her. 'Most of them will be unused to the waltz, and some older people in particular may disapprove. Does it bother you? It shouldn't, you know.'

She did not argue, but they both knew the real reason for the speculation was not just their dance. Adam cursed himself for exposing her to gossip— although he could not regret waltzing with her. Until her father returned he could not speak his heart and propose to her, and the gossips would speculate that he was simply trifling.

How best to protect her?

He had an idea. 'Come with me.'

She complied, and he led her to his great-aunt.

'Miss Wyncroft, I believe you will be comfortable here.'

He seated her beside Miss Langley, and in doing so reminded all the gossips that she was close to the family and it was hardly surprising that they were at ease with each other. Satisfied that he had found a clever solution, he bowed politely—again correcting any misapprehensions about the degree of closeness between them—and left.

Charlotte was confused. Where was her warm, friendly dance partner of five minutes ago? Why was he behaving with such coldness? He had abandoned her with the chaperons, and his bow had been much slighter than his usual courtesies to her.

Anxiety stabbed her, and the glow she had felt during the waltz began to dim. Really, she had begun to rely on him—on their friendship—too much. Now she saw how easily it would disappear. She was leaving Chadcombe the day after tomorrow and would not, despite her dreamy hopes tonight, see much of him again. She watched, helpless, as he crossed the room, petitioning Henrietta for the next dance.

A timely reminder!

Giving the Earl a brilliant smile, Henrietta took his hand and rose.

Murmuring some excuse to Miss Langley, Charlotte slipped through the nearby open door into the blessed coolness of the terrace. Behind her, the musicians struck up a country dance. Charlotte couldn't resist one last look at the Earl and Henrietta.

His attention was entirely fixed on her cousin, chatting and apparently flirting with her. Charlotte's throat swelled with pain, and a film of tears half blinded her. She turned towards the gardens, away from the tender scene, though the image of their togetherness came with her, burned into her inner vision.

The night was mild and dry, and the wind that had whipped up dust along the terrace earlier had now subsided. Charlotte dashed away the unwanted tears. As her eyes became accustomed to the starlight she began to make out shapes and outlines in the gardens. That was the archway of rose bushes over the main path, and that was the top of the fountain of Eros, in the centre of the pathways.

On impulse, she left the terrace to walk in the silver darkness of the rose garden. By now she knew every turn in the paths and found her way easily to the wooden bench where she had enjoyed many happy hours these past weeks, reading and reflecting.

She sat for a while, allowing silent tears to fall. Angry tears…tears of pain and of loss. The fountain burbled and splashed, and an occasional breeze rustled the leaves. Somewhere a vixen called. In the end the tears stopped, and she felt only empty.

It was strange to think she had only one more day at Chadcombe, for she loved the place. She might never be back—unless her cousin married the Earl.

She stood up. She had been out here long enough. She ought to be getting back.

Moving easily back towards the house, she had almost reached the edge of the rose garden when she suddenly collided with the Earl, who was walking purposefully towards it.

'Miss Wyncroft.' He held her arm to steady her. 'So here you are! Is anything amiss?'

He must not know.

She forced herself to speak calmly. 'No, I was just enjoying a short time away from the heat of the ballroom. I am going back now.'

'A wonder I did not take you for a thief, lurking around in the darkness like this.'

The light from the house was behind him, throwing his face into shadow, but she could hear humour in his voice—along with something darker.

'To be truthful,' he continued softly, 'today someone stripped my garden of its most beautiful flowers.'

She shivered, unable to resist the warmth in his voice. She should leave. Right now. Where was the anger and hurt she had felt half an hour ago, when she'd left the ballroom? But she might never have a moment alone with him again. How weak he made her.

She heard herself reply to him, and idly wondered at how calm she sounded. 'And have you caught this audacious thief?'

His eyes were as dark as midnight in the starlight, and the heady scent of roses surrounded them.

'I have caught her now, and I demand a forfeit.'

Slowly, allowing her time to pull away if she wished, he bent his head towards hers.

This time she knew what to expect, and met his lips with an enthusiasm which surprised them both. If this was all she would ever have she would make the most of this kiss.

Seemingly much moved, he put both arms around her and pulled her close, deepening the kiss. She was lost in a dream, where the only reality was him, his kiss, his warmth, his intensity.

'It was just so damned hot in there, and I have had my fill of dancing, Foxley. I— Good God!'

The Captain's voice carried clearly to the Earl, who immediately ended the kiss. Charlotte, greatly confused, looked up to see the Captain and Mr Foxley standing a few feet away.

'Well, dear brother,' said the Captain, recovering his composure. 'Am I to wish you happy?'

He thought they were to be *married*! Mindful of the speculative glances in the ballroom, and now this, Charlotte was horrified. The Earl might be trapped into an unwelcome match with a lady of no great fortune—herself!

She made haste to correct the Captain's misunderstanding. 'Oh, no! Please do not say so! It was nothing— I mean, I was just— I mean—no!'

She stole a glance at the Earl. He looked grim, his face as unyielding as stone. And why should he not? He was close to being trapped for life over what she was sure was for him a light flirtation. She could not do that to him. She loved him too well.

'Please do not speak of this to anyone, for nothing happened.' Her voice cracked, and she looked at them all pleadingly.

'Of course…of course,' said Mr Foxley.

'I must go!'

The Earl did nothing to stop her.

It seemed to Adam he had never seen her so agitated. She had coped with the incident with the poachers with more calm than this. The thought of marrying him was abhorrent to her, it was clear. So he did not protest when she left them, in a flurry of white gauze and distress, to return to the house.

'I thank you, Harry,' he said stonily. 'You have outdone yourself.'

The Captain had the grace to look ashamed. 'Sorry, Adam. But how was I to know you would be in the garden kissing girls at your own ball?'

'Not "girls". Miss Wyncroft.'

'Kissing Miss Wyncroft, then. Though I confess

I would have been mightily shocked to catch you kissing anyone else, for you two have been smelling of April and May these two weeks and more.'

'I shall thank you to keep your opinions—and this incident—to yourself.'

'Of course! Never a word of it shall pass my lips.' He nudged Foxley—hard—in the ribs.

'Er…nor mine.'

'Good!' The Earl stalked off.

'Well. I have never seen your brother so animated.'

'Nor I, Foxley. Nor I.'

Chapter Sixteen

A curious lethargy pervaded Chadcombe on the day after the ball. Not among the staff, who were busy from early morning, clearing up and cleaning. But for the guests—and for some of the family—there was a sense of change, of endings, and the foreboding of goodbyes.

The guests slept late, with most having reached their beds just before sunrise.

Charlotte woke to the hiss of rain and the muted tick of the clock on her mantel. Surprised to find it was almost noon, she sank back on her pillows for a moment's reflection.

She loved him!

Of course she did—it was blindingly obvious to her now. No other man had occupied her thoughts as he did. She felt an affinity and a closeness with him akin to the intimacy she shared with only a few people—her father, Priddy, Juliana.

Yet her feelings for the Earl went beyond warm

friendship. She was intensely attracted to him—the thought of his handsome face and the way his eyes crinkled when he smiled had the power to make her insides melt and her pulse race.

She was not blind to his faults—she still remembered how arrogant he had been towards her at first, and how he had flirted ruthlessly with her as well as courting Henrietta and Millicent. Deep down, though, her heart told her he was a good man, trying to do the best he could with his life.

The reason she was sure beyond doubt that what she felt for him was love was that she wanted only what was best for him. Even if it meant she could not share his life. Caught in a compromising position such as last night's kiss, she was sure Henrietta or Millicent would have created a drama, to make certain they secured an offer of marriage from the Earl.

Charlotte, raised with a sense that honour was higher than self-interest, could not. She had done all she could to reassure Harry and Mr Foxley that what had happened was trivial—no one should be forced into marriage because of a *kiss*, for heaven's sake!

Despite their friendship, he probably viewed their flirtation as a light pastime, to endure no longer than her stay at Chadcombe.

She recalled his tone as he teased her about being a thief and demanded a forfeit… Yes, to him, this was simply an amusing, entertaining way to spend a summer. He would expect her to walk away as unaffected as he would be himself. As she had been, she reflected, after her flirtations with the Italian Count and the young officer in Vienna. She had enjoyed flirting, the thrill of gaining their attention, yet she had kept her heart untouched and had walked away with a smile and a pleasant memory.

Not so this time. Loving him was her fault and her responsibility and she would bear the consequences. She would not accuse him of playing fast and loose with her heart by deliberately trying to make her fall in love with him, as some rakes did. The Earl was no rake, and he could not know the devastating impact of what he would have thought a light flirtation. The fact that she loved him was because of all he *was*, not what he did.

His duty to his family and to Chadcombe meant he should marry someone who could bring increased wealth to its legacy. That was how marriage worked. Charlotte could not be said to be offering anything to Chadcombe, and Adam—the Earl—would be criticised for not marrying well.

'Adam.'

She said his name aloud, just to feel it in her mouth, hear it in her bones. It sounded strange in the quiet bedroom. She suddenly felt sad.

Shaking herself out of it, she rang for a maid and asked to have nuncheon in her room. Today was not a day for the dining room. Afterwards, dressed in the elegant green crêpe dress she had bought in London, she ventured downstairs. The maid—one of the new ones, recently hired in London—was to start packing her trunks, apart from the dresses she would need today and her travelling clothes for the journey to Buxted House tomorrow.

Faith, suffering with burdens of her own, was the only guest interested in walking in the rain. Mr Foxley had gone for a final day's fishing with Mr Buxted.

'Papa insisted,' she said, looking glum. 'Fishermen like the rain.'

Donning long pelisses and stout walking boots of kid leather, the young ladies decided on a turn around the gardens rather than heading for the woods. Following the drama of the poachers, Faith was still nervous of walking without a gentleman to protect them—and Mr Foxley had made her promise she would not venture far without him.

'Shall we go through the rose garden?' she suggested as the footman opened the front door.

Charlotte blushed slightly, remembering last night. 'Er…no. Let's walk along the stream today, for we have not done so in days.'

'Good morning, Lord Shalford!' Faith hailed the Earl.

He was approaching the house on his tall stallion. A misty rain was falling, glistening on his coat and adding droplets to his dark hair. It was not clear to Charlotte if he had heard their conversation.

'Are you well today, ladies?'

The Earl was polite, but distant. His eyes searched Charlotte's face.

Both ladies, lifting the hoods of their pelisses to cover their hair, confirmed that they were in good health. There was a short silence. Charlotte could not think of what to say. The Earl seemed similarly lost for words.

'Thank you for the ball,' offered Faith. 'It was most enjoyable.'

'I am glad you enjoyed it, Miss Faith. Now, if you will excuse me, I must return Volex to the stables. I have much work to do today.'

Faith and Charlotte watched him go. 'Well!' said Faith. 'I wonder what ails Lord Shalford today? He is not normally so curt. And he did not suggest joining us on our walk, as he normally would.'

'He said he has work. The ball may have been keeping him from matters of business.'

'Indeed. I am glad we ladies do not have to worry over such things.'

Charlotte offered a non-committal answer, and steered Faith towards the gardens. They walked along the pretty path bordering the stream. The greenery was more intense in the light rain, and Charlotte marvelled again at England's lush beauty.

They saw a heron, and a brown otter, and glimpsed what they thought was a kingfisher. The rain eventually stopped, so they lingered longer than they had intended. Charlotte was determined to imprint every memory of Chadcombe in her mind. In years to come, she wanted to be able to remember this place—how it looked, smelled and sounded, and how she'd felt. It was all she would have.

She might have meandered through the misty gardens for hours, but Faith had spotted in the distance that her father and Mr Foxley were returning to the house, so they turned back.

They were still a good half-mile away, so it took them nearly fifteen minutes to get there. As they neared the building they noticed an unfamiliar travelling coach outside the main door. The head groom was hurrying towards it to offer assistance, but it seemed its occupants had gone indoors shortly before. Charlotte did not recognise the insignia on the door, but standing with the driver was a young man in regimentals.

'Could it be one of Captain Fanton's friends?' asked Faith.

'Possibly.' Charlotte had had a better thought. Could it be her own, dear papa? It would be so good to see him, today of all days. He would take her to London—away from everything.

Stepping inside, she hurriedly removed her pelisse. The footman brought her slippers, and she swiftly unbuttoned and removed her boots.

'Do we have visitors?' she asked the footman.

He was spared from answering by the arrival of Merrion.

'Miss Wyncroft,' he said, with his usual impassive demeanour. 'Your presence is required in the library.'

Her heart leapt. It *must* be Papa! Leaving Faith behind, she hurried along to the library, failing to notice how Merrion's gaze followed her.

The library, with its comfortable leather chairs, velvet sofas, warm wooden panelling and hundreds of books, was one of her favourite rooms. She had spent many hours there on rainy days, enjoying everything from gothic novels to fables, though she had found some of the more 'improving' texts a little dry.

She opened the door, which creaked slightly. Her first thought on entering was a sense of surprise at the number of people in the library. There was Mr Buxted, his wife beside him, immediately opposite the door. Miss Langley was by the windows, pacing agitatedly. And the Earl dominated the room, standing tall and immobile in its centre. He looked strangely pale. Was he ill?

Facing the Earl, in regimentals, was a man with his back to Charlotte.

'Oh, Charlotte!'

Miss Langley sounded upset. Why was that?

The man in regimentals turned. It was not Papa. It was—

'Major Cooke!' Charlotte was surprised to see Papa's friend and colleague.

The Major approached. 'My dear Charlotte.' Reaching out, he took both her hands, then paused, a crease between his eyebrows.

A dreadful feeling swamped Charlotte. Suddenly

she knew she did not want to hear what he had to
say. Her mind froze, and she was barely aware that
he drew her into the room and seated her on the
edge of the green sofa.

'You must be brave, my dear. I have bad news…
the worst news.'

Her eyes were fixed on his face, which seemed to
grow and shrink as her vision distorted. His voice,
too, suddenly seemed faint and far away.

She picked out some words.

'Died… France…attacked…duty…'

She heard another voice—her own, though from
far away. '*Nooooo!*' It was a high-pitched wail.

The edges of her vision began to go black…

The sharp smell of ammonia filled Charlotte's
nostrils. Confused, she tried to move. She was lying
on the sofa, and Miss Langley was holding hartshorn under her nose. Weakly, she tried to push it
away. In the background she could hear Mr Buxted's voice, and another—Major Cooke's.

'They found two shallow graves in the woods—
four of them were travelling together. The other two
will no doubt be located in the next few days.'

'Shocking, indeed. Do they know who attacked
them?'

'No. Bandits, perhaps, or renegades.'

'Papa!' Charlotte managed, and a rush of shock
filled her again.

Someone was holding her right hand—she could

feel the warmth. She turned her head slightly. It was the Earl. His grey eyes pinned hers, filled with sorrow and truth.

Her hand clutched his, desperation filling her. 'No!' said Charlotte, hoping that he—that someone—would agree with her. The Earl would surely save her. Papa could not be—not be—

'I am so sorry, Charlotte.' His voice was low, deep and sincere.

'Please…this can't be true.'

'Oh, you poor, dear girl.' Miss Langley, visibly upset, set the hartshorn down and took Charlotte's other hand.

Charlotte could not bear it. She directed her gaze to the ceiling above. There, painted in beautiful pastels, was Venus reclining. The goddess was naked apart from a strategically draped sheet. She lay in languorous ease on a golden couch, a slight smile playing about her lips. Her reclined pose mirrored Charlotte's own, which struck Charlotte as absurd.

Nothing was real.

Charlotte struggled to sit up, then wished she hadn't. The room was spinning alarmingly, and her legs felt as though they were made of water. *Shock*, she told herself.

There was a light scratch on the door. A housemaid entered—summoned, it seemed, by Mrs Buxted.

'Bring some tea,' said her aunt briskly. 'Miss Wyncroft has sustained a shock.'

'Yes, ma'am.' The housemaid, after a glance towards Charlotte, left.

Charlotte could imagine the speculation among the servants. It was easier in this moment to concentrate on that, not to think about—

'I shall take your place, Lord Shalford. Dear Charlotte needs me.'

Aunt Buxted sat beside Charlotte, and the Earl gave way.

'Oh, my dear, dear Charlotte…' Miss Langley's tears were flowing.

Charlotte could not bear her distress. 'Please, Miss Langley. You will make yourself ill.'

Charlotte's voice sounded weak and small. Miss Langley wept all the more.

Charlotte kept her left hand in Miss Langley's— to give and receive comfort. The Earl's hand was gone from her right, and Mrs Buxted was awkwardly patting Charlotte's arm. Her aunt looked rather chagrined.

Charlotte could not bring herself to look at the Earl. Of all those present, he was the one she most wanted to console her—and the only person she could *not* expect to comfort her.

The maid returned with tea. Mrs Buxted poured. Charlotte's hand shook as she took it, making the cup rattle in its saucer.

'Tea?' said Mr Buxted scathingly. 'Shalford, what we need here—for medicinal purposes—is whisky.'

The Earl acquiesced to this, and left the library.

As the door closed behind him Charlotte was over-come with a wave of emotion. Her head swam again and she closed her eyes. Unnoticed, her hand slack-ened and hot tea spilled on her dress.

The shock brought her back to herself and she jumped up. Mrs Buxted and Miss Langley fussed around her, lifting the fabric away from her leg in case she should be scalded. She felt some pain on her right leg, but it was brief. Strangely, the intense physical sensation was almost welcome, as for a second it distracted her from her anguish.

The Earl returned with a bottle of golden whisky and a glass.

'What is amiss?' he asked, frowning. He still looked pale.

Miss Langley, with many false starts, explained about the tea. Charlotte sat down again.

'Do you wish me to call the doctor?' he asked, looking directly into Charlotte's eyes.

'No, no—please do not!' said Charlotte. The thought of being prodded and poked and disturbed was distressing.

'He can perhaps give you something…'

'No, I do not wish to have laudanum. I will be well.'

He looked at her intently, then nodded. Without speaking he poured a generous measure of whisky and offered it to her. Their fingers touched briefly as he handed her the glass. She sipped, choking a little as the fiery liquid burned its way down her throat.

Major Cooke cleared his throat. 'Charlotte, I know this is difficult for you, but do you know who your guardian was to be in the event of...?'

She shook her head. 'I do not know, for Papa never said. Perhaps it is Mr Buxted...'

'Yes, yes, of course! I think I am—but I do not recall exactly,' said her uncle. 'Happy to oblige—poor little thing! It really is quite affecting, you know.'

Mr Buxted, as though Charlotte was not present, proceeded to outline how terrible it must be to be orphaned, and that he would do his duty by the child if his name was indeed discovered to be listed as guardian in Sir Edward's will.

Talk of wills and the use of the word 'orphaned' was too much for Charlotte. She begged to be allowed to go to her room. No one stopped her, though Mrs Buxted claimed rank as closest female relative and accompanied Charlotte up the wide staircase.

They disturbed the maid, who was packing the last of Charlotte's possessions into her trunks. Mrs Buxted shooed her out briskly, bade Charlotte lie down upon the bed, then proceeded to express at great length her shock at Sir Edward's death, her own emotional reaction to the news, and her surprise that Charlotte—following an initial fainting fit—should now be so stoical in her response.

'For I am sure if *I* had such bad news—such *terrible* news—I would wail and cry and be unable to function. I declare it is most unnatural to be so quiet and reserved when you have heard your dear father is *dead*!' Wandering to the mirror, she patted her hair. 'I know *my* dear daughters would be unable to contain themselves, for *they* are sensitive, feminine girls. I declare it pains me to think of it—and when I remember how you danced with Lord Shalford, as though you were his *equal*!...'

Mrs Buxted was becoming more animated, working herself up, pacing up and down the room. Charlotte felt pain in her hands, where her own fingernails were digging into the palms.

'I am not a vindictive woman,' her aunt continued. 'Indeed I am full of Christian charity. But I cannot help but think about the wages of sin, and that *"evil pursueth sinners: but to the righteous good shall be repaid"*. Yes, all's changed now. Changed indeed...'

Charlotte, unable to fathom the workings of her aunt's mind, turned her head to one side, closed her eyes and tried to imagine that it was all simply a bad dream.

Chapter Seventeen

Charlotte stared at her own face in the mirror and wondered why she was not crying. The pain inside her was a tight, hard knot. It radiated out from her chest, making it difficult to breathe, to think, to function.

It was two days since they had returned to London, and three since Major Cooke's news. Aunt Buxted had eventually left Charlotte alone, after getting no response to her sermon, and Charlotte had kept to her room afterwards, picking at the food brought to her, wandering aimlessly around the bedchamber and lying listlessly on the bed, struggling with the unreality of it all.

She had been unable to sleep properly, though she had fallen into a light doze once or twice. The coming of dawn seemed a relief—though how, she wondered, could the birds sing and servants rise to their work when her world had ended?

Somehow she had endured the farewells and expressions of sorrow from the Fanton family, their guests and the senior servants. She had been reserved and dignified, and had felt far away from all of them. The part of her mind that still functioned had been able to see that some of them were genuine in their concern for her, but she could not allow herself to *feel* it. She had avoided *him* as much as she could, for fear he would pierce her armour and allow unwelcome feelings to surface.

She could not behave normally. The muscles of her face stubbornly refused to form a smile. Humour meant nothing to her; absurdity had no impact. Even social smiles would not come. She felt hollow—as though she were simply an ornament or a piece of furniture. Everyone else had life and colour, whereas she was flat and grey—a shadow.

The long journey back to London had been as bad as she'd expected. Imprisoned in a jolting carriage with Aunt Buxted, Faith and Henrietta. Trying to shut out their conversation. Giving minimal responses when they spoke directly to her. Surviving it.

Finally, thankfully, they had turned into Half-Moon Street. As soon as she had been able, Charlotte had escaped to her room, where Priddy—dear Priddy—had been waiting for her. Major Cooke, in search of Charlotte, had called at Buxted House first. Priddy, who was no fool, had surmised what his news was likely to be.

Priddy had opened her arms and Charlotte—as

she had done in times of trouble ever since she was six—had sought comfort in her abigail's motherly embrace.

Priddy had shed tears, having had great regard for Sir Edward. Her genuine grief was surprisingly comforting. All the others—the Earl, Miss Langley, Olivia—had felt only sorrow for *Charlotte*, for they did not know Sir Edward. Priddy grieved Papa's loss for his own sake, and Charlotte needed that.

Charlotte herself could not succumb to grief. The tears remained frozen inside her. The song she had sung at Chadcombe reverberated around her head. *Let me weep. Let me weep.*

Yesterday had been Charlotte's birthday. The day would now be associated with this for ever—with pain and loss and sorrow. As a birthday it had meant nothing to her, though she had appreciated the small gifts from the family—some sweetmeats from Henrietta, a friendship sampler from Faith. And Aunt Buxted had given her black gloves and a length of black bombazine.

'You must have it made into a gown, Charlotte, for you cannot be seen until you have appropriate mourning clothes!'

'Mama, since Charlotte's father has died do we also need to go into mourning? Please say we do not! For I should *hate* to wear black and miss the balls and routs all because of some man we barely know.'

'Of course not, Henrietta. Sir Edward was the

husband of your father's cousin—hardly a close relative.'

'Thank goodness! Imagine how terrible *that* would be.'

Mrs Buxted had ignored this. 'Charlotte, your father's lawyer, Mr Ritter, is to call later. Your uncle will send for you when he needs you,'

'Yes, Aunt Buxted.'

Mr Ritter, a small man with eyeglasses and a sympathetic smile, had had more bad news for Charlotte. Seated in her uncle's library, with Mr and Mrs Buxted also present, she had learned that Mr Buxted—as anticipated—was to be her guardian until she reached twenty-five, unless she married first.

She was her father's sole heir, but the state of his finances was not healthy. The house in Shawfield was indeed mortgaged, with the rental income covering the cost of the debt. Mr Buxted and Mr Ritter, as trustees, would jointly manage it to ensure there was no foreclosure. In another fifteen years, the debt would be paid and she might benefit from the income herself.

Until then she would have to rely on returns from the small sum deposited in Child's, along with whatever the Army would give, and any money Papa had banked in Vienna. In the coming weeks, Mr Ritter would write to Sir Edward's man of business there, if Miss Wyncroft would assist in furnishing his name and direction. She had undertaken to do so.

After the lawyer had left, Mrs Buxted had had what she termed 'a kindly word' with Charlotte.

'You know, Charlotte, this means there will have to be changes. It would not be appropriate to ask your uncle to pay for your personal servants, or to stable a thoroughbred horse.'

Priddy and Joseph! But they had been there her whole life. And Lusy! Was she to lose Lusy too?

'Now, now, Louisa…' Mr Buxted had protested. 'She will still wish to ride, and I would not deprive her of that pleasure.'

Aunt Buxted had glared at him, irritated by his lack of common sense. 'She may ride the hack—for you rely on *me* to manage the household accounts, and if you took any interest in them you would know it would not be economical to keep extra horses that we do not need!'

'Yes, but surely—'

'Please…' Charlotte had intervened. 'I do not wish to be the cause of a quarrel between you. I shall be content to ride the hack.'

'I knew you would be sensible, Charlotte. You see, husband, it is all settled.'

Mr Buxted had shrugged his shoulders helplessly. And so, today was to be her last ride on Andalusia.

Mr Buxted had found a buyer immediately on mentioning it at his club, he said, for the connoisseurs of horseflesh had all heard about the stunning Spanish mare belonging to the Buxteds' houseguest.

He had avoided Charlotte's gaze as he'd revealed

that he had been offered a surprisingly high price for the horse. Charlotte had wondered if he had, in fact, supplemented the amount himself, to help her.

So here she was, staring into the mirror and wondering why she was still unable to cry. It was Tuesday, and Papa had been gone since Saturday. No, she had *heard* on Saturday. Papa had died some days ago, while she had been enjoying the pleasures of walking and laughing and dancing—and kissing.

She did not know exactly when he had died, or how. She might never know. She, better than most, knew how chaotic things could be when soldiers died, simply because it was so commonplace. The Army focussed on counting the deaths and informing the relatives, but many soldiers were simply buried where they fell, with no record of the details. Their families would mourn and wonder and carry the lack of knowledge with them for the rest of their lives.

Priddy—an excellent seamstress—was still working on the black gown, so Charlotte had been wearing her plainest clothes. Her riding habit was rather dashing for a lady in mourning, but she would cover it with a dark cloak. She needed to get out of the house, so would risk Mrs Buxted's censure.

She stood up straighter, as if her aunt was already reprimanding her. Charlotte was alone in life now, and every battle to be fought was hers alone. Papa would not be coming to rescue her from Buxted House.

Stop! she told herself. *Do not make things seem worse than they are.*

Most of the time life was perfectly acceptable in Buxted House. But the contrast with the vast expanses of Chadcombe was particularly taxing, as she had become accustomed to freedom, and to spending much less time with Henrietta and Aunt Buxted. Here, they could not be avoided. She would simply have to endure.

She sighed at her reflection and considered what she saw. A slim young woman, pale and haunted, with blue eyes that seemed huge in her face. Her father's eyes.

She slipped down the stairs quietly, avoiding contact. Biddle was there, and indicated with a gesture to the footman that he himself would open the door for Miss Wyncroft. Charlotte thanked him, aware of the honour.

Outside, Joseph was waiting, with Andalusia and his own mount. Charlotte felt a pang as she saw Lusy, sidling impatiently, keen to enjoy the treat ahead. Lusy, too, had missed their morning rides.

Joseph helped her mount.

'Thank you, Joseph,' she said softly, hooking her knee between the two pommels and checking that her skirt was securely taped to her boot. She was conscious that Joseph, too, would be soon gone.

'My pleasure, miss.' His voice was gruff.

She dared not look at him.

He climbed on to his own horse—the staid Bux-

ted hack that would soon be Charlotte's mount—
then they walked together to Green Park. It was
earlier than usual, as Charlotte had awoken before
the sun again. The only people in the park were the
men working on the fortress that would become
the Temple of Concord for the Regent's peace gala.

They spent half an hour enjoying the various
walks around the park, then Charlotte said, 'Joseph,
I should like to gallop one last time on Lusy. Do you
think I could?'

He looked around. About to advise her against it,
he glanced at her pinched, anxious face and changed
his mind. 'Seems to me, Miss Charlotte, there is
nobody here to tell tales of you in society. Let her
have her head.'

He had barely finished speaking before Charlotte
was off. A skilled horsewoman, riding side-saddle
on a spirited mare. They moved together as though
they were one creature.

'Ho, there!' Harry hailed Charlotte's groom as
he and Adam trotted towards him. 'Is that Miss
Wyncroft?'

The groom hesitated.

'Oh, you should not be concerned for her reputation. We would not dream of telling anyone she
was galloping in a London park.'

Thus assured, the man confirmed that it was Miss
Wyncroft, though they already knew it.

'We have just called at Half-Moon Street to ask

if she would ride today, but she was too early for us,' said Harry.

'Yes, sir.' Joseph, loyal to his mistress, would say nothing more.

The Earl, who had not spoken at all, kept his eyes fixed on that small, distant figure.

'She is coming back,' he said. His voice was strained.

Charlotte was indeed returning.

Galloping at full speed was difficult for a man using a traditional saddle. With a side-saddle it was considered dangerous. It was difficult for a lady to signal properly to her horse, as only her left leg was in contact with the animal. If she fell—as ladies sometimes did while galloping—her foot might become entangled in the elaborate side-saddle stirrup, meaning she might be dragged along or trampled by a frightened horse.

All three men watched tensely until she came close, then breathed again as Charlotte slowed Andalusia to a gentle trot.

'Good day, Miss Wyncroft.'

'Captain Fanton.' She nodded to him, then to his brother. 'Lord Shalford.'

'What the devil do you mean, riding like that? You might have been killed!'

All looked in surprise at the Earl. He looked pale and grim. His jaw was set in a hard line, and his mount sidled and pranced as he gripped the reins too tightly.

'But I was not.' Charlotte's voice was quiet and steady.

'You might have been.' He glared at her.

Her chin went up. 'And exactly what business is it of *yours*, my lord?'

He opened his mouth to speak, then clammed it shut. 'None,' he offered, after a pause.

She turned towards home, and they all directed their mounts to follow. Joseph, who was feeling extremely uncomfortable, dropped back a little. As did the Earl a moment later.

Not accustomed to making polite conversation with Peers of the Realm, Joseph did not speak. Ahead, they heard Captain Fanton make a banal comment to Charlotte about the weather. Charlotte replied with an equally ordinary remark. The stilted conversation did little to dispel the tension. They walked in almost silence to Half-Moon Street, and stopped in front of Buxted House.

Charlotte slid off before Joseph could dismount to help, and walked round to nuzzle her horse for the last time. She spoke quietly to the animal, kissed its soft nose, and offered a sweet treat from the pocket hidden under her cloak. Andalusia munched contentedly. Charlotte rested her cheek against the horse's smooth neck for a moment, then stepped away.

'I must go. Good day!' she announced to no one in particular, avoiding everyone's gaze. Shoving the reins at Joseph, she turned and ran—actually ran—up the steps.

The footman, peeping through the glass in readiness, did not anticipate such haste, and she had to wait a moment for him to open the door. As soon as he had done so she entered without looking back.

'The horse is to go today,' Joseph offered, feeling the need to give some explanation for his mistress's behaviour. 'The new owner is to send a groom for her.'

'Er…yes—we know,' said the Captain, glancing at his brother. 'We were in Brook's when Mr Buxted mentioned she was to be sold. A fine specimen.'

'Indeed she is, sir. One in a million.'

Joseph was still gazing at the door. The Earl looked at him sharply.

'We must be gone, Harry. We can call later, when all the family is receiving.'

Captain Fanton assented, and the men rode off. With a heavy heart Joseph led Andalusia to the Buxted stables for the last time.

'Charlotte!'

Aunt Buxted's voice was sharp. Charlotte watched as her aunt descended the stairs.

'Yes, Aunt?'

'I am going to replace the hangings in the green bedchamber. It will therefore be convenient if you could move to a different room. Temporarily, of course.'

'Of…of course. Where am I to stay?'

'In one of the top floor rooms. I have already had your belongings put there.'

'I see.'

Her aunt must have had it done as soon as Charlotte had gone out. Conscious of the footman standing impassively to her right, Charlotte kept her face neutral. Her aunt disappeared down the hallway with a self-satisfied air.

With a sense of foreboding, Charlotte climbed the stairs to the top floor. One of the doors was ajar. Peeping inside, she saw a plain room with two small beds which was clearly being used by the housemaids. Stepping back hastily, she knocked on the next door. When no one answered, she looked inside. Her trunks were in this one.

She stepped in and closed the door behind her. The room was cramped and dim, with a small bed, and her trunks were taking up most of the space. The only other objects were an old washstand, a chamber pot and a tiny cupboard. On the corner of the washstand stood a tallow candle—not wax. There was no fireplace.

The room was completely bare of ornament, and the bed linen was almost threadbare. The only source of daylight was a small skylight above the bed.

Charlotte sank down upon the bed, her knees shaking. This was clearly a servant's room.

She was not concerned with the lack of comfort, for she had been billeted in much worse places during her Army travels with Papa. But the message from Aunt Buxted was clear. She was not worthy of a comfortable room, a fire, or expensive wax candles.

This, now, was her life.

Wearing black was dreadfully strange, Charlotte thought. Priddy—working tirelessly since she had insisted on taking the fabric from Charlotte—had finished making up the dress. Its cut was severe, with half-sleeves, a square neckline and not a single flounce or trim to lighten its plainness.

Priddy had had much to say about Charlotte's new room, and her aunt's cruelty. Charlotte had to ask her to stop, as it was lowering her spirits even further.

It was comforting, though, Charlotte thought, to be marked out as a lady in mourning. It was respectful to Papa, and would give her some licence to be even quieter than usual with visitors. She could not see—although Priddy did—how the tone and severity of the plain black dress accentuated Charlotte's smooth skin and large, expressive eyes.

Mrs Buxted had ordered a second black dress from her own seamstress, to be paid for out of the money Mr Buxted would receive for Lusy. Charlotte was expected to wear only these two dresses for at least the next six months. She tried not to think about the dozens of fashionable outfits packed into her trunks.

Having the black dress meant she was expected to retake her place in the drawing room in the afternoons, on the days when they were known to be At Home to visitors. Aunt Buxted had made it clear that Charlotte should be available, since visitors must know how warm and charitable her aunt was.

Charlotte braced herself to deal with the curious, the sympathetic and the mock sympathetic. If she could maintain a distant poise she hoped visitors would eventually lose interest in her tragedy.

Town was unusually busy for late July, as many of the *ton* had returned for the Peace Celebrations to be held under the light of the next full moon. Their fellow guests from Chadcombe had all travelled to London, and would be expected to call in the next few days.

Mr Foxley, Hubert Etherington and Reverend Sneddon all called that afternoon—though Reverend Sneddon looked almost ready to leave again when he saw Hubert ensconced in the drawing room, holding forth on his planned outfit for the festival.

Recollecting himself in time, the clergyman puffed out his chest, bowed to the ladies, and proceeded to offer a convoluted sympathy speech to Charlotte, who tried to listen to it. It was full of Bible quotes and well-intentioned advice, and Charlotte could not bear it. He had even gone so far as to mark out particular passages in the Old Testament he thought might be of particular help to her, and insisted on giving her his copy of the Bible so she might study them.

Since she had no wish to study his helpful passages, she tried hard to dissuade him from this, but he would have none of it.

'No,' he said stubbornly, 'I insist. So many men have been lost in the wars, and each time—as a clergyman—I have tried to give succour to those bereaved in whatever way is most helpful to each individual. Which reminds me—I must speak with Mr Buxted.'

He bowed and left them, leaving Charlotte wondering what he could possibly want to talk to Mr Buxted about. Her uncle was certainly not grieving. Still, at least he had gone. She took up his Bible and pretended to read, thereby discouraging the others from talking to her.

Mrs Buxted was in conversation with one of her cronies—a Mrs Spenborough, who was unknown to Charlotte—Hubert and Henrietta were chatting by the fireplace, and Mr Foxley was in a *tête-à-tête* with Faith. Charlotte wondered how Faith was coping without seeing Mr Foxley every day. She knew now how it felt to be separated from the man she loved—though the circumstances were different.

She resolved to ask Faith about it later, and then realised that for the first time since hearing her bad news she was able to feel concern for others. In a strange way, she regretted the feeling, for she did not *wish* to heal or to move on as—in her bereaved mind's logic—it might mean forgetting about Papa.

Biddle appeared in the doorway, with more visitors on his heels—the Earl and the Captain. They received a warm and vocal welcome from Mrs Buxted, who insisted they sit with her and Mrs Spenborough as she had just been telling her dear friend of the delights of Chadcombe.

Adam and Harry pulled up chairs and obliged, engaging easily in conversation with all three Buxted ladies as well as Hubert and Mr Foxley. Three weeks together at Chadcombe had eased relations between them all.

Charlotte, after standing for the initial curtsey, had returned to the Bible, seated in the corner. She was conscious of having behaved rudely towards the Earl in the park, but was at a loss to know how to apologise to him. Besides, he had provoked her.

Worrying over this, she was only half aware of the conversation going on between the others. She could hear Mrs Buxted prating on about how beautiful Chadcombe was, and how extensive its grounds.

'There is a beautiful little temple near the woods. My daughters walked there many times. I would have walked too, but for the fact I am crippled with pain in my right knee. But you know, my dear Mrs Spenborough, I am *never* one to complain.'

This was news to Charlotte. Although she had heard Mrs Buxted complain many times, on a range of topics, she had never heard of anything ailing her right knee. Or her left one.

Talk of the woods, though, could only remind her again of the day the Earl had first kissed her, and she felt a slow blush growing. She stole a glance at the

Earl—and found him looking directly at her. Confused, she dropped her gaze immediately.

'Henrietta is an excellent artist. Of course she did not have much time for art while we were at Chadcombe, because our dear host kept us so well entertained. I do recall, though, that she made an excellent sketch of the house. Henrietta, where is your sketchbook?'

Henrietta, with a more accurate notion than her mother of the level of artistic merit in her sketching, was reluctant.

'I do not know, Mama. I have not seen it since we returned.'

'It is on your dressing table,' said Faith innocently, 'for I saw it there this morning when I was looking for my blue ribbon.'

Henrietta glared at Faith.

Mrs Buxted was not to be deterred. 'Faith, ring the bell. I shall ask Sarah to fetch it. No—wait. I have a better notion. Charlotte!'

Charlotte looked up, confused.

'Would you be so kind as to fetch Henrietta's sketchbook? It is on her dressing table.'

Charlotte froze, unable to believe what she was hearing. Was Aunt Buxted *really* asking her to perform a servant's errand?

'Charlotte!' The tone was insistent.

Charlotte, her face burning, set down Reverend Sneddon's Bible and left the room.

She was entirely humiliated.

* * *

Adam was stunned by what he had just witnessed. Mrs Buxted's cruelty had been so casual, yet calculated to inflict maximum hurt on Charlotte. She could not have made it clearer that Charlotte had been reduced to Poor Relation by the death of her father. The fact that she had done it in front of a stranger had made it a very public humiliation.

He glared at Mrs Buxted, but she was serenely unconcerned. Henrietta looked gleeful and Faith shocked. Hubert seemed uninterested in Mrs Buxted's request, and was focused on trying to engage Henrietta's attention again.

Mr Foxley and Harry both looked grim. It was clear all three of them were of one mind regarding the crass insensitivity of Mrs Buxted and their anger on Charlotte's behalf. Adam felt so strongly about it he wished to smash something.

A few moments later, Charlotte returned with the sketchbook. The Earl had in the meantime suddenly remembered an urgent appointment, and he and Harry were preparing to leave. Adam simply could not remain in the same house as Mrs Buxted, feeling powerless. There was nothing he could do for Charlotte.

Charlotte, grateful for the cover provided by their leavetaking, handed the book to Henrietta and made to leave.

The Earl, moving quickly, opened the door for

her. Exiting to the upper hallway before Mrs Buxted had quite finished her farewells, he caught Charlotte by the arm.

'Charlotte—Miss Wyncroft!'

She looked up at him.

'That woman! How can you bear it?'

He took her hand in his and held it without letting go. His eyes blazed with anger.

Something inside her melted—that cold, frozen place. She treasured his warmth as her eyes caressed his dear face.

'Because I must. Please, let me go!' Her voice cracked and her eyes filled with tears.

Reluctantly, he complied. She ran for the second time that day—away from him into loneliness.

He heard her sobs escaping as she climbed the upper stairs, seeking the privacy and security of her chamber. He stood, paralysed and frustrated. If only there was something he could do.

He waited, half hearing his brother exchanging final pleasantries with the Buxteds and agreeing to return tomorrow to walk with the ladies in the park.

A servant came along the corridor. Adam recognised her.

'Miss Priddy?'

'Yes, sir?'

'Your mistress needs you.' He indicated the upper stairs.

Priddy's brow creased in concern, but she thanked him before hurrying upstairs after Charlotte.

He watched, then frowned as he noticed the abigail continue up past the family floors to the attics. He leaned out and clearly saw her hand on the rail as she continued to the top of the house. Why was she going up there?

Harry emerged—finally—from the drawing room, and they left together.

'That woman is outrageous. How *dare* she treat Miss Wyncroft so?'

'She has no breeding, Harry. Charlotte is trapped here. Buxted is the guardian, yet it is his wife who rules the household.'

Harry shook his head. 'Can nothing be done?'

'Something *must* be done, Harry. It simply must.'

Chapter Eighteen

Priddy found Charlotte on the floor. Grief had finally overcome her and she was engulfed by it. Racking sobs convulsed her body, her tears flowed freely and she was incapable of speech. She knew that she might be heard by one of the servants, but she could not stop. She had never felt more alone.

She lay on the cool wooden floor and sobbed in despair. She was not even sure if she was crying for Papa, for Adam, for darling Lusy, or for herself. Everything was lost—her family, her chance for love, the limited independence she had enjoyed, her status in society. She could see no future beyond poverty, servitude and casual humiliation. She was without hope.

Priddy did not hesitate. She sat on the floor beside Charlotte, stroked her hair and laid her hand upon Charlotte's trembling shoulder. She uttered soothing, reassuring words, and Charlotte felt their tone even if she could not truly hear them.

Eventually Charlotte climbed into a half sitting position. She clung to Priddy as she had when she was six, when her mother had died. It took a long time for the storm to subside. In the end, Charlotte knew only a quiet emptiness. She felt hollowed out—an empty, fragile shell.

Priddy encouraged her to stand, then to sit on the bed. Her devoted maid helped remove Charlotte's hairpins, slippers, dress and corset, then fashioned a cover for the skylight, using a thin linen towel. Blessed darkness surrounded Charlotte, and she lay down on top of the bed in her petticoat, closing her eyes.

Priddy secured a small chair from her own room, which she placed in the corner. She would stay, guarding her mistress's sleep.

Charlotte slept right through the evening and the night, and woke early the next morning in some confusion. Where was she? Why was she sleeping in her petticoat? Why was she on top of the bedpane—though with a warm blanket over her?

A second later it all came flooding back.

Papa!

Then the rest.

The Earl. Lusy. Priddy. Joseph. A litany of losses.

There was more.

Aunt Buxted's humiliation of her.

The tears which had so eluded her now flowed again. Memories—layers of them, waves of im-

ages, sounds, emotions—overcame her. They were
so powerful that they escaped from her eyes and
rolled down her cheeks.

Sniffling, she groped around for a handkerchief.
Suddenly she stilled, hearing a soft noise in the
room. A moment later the towel was removed from
the skylight. Early-morning light fell on Priddy, who
was carefully folding the towel and placing it on the
washstand.

'Priddy!' Charlotte's voice was husky. Her throat
felt dry and raw. 'Have you been here all night?'

'Hush, now, child. And where else would I be?'

'Oh, Priddy, I don't know how I shall go on without you.'

'Oh, you poor girl.' Priddy sat on the side of the
bed and offered Charlotte a clean handkerchief.
'You *will* go on, for you know your duty and you
must.'

'But what is my future? What use am I?'

'Now, now, miss! No one can know their future.
We simply do what we can with each day we are
given. This has affected many lives, you know.'

'Oh, Priddy, you are right—as you always are.
I am sorry to be so focused on myself, when you
and Joseph are to go to—goodness knows where.'

'Well, we are servants, Miss Charlotte. When we
are no longer needed we must move on.'

'But I *do* need you. It is so *unfair.*'

'I know…I know.'

'I apologise—again. I must stop crying. And I

shall. Papa would expect me to be brave. But I feel like a lost child, not a lady of twenty.' She blew her nose. 'No, twenty-one. I am twenty-one, Priddy. I wish I were ten again, with none of these grown-up worries.'

'You will endure, Miss Charlotte. You are the daughter of Colonel Sir Edward Wyncroft. That does not change, even though he is gone.'

Charlotte hugged her. 'Again you are right, Priddy. I *will* endure, and I *will* triumph—although I cannot yet see how.'

Priddy poured her a glass of lemonade. Charlotte sipped slowly, relishing its bittersweet freshness.

'I shall miss you and Joseph so much. When will you leave? Will you find positions together in the same household, do you think?'

'Mr Buxted has kindly offered to pay us for two more weeks, which will give us time to find new positions. And it will give you time to adjust before we go.'

Two weeks! Charlotte thought she would never adjust, but did not say so. Instead she sent Priddy to take a few hours' sleep, then sought the security and comfort of her own small, hard bed again.

She lay awake for a while, conscious that she felt a little better after her storm of weeping. It was as if her eyes had needed to be washed by tears for her to see things clearly. Her life so far had been focused on duty, and on trying to make Papa proud. Her future, she resolved, would be no different.

* * *

The black dress was rather crumpled, but Priddy
had done what she could to freshen it. At least Charlotte had the comfort of a clean petticoat. And she
had had a bath in her tiny room. The trunks had had
to be moved out temporarily, to fit it in.

Priddy had insisted a bath would make her feel
better. She had been right.

'There you are, Miss Charlotte. All done. Your
hair is dry and styled neatly, and the dress looks
passable. I will clean and press it properly tonight.
Now you are ready to go downstairs.'

Charlotte did not *feel* ready. She had not seen
anyone but Priddy since yesterday's incident, and
found her heart quickening with anxiety as she descended to the drawing room.

'Ah! Here she is, in all her ghostly beauty.' Reverend Sneddon, slick, black and obsequious, rose
to greet her.

The only other person in the room, which Charlotte found surprising, was Mrs Buxted.

'Good afternoon, Charlotte,' said her aunt, smiling sweetly.

Charlotte's sense of danger increased.

'Good afternoon.' Charlotte walked towards the
small yellow and gold chair near the window.

'Miss Wyncroft—you will be much more comfortable sharing this settee with me.'

She could hardly refuse, and reluctantly sat on
one end of the sofa. Reverend Sneddon and Mrs

Buxted seemed to be sharing an unspoken message. Charlotte intercepted their nods and gestures in some bewilderment.

'Well…' Mrs Buxted rose. 'I must see what has happened to those refreshments.'

Mrs Buxted, instead of tugging the bell-pull, left the room. The door had barely closed behind her when Reverend Sneddon stood.

'You will be wondering, I am sure, why your dear chaperon has left you alone in here with me—with a man. Be assured you have nothing to fear, for you are in the company of a rare creature—a true gentleman.'

He moved to the looking-glass, smoothed his hair and straightened his simple neckcloth.

'I have often thought the word *gentleman* is too loosely applied, and that it should be reserved only for those who display the noble behaviour associated with the term instead of those who think it their birthright. For we receive the due reward of our deeds. Do you not agree, Miss Wyncroft?'

'I am not sure society would agree with you, Reverend Sneddon. I have known many servants, infantrymen and tradesmen who are noble and gentlemanlike in their deeds, but unless their pedigree and their fortune stand up to scrutiny they are condemned to obscurity. For the term *"gentleman"* is used in a particular manner, and with a particular meaning.'

He sighed deeply. 'I fear you are right, Miss Wyncroft. Your perspicacity can only be added to the long list of your virtues.'

Charlotte took this to mean he thought her insightful.

Suddenly agitated, he took a turn about the room, then whirled around—coat-tails flying—to address her dramatically. 'Miss Wyncroft. We have only a few moments together before Mrs Buxted's return, so I shall come to the point.'

Please do, she thought, wondering what this was about.

'Yesterday I left with you my own copy of the Bible.'

Charlotte started, as she had not thought of it since. Surreptitiously she tried to check the side tables to see if it rested on any of them.

'Afterwards I sought an audience with Mr Buxted—a most kindly, intellectual and selfless man.'

Charlotte frowned, hardly recognising this description, then reproached herself for having uncharitable thoughts.

'The two actions—' he raised his left hand, then his right, with precise movements '—were not unconnected.' He brought his hands together.

What was this? A riddle?

'I have been conscious—indeed, we all have—' he indicated the empty room with a sweep of his right hand '—of the terrible bereavement you have suffered.'

Charlotte sat up straighter, bracing herself for his

sympathy. As a clergyman, he would speak to her of Papa. She wished she could instead be with Reverend Welford, the English chaplain in Vienna, who was intelligent, sensitive and compassionate, and had ministered to all of the Army families through difficult times.

She wondered if the padre had been told of Papa's death. When she felt a little better, she would write to him. And to others—their friends in Vienna, Juliana...

'...difficult situation.' Reverend Sneddon was still talking. 'Your uncle has shared with me some of the details, and the thorny issue of your lack of a good dowry.'

Charlotte was suddenly listening. How dared Uncle Buxted share her private business with a near-stranger?

'Now you are wondering, I see, why he should tell me such things.'

'I confess I am, Reverend Sneddon. In fact I am surprised he would do so.'

'Ah, you must forgive your uncle, for he has only your interests at heart. You see, I had a particular question to pose to him. And another—not unrelated—to pose to you. Or, in this case, to *propose* to you!' He laughed lightly at his own witticism.

'I am afraid you are too clever for me, Reverend Sneddon, for I have not the least idea what you mean.'

'Miss Wyncroft. Charlotte.'

Awkwardly he bent one knee in front of her. Her eyes widened.

'May I hold your hand? Ah, I see I may not. Be not concerned, for your maidenly shyness serves to increase my ardour.'

Ardour? Dread flooded her.

'Allow me to tell you of my sincere regard for you, which is long-standing in nature and was inspired by the happy chance that brought us both to Chadcombe at the same time.'

'Reverend Sneddon! Please do not—'

'But I *must*, Miss Wyncroft. I had not dared hope you would consider me, but now, with the unfortunate change in your circumstances—'

'And is that another happy chance?'

'Yes—no! I mean, it is unfortunate indeed that you have lost your father, but I believe I had no hope you would receive my addresses prior to this.'

'Please, Reverend Sneddon, I beg you, do not speak.'

'I have the highest regard for you, Miss Wyncroft, and I ask that you will do me the honour of becoming my wife.'

In shock, she could not immediately respond, and he took the opportunity to lift her hand and plant a wet kiss on it. She pulled her hand away immediately, wishing she could wipe it clean.

'Reverend Sneddon, I thank you for the honour, but I must decline.'

'Decline! But—why?' He sat back on his heels, shocked.

'I—I have no wish to marry.'

'But you must see it would be an ideal solution. Otherwise what is your future, Miss Wyncroft? This way you will have security—a home.'

'I do not wish anyone to offer me marriage out of charity.'

'But I have already indicated how much I admire you, Miss Wyncroft. Indeed, I should be proud to have you as my wife.'

She shuddered. 'I cannot consider it.'

He scrambled to his feet. 'I have spoken too soon. Your father's death is too recent.'

'I do think it is too soon for me to consider making any decision which will have such a profound effect on my life. However—'

'Then I will continue to hope.'

'Please do not, Reverend Sneddon. I do not wish to give you the impression that my answer will be any different in future.'

'Nevertheless, I have erred in speaking too soon. I see that now.'

There was a scratching on the door, then Aunt Buxted peeped her head around it. 'Am I intruding?'

Her voice was playful. Charlotte closed her eyes in horror. Could this situation become any worse?

Aunt Buxted entered, beaming. 'So, am I to wish you happy?'

'Dear Miss Wyncroft is too distressed and her

bereavement too recent for her to think clearly,' said Reverend Sneddon, as though speaking of a child.

'I see.' Aunt Buxted's voice hardened. 'Well, I had thought it would be the very thing. These young girls do not know their duty, Reverend Sneddon.'

'I dare say, Mrs Buxted. But we must make allowances for the loss of her father.'

'It is the loss of her father that should make her see sense. Her chances of making a spectacular marriage were never large, and now—well...'

Charlotte cleared her throat. Reverend Sneddon and Mrs Buxted both regarded her in some surprise, as if they had genuinely forgotten she was present.

'Yes, Charlotte?'

'Er...where are my cousins?'

'They are preparing to go out walking with Lord Shalford and Captain Fanton. You should both join them. Reverend Sneddon—I counsel you to spend some more time with Charlotte. I have no doubt she will eventually see the merits of this match.'

'I do not wish to walk today, Aunt Buxted.'

'There are many things in this life that we do not wish to do, Charlotte, and yet we must endure them. I insist you walk with the others.'

Her cold eyes pierced Charlotte. Conscious that she must not make an enemy of her aunt, Charlotte decided to allow her this small victory, for she was determined that in large matters—such as Reverend Sneddon's proposal—she would be master of her own fate.

'Very well, Aunt Buxted. Please excuse me while I prepare.'

'Unfortunately, I will be unable to join you at this time,' said Reverend Sneddon coolly, clearly still smarting from Charlotte's rejection.

She fled, conscious that she had been running away a lot recently. This time, however, it was a strategic retreat. Papa, she was certain, would have approved.

Quickly donning a pair of stout kid boots and a dark pelisse, Charlotte was soon ready. Avoiding the drawing room, she waited for her cousins downstairs in the hall.

Faith arrived first, and spoke awkwardly to Charlotte. 'Charlotte…yesterday, when Mama—I mean—I don't think she should—I mean, I am sorry that—'

Charlotte hugged her. 'Faith, you are a treasure. Do not say any more, for I know you cannot be disloyal to your family. I appreciate the sentiment, though.'

Relieved, Faith smiled tremulously.

At that moment the footman opened the door to admit the Fanton brothers. Charlotte played her part in the formal greetings, but avoided looking at Adam for too long. She could feel his gaze on her.

Both men turned as Henrietta sauntered down the stairs.

With a stunning smile, she gave her hand to the Earl to kiss. 'I am *so* glad we are to walk out today, for I have heard such exciting things about the Regent's gala.'

'Indeed,' said Adam politely. 'We hear no expense is being spared in the preparations.'

'We had thought to walk to Green Park, to see Mr Nash's work on the fortress. You know he calls his design The Temple of Concord?' said the Captain. 'Then we may continue, if you wish, to the Chinese Bridge in Hyde Park, where they are building a pagoda.'

'How exciting! I shall take your arm, Lord Shalford, if you will permit.'

With a glance towards Charlotte, he offered Henrietta his arm. Charlotte was relieved, for she had not yet fully recovered from Reverend Sneddon's unexpected proposal. She needed time to think.

Like Aunt Buxted, Reverend Sneddon clearly saw Charlotte as little better than a charity case. It was lowering to think that just last week she had been the self-assured Miss Wyncroft, visiting Chadcombe as an equal to her cousins, and engaging in social events with all of the confidence of a typical young lady. Now what was she? Not quite a servant, but not an equal member of the family either.

Her mind was in turmoil.

They walked slowly to Green Park, where a large team of workers were continuing to toil on the transformation of the fortress. Carpenters, painters and labourers were working at an impressive pace, to

ensure that the Temple would be ready for the celebrations.

The bole of a tall fir was being unloaded from
a cart as they watched. A garrulous labourer informed them this was to be the main flagpole for
the upper Temple. He also informed them—though
begged them not to reveal it to another living soul—
that Sir William Congreve had installed a fantastical mechanical device, designed to make the entire
upper level rotate.

Henrietta seemed exceptionally excited by this,
and spoke of her delight at the thought that she had
information that was not common knowledge. She
exclaimed over it all the way to the edge of Hyde
Park, wondering how on earth an entire building
could be made to rotate, and imagining how surprised people would be when they saw it.

The Earl took no part in the speculation, and
seemed preoccupied. When they reached the narrow path that would take them through the copse
towards the water he stopped and bent, seemingly
to adjust his right boot. Assuming he would catch
her up, Henrietta kept walking.

Faith was on the Captain's right arm, and Charlotte had been walking with them. Feeling that she
had the right to be escorted by the highest rank-
ing available gentleman, Henrietta walked a little
faster and slipped her hand into the crook of Harry's
left arm. Squeezed out, Charlotte could only follow
Harry and her cousins.

Like a serving maid, she thought humourlessly.

They continued like that for a few moments, and then the Earl caught up with Charlotte. Speaking softly so as not to alert Henrietta to his return, he asked Charlotte how she did.

'I am well, thank you.' She paused. 'I hope you know I am not normally a watering pot. I apologise for my behaviour yesterday, which you might think overdramatic.'

'Not at all. You were severely provoked. I confess I was much affected myself.'

'It is just because of Papa that I am finding things difficult when normally I should cope with them quite easily.'

'I do not think anyone should have to cope with the cruelty that was shown to you yesterday. And I know what it is to lose a beloved father.'

She glanced at him gratefully. 'It is not as though Papa died in his bed. Normally people have the ritual of the funeral, a chance to say goodbye. But this—'

'Yes,' he said, looking much struck. 'When I lost my father, I was able to say my farewells, to be part of his funeral.'

'I do not even know what exactly happened to Papa, or where he is buried.'

'That is harsh indeed.'

Adam glanced ahead. Harry and the two Buxted ladies were a little way ahead now. This was hardly surprising, since he had deliberately slowed his pace to open up the gap.

Charlotte noticed it too. 'Oh! We should hurry— we have fallen behind.'

'Actually, I had hoped for an opportunity to speak to you.'

She looked at him quizzically. 'Yes?'

This is it, he thought. *Ask her to marry you.*

Chapter Nineteen

He opened his mouth, took a breath, then stopped, trying to find the correct words. How could he express how he felt without scaring her? Propriety dictated that he should ask her father for permission to speak to her, and that had been his intent, but now, with the loss of Sir Edward, he had been forced to act. He simply could not stomach leaving her in the clutches of That Woman any longer than he had to.

Yet, she was recently bereaved. He could see the sorrow in her face, her movements, her air of distance from everyone around her. Now was not the time for a declaration of love that she might not be ready for.

He decided to persuade her of the good sense of his marriage proposal.

Charlotte waited expectantly, musing that today it seemed she was doomed to be in the company of inarticulate men.

'Please do not look at me so, Miss Wyncroft, for I cannot think clearly.'

'Look at you how?' she asked, bewildered.

'Like that. All perplexed and—and...' His voice tailed off.

'Lord Shalford, is there something you wish to say to me?'

'Yes.' He squared his shoulders and tried again. 'When we were in the rose garden at Chadcombe, I kissed you. I enjoyed kissing you, and I think—I hope—you enjoyed it too.'

Her face flaming, she bowed her head. Why was he talking about *that*? Oh, when she thought of how *forward* she had been, and how hungrily she had kissed him that night, she was simply *mortified*.

'Things have changed now. The death of your father has left you in a difficult situation.'

What? *What did that have to do with anything*?

A terrible understanding dawned on her. First her Aunt, then Reverend Sneddon, now him! She was not wealthy, had no real protectors, and she was under the control of her selfish aunt—he felt sorry for her. She already knew that her lack of dowry prevented him from marrying her—even if he had wanted to, which she doubted. And, worse, she had kissed him like a courtesan.

She knew what he was going to say—he was going to offer her a *carte blanche*! Because he pitied her and he thought he could protect her that way. Well, she would not be any man's mistress. She was

Charlotte Wyncroft, daughter of Colonel Sir Edward Wyncroft, and she was a lady.

'I have thought deeply about your situation, and of what I can do to help. I think you know I have a great regard for you. Therefore I would ask you, Charlotte, if you would consent to be my—'

'Do not say it!' The words exploded from her. *How dared he?*

'I—what?' He looked astonished.

And how *dared* he be surprised at her reaction?

'Do not speak. Do not say another word. I do not wish to hear what you have to say.'

'But I—'

'I wish to return to the others.'

She began walking quickly in the direction the Captain had taken with her cousins. Belatedly, he realised she was moving, and sprang to catch up with her.

Adam was mystified. Somehow he had erred. He had not thought his offer of marriage would be spurned so vehemently. His mind would not function—he felt only cold shock.

Once he had decided he could wait no longer and must ask her, he had agonised over every detail. How would he contrive some time alone with her? What words should he use?

In all his plans, all his imaginings, he had never expected a rejection so vigorous, so decided. He was conscious of her vulnerability, the fact that her grief was so fresh, but he had not wished to leave her under the control of that vixen of an aunt. After he had seen how she was being treated, his anger and frustration had made him determined to speak out.

He had decided not to overwhelm her with talk of how much he loved her. He knew she was sensitive and could be skittish. She had also run away from him in the rose garden, when Harry had thought they were to be married. The mention of their kiss—a sign, he thought, of the powerful connection between them—combined with a reminder of the evils of her situation would be a careful strategy.

Well, so much for strategy. So much for his knowledge of the female mind. His first ever proposal and he had made a complete mull of it!

He kept pace with her, trying to marshal his thoughts, attempting to understand how he could mend things.

'Miss Wyncroft.'

She would not look up, but he knew she heard him.

'I apologise if I have offended you. I sought only to help. I do not wish to cause you any further distress.'

On they walked. She did not respond.

'I shall not mention this again.'

'Thank you.' Her voice was low, her words mumbled.

They rounded a bend in the path. Just ahead they saw the Captain, still with a Buxted sister on each arm. Beyond, the trees opened up to reveal the Chinese Bridge. The trio had not, it seemed, noticed that Charlotte and the Earl had been out of sight for a few minutes.

'Here we are.' The Captain indicated the bridge. It was indeed an impressive sight. And a huge pagoda perched on its back, quite four storeys high.

'My goodness!' said Henrietta. 'Look at all the lights hung about it.'

'They are gas lanterns. I think with so many lanterns, this place will be as bright as Vauxhall during the festivities on Monday.'

'Well, I do not know anything about that, for Mama says we are not to go to Vauxhall. She says *vulgar* people go there.'

'I am rebuked, Miss Buxted.'

'Oh…' Henrietta said playfully. 'You know I did not mean to suggest *you* are vulgar, Captain Fanton.'

'I am glad to hear it.'

Charlotte heard their conversation break over her. She was having quite the worst week in her life. Following everything that had happened, and Reverend Sneddon's excruciating proposal today, to have such an insulting offer from the man she— she—

'Shall we turn back?' The Earl's voice was curt.

Henrietta pouted. 'Must we?'

'I fear we must.' He thought for a moment. 'Actually, I had meant to inform you all—I will be gone from London for a while on business.'

Henrietta pouted. 'But it will be my *birthday*

soon. And the peace celebrations. Surely you will be back by then?'

'I cannot say. My plans are not yet fixed.'

The Captain looked surprised, but said nothing.

They all turned away from the Chinese Bridge and its showy pagoda to return to Half-Moon Street. The walk back was long, and—on the part of two of them—extremely uncomfortable.

Next morning, again at an unfashionably early hour, the Earl called at his godmother's house. He had to wait for half an hour in her drawing room, as Lady Sophia had not yet arisen when her maid informed her that Lord Shalford had called and was insisting on seeing her.

She eventually appeared, grumbling but intrigued. Her hair was pinned up in a makeshift chignon, but her morning dress of mauve silk was impeccable. Complaining about the cold summer, she added a long shawl, one end of which trailed behind her and almost got caught in the door.

'Good morning, Godmama.' He kissed her, then retrieved the shawl, offering it to her as she sat in her favourite armchair.

'Heavens, Adam, do not be so loud. It is not yet noon, you know. Why do you always visit so *early*? What do you mean by it? Is all well? Miss Langley? Olivia? Harry?'

'They are all well, as far as I know.'

'Then what is it?' She eyed him keenly. 'Ah, it is *you*, Adam? What ails you?'

'Simply the knowledge that I am a fool, God-mama. I took your advice, you know, in the matter of courtship.'

'Indeed? Has one of the young ladies touched your heart?'

'Touched it?' He gave a short laugh. 'She has stabbed it, more like.'

'Now, Adam, do not pout. It does not become you. Tell me first which young lady has claimed your attention? Not Miss Buxted, surely?'

'Lord, no. It is Miss Wyncroft.'

'Sir Edward's daughter?' She clapped her hands together in delight. 'You have impeccable taste.'

'She is a darling, is she not? I cannot conceive how I did not realise it from the first day I met her.'

'Ah, well, there I have the better of you, for I could see what she was from the minute I met her in this very room.'

'She was here?'

'Yes—before they travelled to Chadcombe. The Buxted mother wished to ingratiate herself with me, I think.'

'That woman!'

'Such loathing! Why, what has she done—apart from being her usual vulgar self?'

'Two days ago she asked Miss Wyncroft to perform a servant's task—in front of me, Harry, Mr Foxley and some woman called Spenborough.'

'Oh, I have met Mrs Spenborough—as vulgar as Louisa Buxted herself! But poor Miss Wyncroft. Why would the woman do such a thing?'

'I fear that—what with death duties and what-not—Miss Wyncroft may not be as comfortably circumstanced as before.'

'Ah. That is unfortunate. Still, with her charm and intelligence, and—yes—her beauty, she will still be sought after.'

'She *is* beautiful, is she not? I think I did not realise at first just how beautiful she is.'

'I like that, Adam. You see her in her essential self, as I do. Some people would see her as pretty, rather than beautiful.'

'Really? I do not think so.'

She let this pass, saying, 'I shall continue my acquaintance with Miss Wyncroft—even if it means tolerating the Buxted woman and her equally vulgar daughters.'

'Oh, the younger daughter, Faith, is harmless. Colourless, and terrified of her mother, but a kind-hearted little widgeon. She will not imitate her mother's cruelty.'

Lady Sophia dismissed Faith with a wave of her hand. 'I have no interest in her. I never did. But—Adam—such a pity my friend Sir Edward is dead. I was never so shocked.'

'Yes. I called at his regimental headquarters yesterday. They know little about his death, save that he was travelling with three others near Reims. So many have died, they said. It is hard to keep track.'

'Shocking. I was looking forward to renewing our acquaintance when he retired. He was one of my admirers, you know, many years ago.'

'You have so many admirers, Godmama, that it is difficult to keep count. But I came to tell you I will be out of town for a short while. I hope to be back for the peace celebrations, though I cannot be sure it is possible.' He frowned. 'It would be good if you could call on Char—Miss Wyncroft. I fear she is suffering.'

She noticed the slip, which suggested an encouraging degree of friendship between her godson and Miss Wyncroft. 'You may trust me. I will do what I can.'

'I…' He hesitated. 'I may have said something that offended her, or upset her. I do not know exactly why—' He ran his fingers through his hair. 'I wish only what is best for her. If she does not want me, then I must do what I can for her in other ways.'

'Not *want* Shalford of Chadcombe! Not *want* the biggest prize on the marriage mart? No, do not look at me like that—you must know that I am funning. But are you sure she does not want you?'

'She said so. I should be honoured to have her as my wife, but I do not think that she sees herself so.' He stared into space for a moment. 'Still, I must not give up hope. If I only knew where I went wrong…'

'What do you mean, Adam? What has happened?'

He would not say more, and refused to be pressed.

He left shortly afterwards, and she thought she must have misheard when she asked him where his destination was.

But it really sounded as though he had said, 'First, Dover.'

Dover? Surely not...

Chapter Twenty

His sense of hearing came back first. An irritating drip, drip, drip. It wouldn't stop. Why wouldn't it stop? Drip, drip, drip. It was slightly slower than his heartbeat, which he could also hear. Or feel. He felt the air in his lungs. Breathe in, breathe out. He was alive, then. For some reason this surprised him.

His head ached. To every beat of his heart, his head answered with a throb of pain. He reached out with his other senses. A smell. Dank air and earth. The metallic taste of his own blood in his mouth. He was lying on a firm surface. His right hand rested on his stomach. He stretched out the fingers carefully, gently. The other hand was twisted slightly underneath him and was painful. He moved carefully to extract it—the arm was sore, but not broken, he thought. He breathed carefully—in, out…in, out. Feeling the space beside him, he touched cool earth, gritty and damp. He was outside, then.

He opened his eyes. No change. Complete darkness. No moonlight, no starlight—nothing. Was he blind? He lifted his right hand close to his face. Close enough to smell it—blood, dirt and sweat— yet he could see nothing. He turned his head—then wished he hadn't. Pain flooded through him. He touched the back of his head with his hand. A sticky mess.

He remembered. Fighting for his life in that field outside Corbeny. Knowing he was going to die. Mercer to his right, fighting bravely.

'La guerre est fini!' he had shouted at the end. 'The war is over!' It had seemed to him the greatest irony that he would die in battle after the war had ended.

They had been French soldiers, not bandits, their attackers. He had realised this as he'd been fighting them, had recognised their weapons, their techniques, the way they'd fought together as a co-ordinated unit. Pockets of resistance remained, and the news had not yet reached everyone. Those men included, clearly.

'La guerre est fini!'

He had tried to look them in the eye as he'd said the words, all the while fighting on, blocking thrusts, staying alive for one more second, one more breath. One man had listened.

'Halte! Arrêtez!'

The French soldiers, well drilled, had immediately begun to pull back. The man who had spoken— their leader—had been a short, swarthy man in his late thirties. He had been bleeding from a wound on his arm, but otherwise unscathed. Both sides had paused, bloodied and panting, their dead all around them.

'Do you tell the truth?' he had asked.

'I tell the truth. I am a man of honour,' Sir Edward had replied, gazing at him steadily.

'He lies, Capitaine Didot!' one of the others had said. 'This is our enemy.'

'I am not your enemy. The war is over.'

'The war is over,' Mercer had repeated.

Didot's eyes had narrowed. 'I have decided,' he'd said, 'that we will take these men as prisoners until we know the truth. Will you come with us as prisoners?' he'd asked Sir Edward politely.

'We will.' Sir Edward had dismounted, and offered his weapons to Didot. Mercer had followed suit.

Didot had taken their swords, along with Sir Edward's pistol and Mercer's Paget Carbine. Their fallen colleagues had already been relieved of their weapons, money and, in Foden's case, his boots.

Sir Edward had looked away.

Didot had spoken to his men. 'Go and bring the cart from the cottage. You—bury the enemy bodies in the wood. Go to the *abbaye* to bury our own fallen comrades, who died for France.'

Sir Edward and Mercer had been marched through the trees to the road. Within minutes a cart had appeared, driven by the scrawny old man. He'd spat with disgust when he'd seen the two Englishmen, still alive.

'Mais les Anglais vivent toujours! Pourquoi? Pourquoi?'

'Do not question me, old man,' Didot had said. 'These soldiers say the war is over. Is that true?'

'Non! La guerre n'est pas fini!'

'We thank you for bringing us food these past weeks, while we awaited orders. But the time has come now for us to seek information from our commanders.' He'd turned to the prisoners. 'Please climb into the cart.'

Sir Edward had alighted, assisting Mercer, who'd been clutching his stomach. He had moved the shirt fabric aside. His wound had been long, but superficial.

Didot had spoken from behind Sir Edward. 'We cannot take the risk of letting you see where we are camped. I apologise.'

Sir Edward had suddenly felt a painful blow to the back of the head and had known no more.

And now he was awake, with a sore head and a dry mouth, and he could not see. He carefully moved his aching head in both directions. *There.* To his left there was a faint glimmer of light. He was in some sort of cave or cellar. He stilled, listening. He could hear, somewhere to his right, the faint sound of someone breathing.

'Mercer? Is that you?' he whispered.

No response.

From his dry throat he managed to produce a low, cracked voice. 'Mercer!'

He was rewarded with a low groan. Moving slowly and carefully, he got himself up into a sitting position.

'Colonel? Are you awake?'

'I am. Where are we?'

'Some sort of cave, I think. They hit me too, so I have no idea where we are. Their Captain—Didot, they call him—asked me to pass on his apologies.'

Sir Edward laughed harshly. 'Well, at least we are still alive. Have they told you their plans?'

'Didot has left us in the care of his troops while he travels to his command centre. He admits to being out of contact for weeks—ever since Reims fell—but I think he suspects we have told him the truth.'

'Good. Let us hope he will return soon, for I have had enough of this war. It still tries to kill us, even after peace has been agreed.'

Charlotte felt as though she was living through a bad dream that refused to end. Papa was gone and she missed him horribly. This was worse than a normal bereavement, though. The limits of her world had unexpectedly narrowed. She felt trapped by her new life, and tortured herself with memories of what had been—Vienna, Papa, long rides on Lusy, and her time at Chadcombe, when she had still had respect from the Earl.

She was struggling to understand the change in him. She had seen the Earl as an ideal man—a man of integrity. Yet, she knew men of the *ton* lived by a rigid set of rules regarding the women in their lives. Society made a clear distinction between the high-born sisters, daughters and wives of the upper ten thousand and those of the lower classes. Charlotte's position, she now realised, was in the grey world between the two.

Although her birth was good, the reduction in status, made so clear by Mrs Buxted, had opened Charlotte's world to other evils—including the offer from Reverend Sneddon which, at least, had been an honourable proposal. That was as high a husband as someone in her position dared to hope for—a clergyman, or perhaps a lawyer, even someone with a background in trade who wished to ally himself with a gentleman's daughter.

If she did not wish to marry, then she would spend the next fifteen years living with the Buxteds as a tolerated Poor Relation. She would survive as best she could until the mortgage was paid off on the Wyncroft property, then rent a cottage with the income. Maybe Priddy would live with her. Priddy would be old by then, if she was still alive.

Perhaps, Charlotte thought, she should have accepted Reverend Sneddon after all. *No!* She shuddered at the thought.

The other offer she'd had that day should not, she reflected, have surprised her. Her abandoned behaviour—the nature of the kiss she had shared with the Earl—had left her open to such an insult. How was he to know she had never behaved in such a way before? The few previous kisses she'd had had been chaste, innocent encounters—including the first time the Earl had kissed her. No, it was that second kiss, in the rose garden, which had clearly given him a different impression of her and made him think a *carte blanche* might be acceptable to her.

She was glad he was away on business. The thought of seeing him again terrified her. Despite what he'd said, would he repeat his dishonourable address?

And yet she missed him, too. Missed the *other* Adam. The one who had walked and danced with her, and conversed with her on every topic imaginable. The one she had thought of as her true friend. But that man was lost for ever. Now she was left with a man who *looked* like her Adam but was interested in her only as his *chère-amie*, not his equal.

Buxted House had never seemed so small. She could not escape her aunt and Henrietta. She was forced to spend hours in their company—doing their bidding, coping with their casual cruelties and inane, self-centred opinions. Henrietta, taking her mother's lead, now frequently asked for Charlotte's 'assistance' when she forgot something, or was 'too tired' to do something. Her manner was becoming increasingly brusque, and she openly sneered at Charlotte at times, finding fault with her behaviour, manner and appearance.

Charlotte found herself each day writing responses to their many invitations, and helping Mrs Buxted by darning pillowcases and counting candles with the housekeeper. The requests were always couched in polite language, but Charlotte was left in no doubt about Mrs Buxted's intentions. Too poor to be a true member of the family, yet too well-born to be treated in exactly the same way as a servant, Charlotte was now doomed to assist Mrs Buxted to earn her keep.

She hated it.

The only time she could feel free and pretend her life was as it should be was when she played music. Thankfully no one had—as yet—stopped her.

She still could not sleep well at night—her room was cold and she was troubled by nightmares. The dreams in which Papa was still alive were the worst, for she would wake with a brief feeling of well-being before remembering.

She usually rose early and made her way to the morning room to play music before breakfast.

She could lose herself in the music. Sometimes it helped her forget. Other times it made her remember. And if tears came that was acceptable, since she generally felt a little better afterwards.

She missed the walks in Chadcombe, and her rides on Lusy. She had always loved being outdoors, and had never truly appreciated the freedom she had enjoyed until it was taken from her. Now she was expected to be always available in case the ladies needed her, so she had rarely stepped outside the door since the day they had all walked to the Chinese Bridge. She had not seen the Earl since.

Today, though, she would have some escape. Faith—dear Faith—conscious of Charlotte's unhappiness, had asked Mrs Buxted if Charlotte might accompany her on a walk to the park after Church, as Mr Foxley was to call to walk with them.

Henrietta, when asked, had not wanted to go. 'Walk with Mr Foxley?' She'd sniffed. 'I should think not!'

Mrs Buxted had politely asked Charlotte if she would chaperon Faith to the park. Charlotte had been only too happy to agree.

They were just going down the steps when they spied Captain Fanton, walking along Half-Moon Street towards Buxted House.

He greeted them warmly. 'I was on my way to see if anyone wished to go for a walk.'

'You may accompany us,' said Faith, 'for we are just walking to Green Park.'

'I should be delighted,' he said, offering Charlotte his arm.

As they walked, they naturally stayed in their pairs. Strolling behind Faith and Mr Foxley, Charlotte was struck by strong memories of the many walks at Chadcombe—only then it had often been the Earl who had walked with her. But she must not think of him.

The day was cool and dry—apart from that one hot day a few weeks ago the summer had been disappointingly cold. That was the day when she and the Earl had ridden together to see the ruined abbey, and Faith had become unwell...

'Is your brother still away on business?' she asked Captain Fanton—her self-control had lasted less than a minute.

'Er...yes. I hope he will return for the festival tomorrow.'

At the park gates they stopped to read a large notice indicating that the celebrations here were not open to the general public, and directing people to the festival fair in Hyde Park. It also announced that at eight tomorrow evening there would be a re-enactment of the Battle of Trafalgar on the Serpentine.

The Captain was fascinated. 'That looks excellent. Foxley, will you be there for the festival?'

'I will. I wonder how they will do the re-enactment?'

Mr Foxley and the Captain discussed the upcoming festivities much in the manner of excited schoolboys, Charlotte thought. She took the opportunity to speak to Faith.

'It is good to see Mr Foxley again. I declare I have missed him these past few days—though not, I imagine, as much as you.'

Faith blushed rosily. 'I am happy to be in his company again.'

'Forgive me—I do not wish to intrude—but has he not spoken to my uncle yet? I was sure he would seek permission to pay his addresses before we left Chadcombe.'

Faith sighed. 'No. We fear Mama will object. Even though he is her godson. I know she hoped I would make a brilliant marriage. But I have no wish for a title, or for great wealth.'

'So why does he not ask?'

'Well, you see, if he is rejected by M— by Papa, it will become difficult for us to see one another. At least this way we can still walk together, and pretend that some day we might be allowed to marry.'

Charlotte noticed her slip—Faith's mama was the true barrier here. 'Faith, I am not the best person to advise you, but I know now how quickly happiness can be stolen away. If you have a chance to be happy you should do all in your power to keep it.'

Faith frowned. 'Do you truly think so?'

'I do—and perhaps your parents will agree to the match.'

'Oh, if only they would!'

They had now reached the Queen's Basin, and Mr Foxley took his customary place by Faith's side. He took her hand and spoke earnestly to her.

'Faith, I have been speaking to Captain Fanton about our situation. I know Miss Wyncroft will not mind if I speak plainly. The Captain recommends I speak to your father.'

Faith looked to Captain Fanton, who nodded. 'I think Mr Buxted holds you both in high estimation, and we all can see how well-suited you are. I believe it might be good to discuss it with him, at least.'

'I have just had a similar conversation with Charlotte,' said Faith. 'Perhaps, then, you *should* speak to him. But what if he forbids you from seeing me again?'

'Mrs Buxted is my godmother. I do not think I will be banned, for I have done nothing improper—save, perhaps, discussing my feelings with you before speaking to your Papa.'

They moved off in the direction of the fortress, heads close together, planning and conspiring.

Charlotte and Harry watched them, before glancing at each other ruefully.

'They are so excited,' said Charlotte. 'I do hope we have advised them correctly.'

'Of course we have.' said the Captain. 'Life is too short to waste in such dithering.'

He offered her his arm and they followed the young lovebirds.

'Since Papa died I have been conscious of how happy I was before, and how I did not even appreciate it.'

'I know what you mean. I have seen so much death, Miss Wyncroft. So many young lives lost too soon. Men who will never marry. These two need to make the most of the happiness they have found.'

She had always wished for a brother, and had unfortunately fallen into the habit during her time at Chadcombe of thinking of the Fantons as family—probably because she had been falling in love with the Earl at the time. It would have been wonderful to have Harry as a brother, Olivia as her dear sister. But she had never deluded herself. Her dowry—even when she'd had one—would not have been enough to tempt the Earl.

'At least that is what my aunt says.'

Charlotte recalled herself to the conversation. 'Lady Annesley?'

'Ah, you are acquainted with my Aunt Sophia?'

'Yes, she knows—she *knew*—both my parents. She called to visit us yesterday. She is very kind.'

Charlotte had been happy to see Lady Annesley again, for she liked the Earl's godmother. Lady Sophia had glared at Mrs Buxted when she had spoken sharply to Charlotte. Her aunt had looked uncomfortable, and had treated Charlotte a little better for the rest of the visit.

'She tells me not to hurry to marry, but to believe I will find the right girl some day. I know she tells my brother the same.'

Charlotte blushed, and mumbled something unintelligible.

'He is a good man, Adam—though I tease him for being a trifle staid at times.'

Was Harry trying to provoke her? Remembering the rose garden kiss—which the Captain had witnessed—she knew one would never describe the passionate Adam as *staid*!

Harry was continuing, his tone entirely serious, so she had to conclude she was being oversensitive.

'He has always had the burden of being the heir, while I have been free to enjoy life more. I have had the easier task in many ways, and if it makes me seem flippant sometimes, then I apologise.'

'Not at all. Your sense of fun becomes you as much as your brother's seriousness suits him.'

'He would not tell me what has happened, you know, but I am sure *something* is amiss between you.' He looked at her directly. 'I am at your service, Miss Wyncroft, if there is anything I can do. My brother is a good man, and he deserves the best of everything.'

What was she to make of this? He clearly had no idea of his brother's dishonourable intentions. Well, she would not destroy his ideals.

'I thank you, Captain Fanton, but I do not require any assistance. Shall we catch up with Faith and Mr Foxley? I am not performing my chaperoning duties very well.'

'Chaperon? *You?* Her chaperon?' He laughed. 'Why, you are barely out of the schoolroom yourself.'

She replied with a tart riposte, and they bickered

contentedly all the way back to Half-Moon Street. It was the lightest Charlotte had felt since she had heard about Papa.

Chapter Twenty-One

Adam stopped to wipe his brow. This was his second time travelling the flat road between Reims and Laon, and the French heat was draining. He believed, though, that he was making some progress. He had started in Reims, and he was now sure the Colonel and his colleagues had not reached Laon. Somewhere in between was the answer to the mystery of how Charlotte's papa had lost his life.

The source who had reported the deaths of four mounted English officers was unknown, as was the location of the 'shallow graves' where they had been buried. It was daunting. No one really cared about four little-known English soldiers and where they'd died.

No one but the Earl. He had to try, for Charlotte's sake. He had to find Sir Edward's grave, or his belongings—anything that might help Charlotte make an end to some of her pain.

He had now adopted the tactic of stopping in

every village along the route. It was not clear whether the soldiers had been attacked soon after leaving Reims, or had stopped for the night before meeting their end. This village—well, it was a hamlet, really—was as likely as any other as a place where the group may have stopped. At the least they would have had to seek regular food and water for their horses, as well as for themselves.

It looked as if there were two inns in this place. He looked more closely at the name over the inn on the right. Charlotte de Valois. His heartbeat quickened. If Sir Edward had noticed the name…

He dismounted, led his horse to the watering butt and tethered him there. Then, trying not to be over-optimistic, he entered the inn.

The place was blessedly cool inside. There were a couple of customers at tables, and more at the long bar on the far side of the taproom. They all turned to look at him when he entered.

Adam ordered a beer, which the innkeeper served without a word. Adam sighed. Another taciturn Frenchman. They were making his task so difficult. Still, he had to persist.

'I am looking for four English soldiers. They passed through here on horseback about two weeks ago. Do you remember them?'

'Hmm… Some Englishmen stayed for one night. They left the next morning.'

'What was their destination?'

The innkeeper thought about this, then shrugged.

'Calais, I think. They were going through Corbeny. Excuse me.'

Frustratingly, he then left Adam to see to another customer—a French soldier. A moment later he returned.

'This soldier may have some information for you.'

Adam thanked him, then walked to the table near the door, where the French soldier was enjoying a savoury stew.

'Pardon, m'sieur.'

'You are seeking information.' It was not a question. The soldier continued to eat the stew.

'I am. Four Englishmen on horseback—'

He looked up. 'Wyncroft, Mercer, Foden and Hewitson.'

'Yes! Do you know what happened to them?'

The Frenchman smiled ruefully. 'You ask the right man. I am Capitaine Didot.'

Henrietta thought she was behaving very well. She told all who would listen that she was having a good birthday. There were an acceptable number of presents—including two posies of flowers from her admirers, and a book of poetry from Hubert. There was nothing from the Earl, who had not yet returned to London. Henrietta had told Faith and Charlotte that he would probably buy her an especially good present for being late. Everyone was being most kind, she said, and even the Peace Gala planned for that night seemed as though it was especially for her.

'Charlotte, I wish to borrow your ermine muff this evening, for the night may be cold.'

Charlotte hesitated.

'And do not say you will be using it, for it is entirely unsuitable for mourning wear.'

Charlotte gritted her teeth. 'I shall endeavour to find it, Henrietta.'

'Oh, do not worry, for I have already sent Flint to fetch it.'

This proved to be the case. When Charlotte returned to her room, Flint was just leaving with the fur hand-muff, an apologetic expression on her normally impassive face.

Charlotte said nothing, but was moved to punch her pillow when she was safely alone. Henrietta had already ruined a shawl and two pairs of Charlotte's gloves, having 'borrowed' them. Really, Henrietta was the most frustrating, the most *spoiled*—

She forced her mind to be calm. She must endure. She was hoping tonight's Gala would divert her spoiled cousin, for today Henrietta had been even more demanding than usual, and Aunt Buxted had indulged her daughter's every birthday whim.

Charlotte donned her cloak and joined Aunt Buxted, Henrietta and Faith downstairs. Mr Buxted would view the festivities with his own friends, he said, for the ladies would wander around the fair for hours and forego a proper supper. He would eat at his club.

They travelled by carriage to Hyde Park for the re-enactment—which was cleverly done with rowing boats—then went on to Green Park for the unveiling of the Temple of Concord. As promised, the upper level did rotate, and the spectacle was made even more exciting by the addition of eight mechanical fountains, two on each side of the temple. The paintings—which became difficult to see after sunset—showed allegorical scenes of England's triumph under the Regency.

The evening finished with the anticipated walk around the fair and an impressive firework display. They met many friends and acquaintances at the various events—including Mr Foxley and the Captain, who stood together at the re-enactment—and returned to Buxted House weary but content.

Charlotte, while relieved that she had been asked to attend with the family, had struggled to find enjoyment in this celebration of war. She had eaten nothing all day, and could not wait to find her bed.

'How exciting! What a wonderful birthday I have had!' Henrietta exclaimed.

'Yes, dear. But it is late now, so you must calm yourself or else you will not sleep tonight.'

'Oh, Mama. As if anything could stop me from sleeping. Why, you have said yourself that I could sleep the clock around if I were allowed to.'

'That is true. Would anyone like some hot milk before bedtime?'

'No, thank you, Mama.'

'In that case, I shall retire. Is Mr Buxted home?'

The footman on duty nodded. 'Yes, madam. He has already retired.'

'Very well—you may lock up.'

As her aunt and Henrietta mounted the stairs Charlotte took the opportunity to have a quiet word with Faith.

'I saw you speak to Mr Foxley at the fireworks. Has he approached my uncle?'

Faith nodded miserably.

'*Never* say he rejected Mr Foxley?'

'No…but he has not given his approval either. Papa has said he must consider the matter.'

'I see… In that case, perhaps he will say yes.'

Faith's eyes misted. 'I cannot believe so. I know Papa. He is a wonderful man, but it is difficult when Mama has her mind set.'

Charlotte hugged her. 'Do not give up hope. Things may yet work out well.'

Twenty minutes later, sitting on her bed, she repeated her thoughts to Priddy.

Priddy was brushing out Charlotte's long hair, having waited up to attend to her mistress despite Charlotte's earlier instructions to the contrary.

'Mr Foxley is a fine young man, but Miss Faith's papa must do what he believes to be best for her.'

'I think he would be just the husband for her.'

'Now, Miss Charlotte, it is not for you to interfere.'

'I do *so* wish to interfere in this case, but you are right. I just—'

She broke off, for there was a sharp scratching at her door. Priddy opened it, and Charlotte heard the footman's voice.

'Miss Wyncroft is wanted downstairs.'

'Why? What is happening?'

'As to that, I cannot say. I was told by the mistress to fetch her.'

Charlotte rose as Priddy came back. 'Perhaps Henrietta is upset about something. But why would they return downstairs?'

Priddy handed Charlotte a light robe to wear over her thin nightgown. 'Shall I accompany you?'

'No, you should go to bed. If Henrietta is having a tantrum this could take hours. I am surprised, though, for she seemed in excellent spirits not half an hour ago.'

As she descended the stairs, barefoot, Charlotte slipped her arms through the light muslin robe. There were voices coming from the small parlour. Her aunt—exclaiming. Then a man's voice. Was Mr Buxted also awake? It was extremely odd.

She reached the hallway and Biddle was there. 'What is amiss, Biddle?'

He looked strangely shaken. 'Miss Wyncroft...' His voice shook. 'We have unexpected visitors. I—' He composed himself and opened the door for her. 'The Earl of Shalford and...and Colonel Sir Edward Wyncroft.'

Charlotte felt as though she were in a dream. The Earl was there, looking weary, but smiling, and beside him, was—

'Papa?' Her voice was little more than a whisper.

'My little Lottie! My darling girl. I am so happy to see you.'

Was this real? How could this be real?

She wanted to run to him, but her feet would not move, and now everything was starting to go black. Just like...

She saw the Earl's expression change as he stepped forward urgently to catch her as she fell.

This time she came round to find herself being carried in the Earl's strong arms to the nearest settee.

'Papa?' she asked him as he gently laid her down. 'I thought I saw Papa.'

'I am here, Daughter.'

He was beside the Earl. Both looked concerned.

Charlotte sat up, and reached out to hug her father. 'Papa! *Papa!*'

They hugged for some moments, while the Earl covertly wiped a speck from his eye.

Charlotte finally regained the ability to speak. 'But I do not understand! How can this be? They told me— Major Cooke told me—'

'Yes, yes, but we cannot blame the Major, for I was *nearly* dead. Two of the men who travelled with me were killed, and it is only by good fortune that I and Mercer survived.'

He looked older, and pale and tired. His left arm was bandaged, and he was definitely thinner than he should be. But he was *alive*. Charlotte had the same sense of unreality that she had felt in the Earl's library, when Major Cooke had spoken to her, but this time it was a beautiful, wonderful, fantastical unreality.

And the Earl was here too. Why was he with Papa?

She looked towards him in some confusion. 'How has this come about?'

'Ah,' said Papa, 'I think you know Lord Shalford. Well, he has been my rescuer.'

'Hardly that,' said the Earl. 'Captain Didot was already on his way to release you when I met him. He would have done it sooner, only he was feverish with an infected wound and had to stay in Reims for near a sennight.'

'Yes, but he would have brought me only as far as Reims, and I would have had the devil's time of it trying to arrange for clean clothing and funds and my passage home. The Earl organised everything for Mercer, too—got him to the Commissioner's building, where he could be looked after, and left him funds to manage everything—Mercer told me. I must admit it was all much easier with an earl making the arrangements. We were home in two days.'

He twinkled at the Earl, who threw his head back and laughed in response.

'Now, Sir Edward, you will make me sound like an autocrat, who uses his title unfairly.'

"'I am the Earl of Shalford!'" said Sir Edward, in a mockingly haughty tone. "'I wish to cross the Channel *today*, not tomorrow.'"

The Arrogant Earl! thought Charlotte, remembering her first—wrong—impression of him.

'You have me there. But it had the desired effect, did it not?'

'It certainly did—for here we are. We started out Sunday morning, near Laon, and I hardly know what day it is now! That was yesterday, I think.'

'Oh, Papa, you must rest. Aunt Buxted, perhaps…?'

Mrs Buxted, who had been sitting in unaccustomed silence in a rather shocking lilac nightgown, with her hair half unpinned, suddenly came to attention.

'Yes, of course. Sir Edward—you must stay with us. I shall ask Biddle to call Mrs Walker.'

Biddle, when called, had already anticipated the need. 'Mrs Walker is preparing a room for Sir Edward at this moment. I presume—' he bowed to the Earl '—Lord Shalford would prefer to retire to his own townhouse?'

'Indeed, and I shall leave right now,' said the Earl.

Sir Edward shook his hand warmly. 'Thank you, my boy,' he said, in the tone normally reserved for his best officers. 'Shall I see you on the morrow?'

'I think I can safely promise it,' said the Earl.

He bowed to the ladies—smiling warmly at Charlotte, who beamed back—and left them.

* * *

As he travelled home in the hired coach, the Earl reflected that, despite his tiredness, he might not get much sleep tonight. Charlotte's reaction had been all he had hoped for—and he had anticipated it many times since Didot had taken him to the cave where Sir Edward and his colleague had been held.

It had been odd to see Didot and Sir Edward dealing with each other so politely. The former enemies had accepted each other's apologies—Sir Edward for the deaths of Didot's comrades and Didot for attacking the group in the first place, for the deaths of Foden and Hewitson, and then for keeping Sir Edward and Mercer captive for so long.

The infected wound which had so delayed Didot's return had been inflicted, ironically, by Sir Edward himself. The adversaries had parted with a sense of mutual respect which Adam had found curiously noble.

He had been busy afterwards, seeing to Mercer and Sir Edward, who both carried injuries. Initially they had hired a cart from a local aged man who, it seemed, had been the cause of the trouble. It was he who had fed Didot misinformation, motivated by revenge for the death of his only son, killed in battle by an English bayonet.

Adam had brought the two injured soldiers to Reims, where they had enjoyed good food and comfortable sleep for the first time since they had left the city. The following day, he had sorted out the necessary funds for the three of them, organised Mercer's safe passage to Paris, where his brother would meet him, and finally, hired a coach to take himself and Sir Edward to Calais.

Through it all, thoughts of Charlotte had sustained him.

His likely insomnia tonight, however, was not due to Charlotte's undoubted happiness, but had quite another source. The unexpected sight of his beloved *en déshabillé*, wearing nothing but thin nightrail, and with her glorious hair unbound, had affected him profoundly. It would surely be almost dawn before he would successfully eliminate the enchanting image—and the feeling of holding her in his arms—from his mind.

Chapter Twenty-Two

⦿~~~~~~~~~~~~⦿

Charlotte's joy on waking the next day was immediate. Her heart, which had struggled to become accustomed to the loss of her father, now thrilled at his return. She donned her favourite morning dress of lemon figured muslin, and shared her delight with Priddy, who was dressing her hair.

'I am so glad I stayed up last night, Miss Charlotte, for you gave me the best possible news.'

'It is wonderful, is it not? I cannot wait to see Papa today—to talk to him and to hug him and hear his tale.'

'He is still abed at present, but the servants, as you may imagine, are agog with curiosity.'

Charlotte giggled. 'I am hardly surprised, for it seems amazing to me that he is alive.'

'Yes—and have you thought about what this means for yourself? You will not be living here as an orphan, but instead you will be with your father.'

'I know. Oh, Priddy—I expect he will have an

Army pension, or work for the Foreign Office, and we shall get by. I hope also that you and Joseph can be part of our household.'

'Well, as to that, I am sure Sir Edward will let us know—though we would not wish to be a burden.'

'Oh, Priddy, of *course* he will find a way, for everything is perfect now.'

Well, nearly everything, she amended in her head.

In the event, Sir Edward slept until mid-afternoon. Charlotte had asked that a bath be offered to him, to which Mrs Buxted had agreed with alacrity. Her aunt seemed fascinated by Sir Edward's tale, and had talked of the notoriety to be gained by hosting one whose story would earn him the status of hero among the *ton.*

She had already written excited letters to two of her closest friends, her crossed and re-crossed lines detailing the heroism, endurance and good fortune of her illustrious relative. Unfortunately London society was preoccupied today, with the news that the Chinese Pagoda had caught fire after the Buxted party had left the park, and two men and some swans had died.

The crowd had clapped and cheered, thinking the conflagration a planned part of the celebrations. Mrs Buxted had said, to Charlotte's amusement, that she was sure *she* would not have been so stupid.

So Sir Edward had a bath, and the services of Mr Buxted's valet, who shaved him, cut his hair and helped him dress. The Colonel was rather limited by the injuries to his arm and the back of his head, though both wounds were healing well.

Charlotte's things had quietly been moved back into her old room—which still had the original green hangings—and Priddy had taken great delight in unpacking Charlotte's trunks and returning her hairbrushes to the dressing table.

The Colonel finally appeared in the drawing room late in the afternoon, looking much more like his old self than when Charlotte had seen him last. She jumped up to embrace him, then held his hand as Mrs Buxted introduced him to her daughters, her friend Mrs Spenborough, and to Mr Foxley, who had called for his usual visit.

Mr Foxley and Faith still seemed quite forlorn, and Charlotte surmised that Mr Buxted had not yet given Mr Foxley his decision.

Sir Edward contentedly endured the attentions of the group and told his story in full—though playing down some of the more distressing details. His audience were fascinated and amazed. Mrs Spenborough could hardly wait to spread the story far and wide, and pressed Sir Edward for every detail she could think of, including whether he had been tortured in captivity.

'No, not at all.' Sir Edward laughed. 'I do not say living in a cave is to be recommended, but we were well-treated. There was not much food, and it was cold at times, but better that than being held somewhere that exposed us to the hot French sun.'

The Earl and Captain Fanton called shortly afterwards, along with Lady Annesley, who was delighted to see her old friend looking so well after his ordeal. The Earl also found himself being interrogated by Mrs Spenborough, but was much more reticent than Sir Edward, repeating only that he had found Captain Didot by the merest chance.

'Yet, you had been searching for information about me, I know. I gleaned as much from Didot, and from the Army men in Reims.' He looked at the Earl keenly. 'There is one thing I do not yet understand, Lord Shalford.'

'And what is that?'

'What made you travel all the way to France in search of a man you had never met?'

There was a sudden charged silence in the room. Mr Foxley, Lady Annesley and the Captain all looked at Charlotte. Her face burned, and she did not know what to say.

'The Buxted family—along with your daughter— were my guests at Chadcombe for a number of weeks,' said the Earl smoothly. 'In fact, Major Cooke came to my house to break his bad news to Miss Wyncroft. It was the least I could do—though I confess I did not expect to find you alive.'

Sir Edward looked a little sceptical, but did not challenge the Earl. Lady Annesley smiled a secret smile and had a decided look of satisfaction on her face.

Charlotte did not know what to make of it all.

* * *

Later, Mr Buxted found Charlotte and Sir Edward in the morning room. They had gone to escape the attentions of the steady stream of visitors that had arrived at the house as news of their guest spread. Mrs Buxted and Henrietta, delighted with the attention, were quite happy to be the ones to relate the tale, while Faith was content to listen to it time and time again.

Sir Edward, tired of talking about himself, took the opportunity to ask his host about Mr Foxley. Mr Buxted summarised Foxley's family background, and his link to Mrs Buxted.

'Actually, Edward, I should welcome your advice about Foxley. You see, he wishes to marry Faith.'

'Does he? Seems a good sort of fellow. What's his fortune?'

'Modest, for he is a second son—enough for them to have a comfortable life. He is, as you say, an excellent young man, and I think they would deal well together.'

'Hmm… Charlotte, what is your opinion?'

'I agree that he is a good man, Papa, and their regard for each other is, I believe, sincere and enduring.'

'Splendid. Then there should be no problem. It seems to me you should approve the match.'

Mr Buxted looked dubious.

'Why, what is the problem, Freddy?'

Mr Buxted spluttered a little. 'Well, Louisa might not like it...'

'Louisa? I thought you said he is her godson. And besides, what has *she* to say about it? It is *your* decision, is it not?'

Mr Buxted regarded him with all the malevolence of a man who had been married for more than twenty-three years. What would Edward know about it, when he had been a widower these fourteen years and more?

'What is it that you wish for Faith?' Charlotte asked her uncle softly.

'I wish her to be happy.'

As soon as he said it, his expression changed. Charlotte saw in him a sudden firmness, a resolution, which had been missing before.

He stood. 'I will speak to Louisa immediately—yes, and Faith too. For I know my courage will fail me if I wait too long.'

In the five minutes or so that it took for his wife and daughter to come to his study, as requested, Mr Buxted's resolve began to leach away.

Perhaps Louisa *did* know best. It was certainly traditional for a girl's mother to have a good deal of influence when it came to a decision about marriage. The habits of twenty-three years—and disquiet at the notion of standing up to his formidable wife—had him pacing the room in apprehension.

Louisa and Faith arrived together. Mr Buxted

composed himself, and invited them to be seated. They sat together on a heavy oak couch, straightened their skirts, and waited.

Mr Buxted chose the large leather chair near the fireplace. It was an imposing chair, and gave him a sense of security at his back. He had inherited it from his father, and had often speculated about the weighty matters his pater would have considered, while seated there. Mr Buxted found it a comfortable seat for an afternoon doze...

'What is this about, Frederick?'

His wife sounded cross. She was not, it seemed, in a particularly amenable mood. But then, she was rarely in an amenable mood.

'I hope you know I was busy with Cook, confirming tonight's menu. Lord Shalford is to dine with us, and I thought we could prepare some of the dishes he particularly likes, as well as a few special dishes to tempt poor Sir Edward. Such *trials* your dear cousin has been through.'

'Ah. I hope you will include a nice game pie. For not only does Lord Shalford enjoy it—as we both know from our time at Chadcombe—but it is also one of *my* particular favourites. Not that this is anything to do with the matter in hand. I did not ask you here to speak of game pie—or that dish with shallots, leeks and cream, which is also particularly delicious and is an excellent accompaniment to game pie.'

'I had not planned on game pie, but I may mention it to Cook.'

There was a pause. Both ladies looked at him expectantly. He stood up and took a turn about the room.

'I have received an offer of marriage for Faith. From Mr Foxley.'

His daughter looked directly at him, hope filling those damned blue eyes of hers.

'Well,' said Louisa, 'I hope you refused him. He is my godson, of course, and of good family, but I hope we know better than to throw away a daughter on a near-penniless second son.'

'Actually, I told him I needed time to consider the matter.'

'There is nothing to consider—he is not good enough for a Buxted. I hope you know what is due to the Buxted line, to the tradition and history of the name. Why, there were Buxteds came with the Conqueror.'

In this, she had miscalculated. Having been frequently irritated by the sense of superiority she had gained through their marriage, Mr Buxted suddenly found the courage he needed.

'You forget something, Louisa.'

She looked at him, a perplexed frown between her eyebrows.

'You are not a Buxted.'

She gasped.

'If I remember correctly, you are a Long by

birth, and therefore cannot truly know what it means to be a Buxted.'

Avoiding her eyes, he continued headlong with his rash course.

'Despite what has been happening these twenty years and more, *I* am still master in this house. To marry for money and position is all very well, but Faith has the chance to marry a sensible man who enjoys fishing. I mean, not that he is sensible *because* of the fishing, but rather he is sensible *and* he enjoys fishing. In short, an ideal sort of man. If Faith wants him, then Faith shall have him—for he is a good man, not a snivelling fool.'

'I hope, even if *you* have lost all sense, Husband, that my daughter has not.'

Louisa turned to Faith, whose eyes blazed with hope—and fear that her mother would prevail.

'Oh, Mama, *please* do not ask me to reject Mr Foxley, for indeed I *wish* to marry him.'

Mr Buxted nodded approvingly. 'If you think to make Faith unhappy, Louisa, by telling her to reject him, then I say this—you shall not. For I know when my Faith is unhappy, and I insist that she is happy. Yes, I *insist* on it.'

Unaccustomed to such passion from her husband, Mrs Buxted could only concede. 'Well, if you truly insist, then I dare say I must submit. But I do think my views should have been heard.'

'I am aware of your views on the matter, but I

am the head of this family and the decision rests with me.'

His wife inclined her head.

'Very good. Faith, my dear, I wish you happy.' He kissed his daughter on the cheek, and was moved when she threw her arms around his neck.

'Thank you, Papa. Oh, *thank* you!'

'Yes, yes. You are a good girl. Now I will leave you to your mother, for no doubt you will wish to talk of bride clothes and such things.'

'She will be married at St George's in Hanover Square, and we shall have a Venetian Breakfast here afterwards,' said Mrs Buxted, already imagining how to make the best of this wedding. 'I know a particular modiste who makes beautiful dresses suitable for a wedding. She is expensive, but—'

'You may pay whatever she demands, my dear. Our daughter's wedding is to be celebrated.'

Mollified, his wife began planning in her head. Though she was disappointed, she would soon convince herself that this match was what she had wanted all along. She was however, still displeased by her husband's new-found assertiveness.

'I shall be at my club,' Mr Buxted announced, seeing an opportunity to escape. 'I shall return for dinner.'

His wife did not reply.

As he left Mr Buxted reflected that the likelihood of game pie tonight was probably close to nought.

* * *

Lady Sophia Annesley had a plan. Well, she *almost* had a plan. Having seen Adam and Charlotte together in the same room for the first time, she was convinced that Charlotte had indeed developed strong feelings for Adam, but the two of them were separated by some misunderstanding. Charlotte had watched the Earl constantly yesterday, and blushed when caught doing so. Adam had been his usual urbane self, but Sophia knew her godson well enough to know when he was deeply unhappy.

She sent a note round to Buxted House, inviting Edward and Charlotte to call on her at three, and summoned Adam to visit her half an hour earlier.

He came promptly, engaged with her in his relaxed way for twenty minutes, then signalled his intention to leave.

'Oh, no, you cannot go yet.'

'Why ever not?'

'Because Sir Edward is to call, and I wish you to converse with his daughter so that I might enjoy his company properly. Charlotte is a delightful girl, and is clearly overjoyed to have her father back, but she will hardly leave his side for an instant.'

His eyes narrowed. 'Godmama, what is your game?'

She opened her eyes wide. 'I'm sure I do not understand you. I wish to speak to Sir Edward, that is all.'

* * *

She would not be moved, and since he lived
for any opportunity to spend time with Charlotte,
Adam could not argue.

He was sure of Charlotte's gratitude for his part
in her father's recovery, for she had told him so
many times over the past two days—including at
dinner last night. Since she clammed up when he
tried to engage her in any meaningful conversation,
though, he could only conclude that she had not
changed her mind about rejecting his suit.

He had some hope though—he felt that she liked
him, and that there might be another chance for him
some time in the future.

His heartbeat quickened when his godmother's
butler announced the arrival of the Wyncrofts,
though he greeted them with composure.

Within minutes, when Sir Edward and Charlotte
were barely seated, his godmama surprised them
all by saying brusquely, 'Adam, please take Sir
Edward to the library to show him that portrait of
my mother, for he will enjoy seeing it. My mother
did not approve of Sir Edward,' she explained to
Charlotte as an aside.

'Should we not *all* go to see it?' asked Adam,
slightly confused.

'No, no. Besides, I wish to speak to Miss Wyncroft.'

Sir Edward, not one to question the whims of a
lady, assented immediately. Adam was rather more

reluctant, and sent her a suspicious glance. She returned his gaze steadily, all innocence, until he turned and followed Sir Edward out of the drawing room.

'Now, Miss Wyncroft, you and I shall have a comfortable coze. Tell me—are you happy to have your father returned to you?'

'Oh, yes, it is like a fairytale. I could not believe it when I saw him standing there—I still have to remind myself that it is true, and he is alive.'

'And yet, there is some unhappiness that still shadows you. No—do not deny it, for I have seen it in you. It is something to do with Adam, is it not?'

Charlotte looked at her helplessly.

'He will not tell me either, but I know he is unhappy. Have you had a falling out? For I understood you had become…good friends.'

'I—we had—we were—but then—'

'Yes? But then…?'

'Oh, I cannot tell you.'

'Yes, you can, my dear.' She moved to sit beside Charlotte. 'You will feel much better when you do.'

Charlotte looked at her uncertainly. 'It was—something he said to me—in the park—he wanted me to be his—his…' She faltered.

'His what?'

Charlotte looked down at her hands, blushing.

Lady Sophia's eyes widened. '*Never* tell me

you think Adam Fanton was offering you *carte blanche*?'

Charlotte nodded miserably.

'Nonsense.'

'But he said so.'

'What *exactly* did he say?'

'Well, I can't remember exactly. He said I was in a difficult situation. That he enjoyed…kissing me.' Her voice fell to a whisper.

Lady Sophia snorted. 'Good gracious, he made a mull of it, indeed. Made you think he was offering to set you up as his mistress. Lord, young men. Hopeless!'

Charlotte stared at her. 'But—surely you do not think he planned to offer me *marriage*?'

'I know my godson, and I know he would never dream of offering an insult to a well-bred young lady.'

Charlotte looked stunned. 'But—it is impossible. Why should he offer for me? I have no fortune.'

'And what is that to say to anything?'

'But he must marry well—for Chadcombe and for his family.'

'I think his idea of marrying well may have altered when he met you. Oh, I do not mean he would marry a chambermaid, or an actress or some such, but he has learned to appreciate the difference between the *theory* and the *reality*.'

'So you think—?' Realisation dawned. 'Then

I have insulted him in the worst possible way by thinking him capable of such baseness. Oh, *no!*'

She held her face in her hands—then jumped up as Adam and Sir Edward re-entered the room.

'Papa. We must go.'

'Why should we go, Charlotte? For I have not seen Lady Sophia in an age, and had thought to enjoy a quiet hour here. Though if you are unwell then of course—'

'She is not unwell, Edward. She merely needs to speak to my godson. Edward—you and I shall retire to the parlour.' She turned to the Earl. 'Adam, you made a mull of it, but you can yet set everything to rights. Do not let me down.'

With that, she ushered a confused Sir Edward out of the door, saying 'Let us go. I shall explain the whole to you, Edward.'

A tense silence grew in the drawing room. Charlotte—in an agony of regret and anxiety— moved to the fireplace and stared fixedly at the little ormolu clock that stood on the mantel. Why was it, she wondered, that she had faced the poachers calmly and yet could be slain by her own mortification?

The Earl—unclear about why Charlotte was upset—took a moment to collect his thoughts. The message from his godmother had been clear: he should speak to Charlotte again. But he had ruined everything on the first occasion. What could he do or say differently this time?

He caught himself up. Thinking too much had been his downfall that first day. Today he would have to speak from the heart and hope that she felt something for him.

'Charlotte.' He spoke to her back. 'I am sorry for causing you distress in the park. You were overwhelmed with grief, and I crassly tried to make you an offer at the wrong time. I also failed to speak to you in the right way.'

Charlotte, distressed, turned to face him and made as if to speak, but he would not be deterred.

'Ever since that day I have been trying to make things right—doing whatever I could to regain the regard I once thought you held for me. Those weeks in Chadcombe—up until Major Cooke's arrival—were the happiest in my life. Seeing you every day, watching your kindness to others, I came to appreciate your beauty, your intelligence and your compassion—all of those things meant I did not want your visit to end. I want to be with you every day, for the rest of my life.'

Daringly, he took her hand, and she did not resist.

'I love you, Charlotte—and I never thought I would marry for love.'

'But I have no dowry. You cannot truly wish to marry me.'

'I do not care about a dowry. I know that Chadcombe will be better with you as its mistress, by my side, than any other woman. I had not been long in your company before I knew how much above me you are, how infinitely better than every other maiden I have met.'

He took her other hand.

'It must be you, Charlotte. Will you have me?'

A thousand thoughts went through her mind— chief among them a sense of how lucky she was. This man—this beautiful, wonderful man—actually wanted to marry her. She could barely take it in. Everything she had suffered, all she had believed, the many tears she had shed—

'Charlotte?' He looked anxious. 'Will you marry me?'

'Yes. Yes. I will! I—'

He reached for her before she could say any more and they shared a ferocious kiss, continuing from where they'd left off in the rose garden on the night of the ball.

After a long moment they broke off to look at each other and smile.

'I cannot believe it. You really will be my wife?'

She nodded happily, lifted his hand, and pressed it to her cheek adoringly.

'Charlotte—' he said, his voice cracking.

'I must tell you before too much time passes— No, let me speak, my lord!' He was covering her face in kisses.

'My lord?' He raised an eyebrow. 'I think you should call me Adam, don't you?'

'Adam—'

He kissed her.

'Say it again.'

'Adam.'

He kissed her again, this time pulling her close.

Happily, she wrapped her arms around his neck and pressed even closer to him.

He groaned and broke off the kiss. Stepping back, and breathing rather hard, he led her to the settee. then sat down beside her. 'We will be married extremely soon.'

'Yes. But I *must* tell you— No, listen! When you spoke to me in the park—'

'How I have regretted that day. I should have waited, or spoken differently. When you rejected me I felt lost. I have never experienced anything like it. That is why I went to France—to get away from the pain and to find news about your father's death to comfort you. Of course, the pain came with me to France—though at least by assisting Sir Edward I was of some use to you.'

'And I will thank you for it always. But when you spoke to me that day I confess I did not believe you thought of marriage.'

'What? You thought me capable of offering you such an insult?'

'I know—I am sorry. But my lack of fortune— the fact we had…kissed. You said I was in a difficult situation—'

'I meant only to explain why I had not waited until you were out of mourning.' He reflected, trying to remember his own words. 'Lord, I *did* talk about your situation—and our kisses—but I was simply trying to show you we would make a good pair.'

'To think such a thing of you when I know how honourable you are. I cannot say how sorry I am.'

'Hush, my love, it is forgotten.'

A noise in the hallway told them Lady Sophia and Sir Edward were returning. Though Charlotte would have jumped up and moved away from him, he held her hand firmly and smiled reassuringly.

Sir Edward and Lady Sophia took in the situation at a glance—the joined hands, the happy smiles, the glow surrounding the young couple.

'Well,' said Lady Sophia, 'I shall be the first to wish you happy.' She kissed both of them. 'And I shall tell everyone it is all *my* doing.'

Sir Edward looked rather shocked—though clearly Lady Sophia had prepared him. 'My little Lottie. Do you wish this?'

'I do, Papa. He is the best of men—apart from you, of course.'

'Then I am happy for you.' He kissed her cheek. 'Young man, in my day it was customary for a gentleman to seek permission if he wished to pay his addresses to another gentleman's daughter.'

'Sir Edward, you are right. I apologise for being anticipatory. My godmama…er…was most insistent. If you have no objections, might I call on you tomorrow to discuss—arrangements?'

'You may.'

Charlotte squirmed uncomfortably. Would Papa be embarrassed at the lack of dowry for his daughter?

'I shall ride across at around eleven o'clock, if that would be convenient?'

'That would be acceptable. And perhaps,' said Sir Edward, unbending a little, 'you and Charlotte could ride out to Green Park afterwards. My Lottie is a fine horsewoman, you know.'

'I *do* know. I have seen her gallop side-saddle.'

'Ah, on Andalusia? A fine piece of horseflesh. I got her in Spain, you know.'

Charlotte's discomfort increased. *Lusy!* 'Papa, I must tell you—'

The Earl shook his head slightly.

'Sir Edward, finally our families are to be joined.' Lady Sophia beamed happily. 'This surely makes us cousins by marriage, or some such thing.'

'Ah, but, Sophia, I have no *wish* to be your cousin.' He kissed her hand gallantly and she giggled.

Adam and Charlotte watched, open-mouthed.

'I declare I believe that I will enjoy my retirement,' said Sir Edward, with a wink towards his future son-in-law.

In the carriage, on their way back to Buxted House, Charlotte thought of something. 'Papa, please don't tell the Buxteds yet. About my—my betrothal, I mean.'

'Why ever not? You are making a spectacular marriage, as the *ton* would have it. Though I am more interested in the fact that you have chosen a good man. I spoke to him just now, when you were saying your goodbyes to Lady Sophia. He mentioned that I should consider living at Chadcombe after you are married.'

'Oh, that would be wonderful.'

'Yes, well, I should not wish to intrude.'

'Of course you would be welcome. And, besides, you have not seen just how large Chadcombe is.' Her eyes danced. 'Why, if you wish to avoid us we may not see you for a week.'

He laughed at this. 'Then let us rent some nice townhouse for a month or two, until you are wed, and afterwards we go to Chadcombe.'

'Papa, I believe Faith has just become engaged to Mr Foxley. They have not announced it yet. It would be better, I think, if we waited with our announcement until a little time has passed.'

And until I am not living in the same house as Henrietta! she added privately.

Sir Edward agreed, and Charlotte was glad he had done so, for Henrietta was in a foul mood today. And Mrs Buxted had still not told her elder daughter of Faith's news.

Nothing had been said at dinner last night, although Charlotte had realised by the change in Faith's demeanour that she had good news. They had talked briefly afterwards, and hugged, and Faith had declared that nobody could be as happy as she was.

Today Charlotte, with Papa restored and the Earl in love with her, would beg to differ.

As Charlotte mounted the stairs she could already hear Henrietta's litany of complaints. She was disappointed with her new dress—and her hair, she said, was not styled properly.

'There you are, Charlotte. May I ask Priddy to help me with my hair? Flint has made it look ugly.'

This was a change. Last week she would not have asked Charlotte's permission, but ordered Priddy around as if she was her own personal servant.

'I do not think you look ugly, Henrietta,' said Charlotte. 'But of course I shall ask Priddy to attend you.'

In truth, she was glad of a reason to go to her room and call Priddy. Her maid was delighted to hear that Charlotte was to be married, and that she and Joseph would be moving to Chadcombe.

'Oh, Miss Charlotte, I am overcome. This is wonderful news. He is the very man for you. And an earl. You are to be a *countess*—Lady Shalford. This will likely cause apoplexy for Miss Buxted—*and* her mother.' Her tone was scathing as she mentioned the two ladies who had caused her darling such pain. 'May I tell Joseph?'

'Of course—though you must ask him to tell nobody for now. Oh, and Miss Buxted wishes you to dress her hair.'

'Well, I will, of course—though I wish I could be there when she discovers you are to marry the Earl.'

Priddy left, still muttering about Henrietta.

Charlotte waited for the door to close, then waltzed around the room, unable to contain her happiness. He *loved* her! She was to *marry* him. Papa was alive.

Everything was wonderful, and the contrast with her feelings only a few days ago was difficult to encompass.

'Adam,' she said aloud, as she had once before. *'Adam.'*

Chapter Twenty-Three

❦

The next day, in the drawing room, Mrs Buxted finally broke Faith's news officially to Henrietta and Charlotte.

'Girls,' she said bluntly, 'you are to wish Faith happy. Your father has decided she is to marry Mr Foxley.'

Henrietta caught her breath. '*What?* Faith and Mr *Foxley*?' Her voice rose to a screech. '*Married!* But—he is a *nobody*! Why would Papa do such a thing? Why, *I* am not even engaged yet. And I am the *elder*. This cannot be true.' She stood up and began to march around the room in an agitated manner. 'I must speak to Papa.'

Faith looked panicked. 'Henrietta, please do not. I *wish* to marry Mr Foxley. Papa has said I shall. And,' she added with defiance, 'he is *not* a nobody.'

Charlotte rose and hugged Faith, glad she could finally congratulate her publicly. 'This is wonderful news. Mr Foxley is an admirable man and will make an excellent husband for you, Faith.'

Mrs Buxted sniffed. 'I confess I had hoped for more. But he is my godson, and of good family. He is, of course, fortunate to be allying himself with the Buxted name.'

'Why is nobody listening to *me*?' Henrietta appealed to all three ladies. 'I have been *wronged* by this. Mama, how can you not see how *unsuitable* Mr Foxley is? And for a younger daughter to be married first—it will make it seem as though—as though—'

'As though you could not get a husband? Yes, Henrietta, it will. But you had every chance. The Earl has not yet come up to scratch, and so you must give way to your sister, who has found a fine husband.' Mrs Buxted smiled benignly at Faith, who looked extremely nervous at this turn of events. 'Now, pass me the *Morning Post*, for I must copy the correct words to announce the engagement.'

Faith passed her the newspaper and she began to search its pages for the announcements.

Henrietta stamped her foot. 'Mama. I *insist* you listen to me.'

Mrs Buxted continued to turn the pages.

'If Faith marries first she will have Monkton Park. And Monkton Park was to be *mine*!'

Faith looked startled. 'Monkton Park? I had not remembered. Mama, perhaps Henrietta could still—?'

'Indeed not. It is clearly stated that the property

is for whoever marries first. Monkton Park will be yours, Faith.'

'That *cannot* be. It was to be *mine*.' Henrietta's voice became even more strident. 'I believe Mr Foxley does not really *wish* to marry Faith, but just wants the property. He is a fortune-hunter.'

Charlotte, seeing Faith's hurt expression, intervened. 'No one can doubt the true feelings that Faith and Mr Foxley share.'

Faith smiled weakly.

'What? *What?*' Mrs Buxted, ignoring her daughters, stood up in some agitation. 'The *Morning Post* has made a terrible mistake.'

'What is it, Mama?' Faith looked at the newspaper. Her mother was pointing to one of the announcements, seemingly unable to speak further.

They all stood, concerned. Faith took it from her and read aloud.

'"The engagement is announced between Adam Arthur Charles Fanton, fourth Earl of Shalford—"'

'What?' Henrietta shrieked, immediately distracted from the loss of Monkton Park. 'It cannot be true. Is it *Millicent*? That hateful, deceitful—'

Oh, no, thought Charlotte. *The Earl must have put the notice in already.*

At that precise moment the door opened, admitting Mr Buxted, Sir Edward and the Earl.

Faith, oblivious, continued. '"To Miss Charlotte Wyncroft, only daughter of Colonel Sir Edward Wyncroft—"'

'*Noooooo!*' Enraged, Henrietta lunged at Charlotte with hands outstretched. It was unclear if she intended to wrap her hands around Charlotte's throat or rake her face with her fingernails.

Charlotte instinctively took a small step to the side, bent slightly to brace herself, and knocked Henrietta's hip with her own. At the same time she brought her left arm up to protect her face and neck.

Henrietta's momentum caused her to crash headlong into Charlotte's elbow, bounce back and tumble to the floor. It all happened lightning-quick, before any of them—least of all Charlotte—was fully aware of what was taking place.

Confused, Henrietta lay there for a second. Her dress, unfortunately, had ridden up, exposing her thin white legs. Shock kept her still for an instant, before outrage claimed her. Realising what had happened—though not exactly how—she began to wail dramatically.

The ladies immediately rushed to her. Charlotte, who was closest, was met with resistance and a look of fierce anger. Henrietta was furious.

'Mama! Did you see how Charlotte hit me with her elbow and pushed me over? She is vicious—*vicious*!'

Mrs Buxted briskly rearranged Henrietta's skirts and gave her a hand to rise. 'Come now, Henrietta, stand up!'

Henrietta complied, putting a hand to her face where, in truth, a red mark *was* beginning to form.

'*You* attacked *her*, Henrietta. Charlotte only stopped you.' Faith was extremely agitated.

'No! *She* did it. She *stole* the Earl from me. She has been flirting with him behind my back. She has *betrayed* us, Mama. She—' Henrietta, finally taking in the presence of the gentlemen, stopped.

The Earl, who had noted Charlotte's pallor, was livid.

'Permit me to tell you, Miss Buxted, I was never yours to steal—except perhaps inside that dull, vain, self-centred little head of yours. Miss Wyncroft—who is to become my beloved wife—is worth a hundred of you. I have watched you slight her and be unkind to her—and to your own sister, who is also higher in my estimation than you are. I should pity *any* man who marries you, unless you learn self-control and some consideration for others.'

Henrietta, confident in her own worth, sneered contemptuously. 'You are *nothing* to me. I never wished to marry you anyway. I just did not like to think of Charlotte abusing my dear mama's trust. You are a dishonourable rake, and Charlotte is nothing better than a—' She used a term that made all the ladies gasp.

'That is *enough*, Henrietta!' Mr Buxted's voice was harsh. 'You will apologise to Charlotte and to Lord Shalford.'

'I shall not.'

'Then you shall be confined to your room. Mrs Buxted?'

'Indeed, Mr Buxted! I am shocked that any daughter of mine should behave with such little decorum. Henrietta, I am extremely disappointed in you. Go to your room this instant.'

'Well, I shall—but only because I wish to.'

Defiant to the last, she stalked out, her head held high.

'Lord Shalford, Charlotte, Edward—I apologise sincerely for my daughter's actions. I knew she was spoiled and silly, but I never realised to what degree.' He glared at his wife. 'From now on I will take a closer interest in her doings. She has been over-indulged. That will change.'

Mrs Buxted, shaken, agreed. 'I am truly shocked by her actions. Though you must understand she was already distressed, my lord, for Faith is also to be married—to Mr Foxley.'

'This *is* good news,' said the Earl, nodding at Faith.

He crossed to Charlotte and took her hand, his expression one of concern.

'Charlotte? How do you?'

'I am well. No, really, I am quite well.'

'This is my fault.' said Mr Buxted, still agitated. 'I am aware I have failed in my duties as a father.'

No one could disagree. There was an awkward silence.

'Well,' said Sir Edward. 'I had forgot we'd agreed yesterday that you would put a notice in the *Morning Post*, my lord. I did not even remember to tell Charlotte.' He addressed the Buxteds. 'But, yes, Charlotte is to be married.'

All three exclaimed and wished them happy—two with warm enthusiasm, one with resigned equanimity.

'At least,' said Aunt Buxted, 'our two houses will be allied. When is the wedding to be?'

'Soon,' said the Earl, smiling at Charlotte, 'though we have not yet had the opportunity to consider the details.'

'Faith and Mr Foxley will also be married soon,' said Mrs Buxted, seeing an opportunity. 'Perhaps a double wedding?'

'Unfortunately,' said the Earl quickly, 'that will be impossible. Fanton tradition, you know.'

He did not elaborate, and his knowing air was enough to deter her from pressing further.

'Then perhaps the future Countess would stand with Faith as her witness? You would like that, girls, would you not?'

'Mama, *Henrietta* may wish to be my witness.'

'Henrietta is not in my consideration. I have more important priorities now. I am sure Lord Shalford will not object?'

'I will discuss everything with my bride and her father,' said the Earl glibly.

'Yes, yes,' agreed Sir Edward. 'One thing I am clear about, though—no expense will be spared for Lottie's wedding.'

Charlotte looked confused. 'But, Papa. Can you afford it?'

'Afford it? Why I am as rich as—well, perhaps not quite as rich as Croesus, but Herr Lenz and I have made excellent investments these many years.'

'Rich?' Charlotte was stunned. 'But Mr Ritter said—'

'Ritter? But he knows nothing of my business affairs—everything is based in Vienna. Ritter only deals with that old mortgage on the Shawfield house—which I plan to redeem as soon as I may find the time.'

'Rich…? I cannot believe it.' She put a hand over her eyes and her shoulders shook.

The Earl frowned. 'Do not be upset, my love. I know you went through some trials for a time, but that is finished now.'

She removed her hand to reveal a face alight with laughter. 'I am not upset. I just find it amusing that I worried over how I was to afford mourning clothes.'

'Eh? What's that? Did that old fool lawyer tell you there was no money? I think he was confusing me with your grandfather, Charlotte.'

'So I have a dowry?'

'Of *course* you have a dowry—an excellent dowry. It is what I will talk to the Earl about today— if he will let go of your hand for long enough.'

Undaunted, Adam retained his darling's hand. 'At least you know by this that I would have married you with no dowry.'

Charlotte thought of something else. 'Oh, no. Andalusia!' Sir Edward raised a brow. 'I had to sell her, Papa. I thought I had no money.'

'Fear not, my love.' Adam shook his head. 'I bought her—for you. She will be your wedding present.'

'Really?' She took his other hand. 'She is safe? I cannot believe it. I thought her gone for ever.'

'I told Buxted at the time I would pay more than any other bidder. How could I let someone else buy her when I know how important she is to you?'

This time Charlotte, overcome, did cry a little.

Two days later, Charlotte was sharing a light nuncheon with her papa, her aunt and uncle and Faith, when Mrs Walker asked to speak to her mistress. The housekeeper was wringing her hands in some agitation, and seemed distressed.

'You may speak to me here, Mrs Walker. What is it?'

Mrs Walker swallowed. 'It's Miss Henrietta—she is not in her room.'

'Not in her room? I had thought she was still sleeping, for she can sleep for half the day when she chooses. Do you mean she has gone out shopping? She went yesterday, to find a betrothal present for her sister, but came back empty-handed. Nothing was quite right, she said, and she wished to buy something special to show Faith she was sorry. I thought it most generous, and a good sign.'

'Perhaps, but…all of the footmen and housemaids are here, so I do not know who could have accompanied her…'

'Oh, Mrs Walker, you are likely panicking over nothing. One of her friends must have called to take her shopping.'

'I have checked with Biddle and he says there have been no visitors this morning. He also says…'

'Well?'

'The front door was unlocked this morning, though the footman swears he locked it before retiring.'

Charlotte felt a cold fear in her stomach. What had her headstrong cousin done?

Charlotte had been the only one unconvinced by Henrietta's show of contrition yesterday. She had accepted Henrietta's stilted apology and had been glad to see how happy Faith was to be reconciled with her sister, but she had seen a familiar calculating gleam in Henrietta's eye. She had known something was amiss, though she had never thought Henrietta would leave the house.

An hour later the story was a little clearer. Henrietta had *not* gone shopping yesterday, but had met A Man in a quiet area of the park. Jane, the housemaid involved, had thought it exceedingly romantic, and had kept Miss Henrietta's secret as requested—until questioned by Mrs Walker, Biddle and Mr Buxted. Then she'd broken down in tears, confessing she had indeed helped the girl.

Jane had no idea who The Man was, but said he had been compassionate towards Miss Henrietta, and had exclaimed at the bruise on her cheek, claiming he would protect her from those who were abusing her. Jane had not overheard any more of their conversation, but had agreed that after the house was quiet she would sneak out of bed to unbolt the door, for Miss Henrietta did not know how.

'She has eloped with some madman or vile seducer. Oh, my poor Henrietta. You foolish, *foolish* girl!' Mrs Buxted was becoming extremely upset, causing Faith and Mrs Walker immediately to go to her aid.

Charlotte went to the assistance of her uncle. 'Can she be recovered, do you think?'

'I do not know, but I must try. I cannot think where to start.'

'Perhaps Mr Foxley and Lord Shalford may help?'

'Charlotte, you are a treasure. Biddle, I wish to write notes to Mr Foxley and Lord Shalford. See that they are delivered.'

'Yes, sir.'

In the end, it was almost four o'clock before the Earl left, along with Joseph, to follow Henrietta. He and Mr Foxley had spent hours making enquiries at various coaching inns, and had finally met with success at the Red Lion, in Barnet. A young couple—the lady with a bruise on her cheek—had left early that morning on the Great

North Road. The lady had seemed agitated, and had been urging the gentleman to hurry.

'Looks like Gretna, at least,' said Mr Buxted.

He had seemed to age years as the day went on, and Charlotte's heart went out to him.

'You may trust Lord Shalford to find them.'

'I can do nothing else. I have been singularly inept in everything.'

'Never say so. It's just that Henrietta is a—a wilful person. That can be a *good* thing.'

He patted her hand, saying sadly, 'Not in this case—though I thank you for trying to give me comfort.'

They waited for news all through the evening, though they knew, with eight hours' head start, that Henrietta would not be recovered that night.

The next day, too, passed without any information. They did not go to Church, for fear of being questioned about Henrietta's absence.

Thankfully they had no visitors—apart from Mr Foxley, who came to take Mr Buxted out for distraction. Charlotte and Faith did what they could to comfort poor Mrs Buxted, who vacillated between concern for Henrietta and rage at The Man who had taken her.

On Monday afternoon, they heard the sound of a coach stopping outside the house. As one, the ladies rushed to the window—to see Henrietta alighting, along with an unknown serving maid. Joseph, along with a grim-looking Lord Shalford, were accompanying the coach on horseback.

The women hurried downstairs, sending a footman to alert Mr Buxted and Sir Edward, who were in the library.

Henrietta stomped in through the front door, her expression stormy.

'Thank goodness you are alive,' said Mrs Buxted. 'But how could you *do* such a thing, Henrietta? Where have you been? And who with?'

Henrietta tossed her head. 'It is of no matter—save that I must be married now. And Monkton Park will be mine.'

'I thought as much.' Mr Buxted looked angrier than his family had ever seen him. 'I have had much time to reflect these past two days—on my failures as a father and on the likely reasons for you to run away. I am, I admit, not the cleverest man in England, but it occurred to me that Monkton Park and the status of being first-married was your aim.'

'I am the elder. It is only fair.'

He continued as if she had not spoken. 'I have therefore organised a licence for a marriage to take place this week—'

'I *knew* it. This is what I planned. What do I care for my reputation, when I will be living in Monkton Park as a married lady?' Henrietta was gleefully unrepentant.

'Henrietta! Have you no shame?' Mrs Buxted was grey with shock.

'A marriage licence for Faith and Foxley,' concluded Mr Buxted.

'For Faith? *Faith!* But—I *must* be married. I spent an entire night with a man.'

'You will spend your life with him—whoever he is. I care not. But Faith will marry first. Mr Foxley assures me he has no objection to a quiet wedding. In fact he says he and Faith would prefer it.'

'I am quite *sure* he has no objection,' snarled Henrietta. 'For Monkton Park is the only thing he is interested in.'

At this, Faith could take no more. She marched up to Henrietta and slapped her face. 'You must stop saying these things about him. *Stop* it, do you hear? *Stop!*'

Henrietta was so shocked at this she forgot to shriek or carry on. Mrs Buxted took the opportunity to usher her prodigal daughter up the stairs.

As they passed Mr Buxted he said, 'Make sure she does not leave this house tomorrow unless a member of the family is with her. Once Faith is safely married, the next day she may do what she wills.'

Henrietta did not respond.

When she was nearly at the top of the stairs he spoke again. 'Henrietta?'

She stopped.

'Who is the man?'

'There is only one person in the world who cares about me. And that is Hubert!'

Epilogue

The day the Earl of Shalford married Miss Charlotte Wyncroft was a joyful one—and not just for the couple themselves. Adam's family were delighted to gain Charlotte as their new Countess, and Sir Edward—happily—already had good reason to know the Earl's good qualities. Mr and Mrs Buxted were pleased too—Charlotte's uncle held a genuine affection for the bride, while her aunt had already gained some of the advantages that the alliance offered to her own social standing.

Charlotte's cousins were also content—one because she counted both Charlotte and the Earl as friends, and the other because today's invitation was the first sign of her rehabilitation within the family. Charlotte had insisted Henrietta be invited, despite the reservations of the Earl—and of Mr Buxted, who still struggled to understand how he had nurtured such a daughter.

The newly married couple themselves had no

doubt of their being the luckiest creatures in England, and their felicity was plain to see.

The Earl looked tall and handsome in a new coat of his favourite blue superfine, paired with elegant knee breeches and a snowy-white neckcloth tied in a complicated Waterfall. His bride wore an elegant dress of blue and silver, with lace sleeves and fine silver embroidered rosebuds.

The wedding was a traditional, quiet affair, with only close family present. Afterwards, a few select guests had been invited to the wedding breakfast at Chadcombe, there to exclaim at the happiness of the newlyweds and to speculate about the other family members.

Mr and Mrs Hubert Etherington attracted much attention. They had been married recently in London, it was said, though rumours persisted that they had been seen in an inn in Stamford together before they were wed.

The new Mrs Etherington was wearing an unusual gown in purple silk, with a matching turban and three ostrich feathers. Her fashion-conscious husband had declared it all the crack, though in truth the colour did nothing for her complexion, and the style was not really appropriate for a young married lady.

Mr Hubert Etherington, meanwhile, was attired in a vibrant red velvet coat, worn with a pink waistcoat and wine-coloured small-clothes—a combination which drew much attention, not all of it favourable. He and his wife spent the day bickering and being

critical of one another, then coming together to crit-
icise others.

Mr Buxted, sitting with Sir Edward in a quiet part
of the room, averted his eyes from his flamboyant
son-in-law. Instead, he sought out Mr and Mrs Foxley, who were sitting quietly together near the middle
window. They were dressed soberly but stylishly—
Mr Foxley in a close-fitting Weston coat and his wife
in a pretty pink gown. They had recently taken up
residence in Monkton Park, and were expected to
be frequent visitors at Chadcombe. As Mr Buxted
watched the bride moved to sit with them, and she
and Mrs Foxley embraced warmly. The Earl soon
joined them—he and Charlotte were never apart for
long.

Mr Buxted and Sir Edward, while sipping an
excellent red wine provided by Merrion, reflected
on the nuptials with satisfaction.

'I approve of my new son-in-law more and more,
Freddy,' said Sir Edward. 'Yes, and yours too. Young
Foxley is a sensible fellow.'

Neither mentioned Mr Etherington, currently battling a confused but persistent wasp who thought he
was a hollyhock.

'You know, despite the title, I think my Faith has
got the better deal.'

'And why is that?'

Mr Buxted delivered the clincher. 'Well, you see,
my son-in-law—unlike *yours*—likes fishing.'

Adam whispered in Charlotte's ear and a moment

later they slipped away to the rose garden, to enjoy a quiet moment together. They wandered among the late-blooming flowers, hand in hand, until the sounds of the party faded behind them.

'Oh, Adam, I cannot tell you how happy I am! When I think of how low I felt, with Papa gone and no hope of being with you, it seems like another world.'

'I will never forget how your aunt belittled you and insulted you,' he replied, looking grim. 'I sent Priddy to find you that day.'

'That was you? Thank you. That was, I think, my lowest point—crying in that attic room.'

'Yes, why *did* you go to the attic that day? Was it to find Priddy's room?'

'No, mine. My aunt had moved me to a servant's room.' She shuddered at the memory.

He looked thunderous. '*What?* How *dare* she?' He stopped and drew her into his arms. 'That woman!' he said, with loathing.

'Hush!' She stood on tiptoes and planted a feather-light kiss on his lips.

'Charlotte!' He returned the kiss with fervour.

After a few moments they stopped to look at each other and catch their breath.

'I had planned to speak to your father on his return, to ask permission to pay my addresses to you. While he was lost *I* felt...lost. To see you entrapped by your aunt when I was unable to help you—and then you turned down my proposal...'

'Please don't remind me! I was so cruel to you that day! I had no idea you wanted to marry me.'

He smiled. 'We nearly made a complete mull of it, between us, didn't we?'

They walked on a little further, arms now entwined around each other's waists.

'Let's remember happier times,' he murmured. 'I recall the night I kissed you here, during the ball. I had already decided I would marry you even then.'

'I had no clue about your intentions, Adam. We had just danced the waltz together, and it was such a wonderful moment. I saw everything slipping away, and I believed we would never dance together again. I was so unhappy afterwards.'

'As was I—you ran away from me that night.'

'I thought only to spare you from being trapped into marriage!'

'It is no trap, my love,' he said, taking her hand and putting his arm around her in a waltz hold. 'I am happy to be your husband. In fact I suspect I am the luckiest man in the world, for I have *you*.'

They began to move together, to music unheard.

'And I am happy to be your wife.'

'I love you, Charlotte.'

'And I love *you*, Adam.'

He bent his head towards hers. 'And we will waltz together whenever we choose.'

'Yes, we will,' she whispered as their lips met.

* * * * *

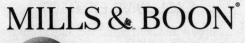

MILLS & BOON®

 HISTORICAL

AWAKEN THE ROMANCE OF THE PAST

sneak peek at next month's titles...

In stores from 23rd March 2017:

Claiming His Desert Princess – Marguerite Kaye
Bound by Their Secret Passion – Diane Gaston
The Wallflower Duchess – Liz Tyner
Captive of the Viking – Juliet Landon
The Spaniard's Innocent Maiden – Greta Gilbert
The Cowboy's Orphan Bride – Lauri Robinson

Just can't wait?
Buy our books online before they hit the shops!
www.millsandboon.co.uk

Also available as eBooks.

MILLS & BOON®

EXCLUSIVE EXTRACT

The Earl of Penford knows his passion for Lorene
Summerfield is scandalous, but when he's accused of
her husband's murder, he must clear his name—and
win her hand!

Read on for a sneak preview of
BOUND BY THEIR SECRET PASSION

Her old romantic dreams burst forth. Why hold back?
Dell's kiss was even more than she could have imagined.
Why not give herself to it?

She pulled off her bonnet and threw her arms around
his neck, answering the press of his lips with eagerness.
He urged her mouth open and she readily complied,
surprised and delighted that his warm tongue touched
hers.

He tasted wonderful.

She plunged her fingers into his hair, loving its soft-
ness and its curls. She liked his hair best when it looked
tousled by a breeze. Or mussed by her hands.

He pressed her body against his and the thrill inten-
sified. How marvelous to feel his muscles, so firm against
her. And more. One hand slid down from his hair to his
arm to his hip. How wanton was that?

But she was a widow, was she not? Was not everyone
telling her she had license to do as she pleased? It pleased
her to touch him. Although she was not quite brazen

enough to touch that hard part of him that thrilled her most of all.

'Lorene,' he groaned as his hands pressed against her derriere, intensifying the sensations in all sorts of ways. 'We should stop.'

She did not want to stop. 'Why?' She kissed his neck. 'I am a widow. Are not widows permitted?'

'Do not tempt me,' he said, though his hands caressed her.

She moved away, just enough that he could see her face. 'If you do not want this, then, yes, we should stop, but I do desire it, Dell.'

For a long time, she realized. Since she first met him. He was the man she had dreamed about in her youth, a good man, kind, honorable, handsome. But something more, something that made her want to bed him.

Don't miss
BOUND BY THEIR SECRET PASSION
By Diane Gaston

Available April 2017
www.millsandboon.co.uk

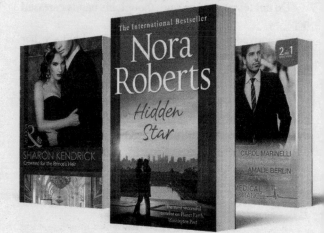

MILLS & BOON®

Read on for an exclusive extract

How did she walk away? Lydia wondered.

How did she go over and kiss that sulky mouth and say goodbye when really she wanted to climb back into bed?

But rather than reveal her thoughts she flicked that internal default switch which had been permanently set to 'polite'.

'Thank you so much for last night.'

'I haven't finished being your tour guide yet.'

He stretched out his arm and held out his hand but Lydia didn't go over. She did not want to let in hope, so she just stood there as Raul spoke.

'It would be remiss of me to let you go home without seeing Venice as it should be seen.'

'Venice?'

'I'm heading there today. Why don't you come with me? Fly home tomorrow instead.'

There was another night between now and then, and Lydia knew that even while he offered her an extension he made it clear there was a cut-off.

Time added on for good behaviour.

And Raul's version of 'good behaviour' was that there would

be no tears or drama as she walked away. Lydia knew that. If she were to accept his offer then she had to remember that.

'I'd like that.' The calm of her voice belied the trembling she felt inside. 'It sounds wonderful.'

'Only if you're sure?' Raul added.

'Of course.'

But how could she be sure of anything now she had set foot in Raul's world?

He made her dizzy.

Disorientated.

Not just her head, but every cell in her body seemed to be spinning as he hauled himself from the bed and unlike Lydia, with her sheet-covered dash to the bathroom, his body was hers to view.

And that blasted default switch was stuck, because Lydia did the right thing and averted her eyes.

Yet he didn't walk past. Instead Raul walked right over to her and stood in front of her.

She could feel the heat—not just from his naked body but her own—and it felt as if her dress might disintegrate.

He put his fingers on her chin, tilted her head so that she met his eyes, and it killed that he did not kiss her, nor drag her back to his bed. Instead he checked again. 'Are you sure?'

'Of course,' Lydia said, and tried to make light of it. 'I never say no to a free trip.'

It was a joke but it put her in an unflattering light. She was about to correct herself, to say that it hadn't come out as she had meant, but then she saw his slight smile and it spelt approval.

A gold-digger he could handle, Lydia realised.

Her emerging feelings for him—perhaps not.

At every turn her world changed, and she fought for a semblance of control. Fought to convince not just Raul but herself that she could handle this.

Don't miss
THE INNOCENT'S SECRET BABY
by Carol Marinelli
OUT NOW

BUY YOUR COPY TODAY
www.millsandboon.co.uk

CM0317_2